REQUIEM FOR THE DEAD

BY KELLY MEDING

Requiem for the Dead

Copyright © 2013 by Kelly Meding

First Print Edition, 2016

ISBN: 978-0-9899188-2-4

www.kellymeding.com

Cover Art by Robin Ludwig Design, Inc.

For every Dreg City fan who has supported this series since day one, this book is for you. It wouldn't have happened without you.

CHAPTER ONE

Sunday, August 31
1:15 a.m.

I don't like morgues. Never have, never will. My life started over again in a morgue, so naturally I have a pretty negative association with them—and with this one in particular, since it's where I was reborn. In the basement of St. Eustachius Hospital, not twenty feet from where I was standing, right behind that solid metal door.

Plus morgues smell to high hell and that's just never pleasant for anyone, especially a half-human, half-werewolf with an extra-sensitive sense of smell.

Not me. I'm completely human (well, kind of). The half-and-half I live with (he despised the word half-breed, so I gave him a nickname he despised just a little bit less) would be Wyatt Truman, my boyfriend, work partner, and also the guy creeping into the morgue with me late on a Saturday night. We never seemed to manage anything normal couples did together, like dinner and a movie, or even just a long walk in the park on a sunny afternoon. Our "dates" usually included any combination of hunting, capturing, questioning, killing, and breaking-and-entering. Normal has never been in our relationship description.

This particular morgue wasn't providing us with much of a challenge in regard to breaking and entering. The lower level of the hospital was nearly deserted at this hour, the corridor barely lit, and the only way I imagined we'd be interrupted during our little job was if a pileup on the city bypass resulted in a mad rush of casualties into the ER. And even then, our eyes and ears on the outside would give us ample warning.

Getting access to our objective was as easy as using the keycard we'd had copied for us the day before. In the dim corridor of the hospital basement, I slid the card down the door lock while Wyatt waited behind me, every muscle in his body tense and alert. Shadows made his black hair seem impossibly darker, and the telltale ring of silver around his otherwise black irises glimmered in the light of a nearby overhead. The silver was the only outward sign that he was no longer human—hadn't been for five weeks.

The lock light turned from orange to green, and something inside the door popped. I grabbed the handle, but didn't pull.

"Evy?" Wyatt said softly, his voice strangely loud as it burst the silence.

"Just reflecting," I said. "A few months ago, I was sneaking out of this place in sweats eight sizes too big and with every intention of stealing a lab tech's car."

"And now you're breaking back in."

"Yeah. Funny how life comes full circle." Usually right before it turned around and bit you on the ass, but I was trying to stay positive about tonight's adventure.

I pulled the door, and Wyatt and I slipped inside. The familiar smells stung my nose—formaldehyde and industrial cleaner and a deeper, darker scent of death. I felt along the wall to my right until I found a switch, then blinked as my eyeballs were assaulted with light. It took a minute for the room to come into focus.

Same plain gray walls and yellow tiled floors, with two beds on either side of a floor drain. Instrument tables stood clean and organized, waiting for their next victims to be brought in for autopsy. Just past those tables was the wall of doors that held individual trays, and some of those trays held bodies. My body had been in one of those for a few hours, until being put out for autopsy. Fortunately, I came back to life before they could cut me open, and I scared the hell out of a lab tech named Pat.

I was forever grateful I hadn't woken up still locked in one of those little cubicles; I'd have probably lost my shit completely and never adjusted to life in someone else's body. Or simply frozen to death before anyone knew I was back, and then Wyatt's sacrifice would have been for nothing.

The mental image of me, blue and cold, zipped up in a black bag, burrowed into my brain like a tick and refused to let go. I took a deep, steadying breath so the macabre thought didn't show on my face.

Keep it together, Stone.

"It's in number four," Wyatt said.

He crossed to the wall of doors and stopped near the top one, far right. He pulled the door lever and it creaked open with a hiss and burst of cool air. I waited a few feet away while he pulled the tray out, along with the black bag on top of it. It put the body at about chest-level.

"Evy, is this freaking you out?"

A snappy "no" resisted passing my lips. Wyatt would know I was lying. Even before he was infected by a Lupa bite and gained a few enhanced senses, it had been hard to lie to Wyatt. He knew me better than anyone, and despite all of the bullshit we'd dealt with in the last few months, he still loved me. And I loved him back in the best, fiercest possible way, so I decided to go against type and be honest.

"Yeah, a little bit," I said.

"I'm sorry I wasn't there when you woke up."

"I know. You've apologized for that already, and you're forgiven. It's just seeing everything again is giving me this bizarre sense of déjà vu."

"We didn't have to take this assignment."

"Yes, we did."

In the last two weeks, we'd been monitoring and investigating a sudden rise in goblin-related attacks—not only on innocent humans, but also on the occasional Therian and half-Blood vampire. The goblin Hordes hadn't been a threat for months, not since a mountainside battle at an old nature preserve killed one of their queens and a huge chunk of her forces. No one expected them to go underground forever, but we hadn't been prepared for the sheer number and viciousness of the new attacks.

With the loss of the vampire Families and their support of the Watchtower, our combined forces had been drained by nearly a third, and we had a difficult time finding new humans and Therians to join our ranks and help protect the city. Adding humans meant finding trustworthy people who could keep their big mouths shut about the existence of shape-shifters, vampires, goblins, gremlins, and various kinds of Fey. Not to mention possessing the necessary skills to track, fight, hunt, and kill.

The Therians...well, they were dealing with a few internal crises of their own, which made it hard to get support from more than half of the thirteen Clans on the Assembly. And without Clan Elder approval, an interested shape-shifter wasn't allowed to join.

Assembly politics made my head hurt.

So what had once been five-person squads (four members and a squad leader) were shrunk into four-person quads, managed from the Watchtower by three people who'd become the brains of our operation: Astrid Dane, a were-jaguar and granddaughter of the Felia Clan Elder; Adrian Baylor, a former Triad Handler with the build of a linebacker and the temper-control of a Buddhist monk; and Rufus St. James, another former Handler who'd finally agreed to work with us instead of sulking over an injury that had left him unable to walk without assistance. The three of them handed out quad assignments, and they made decisions based on the intel we returned to them.

So far the system was working. A few of us referred to our three esteemed leaders as Cerberus, the multi-headed dog that guards the gate to Hades. Considering we basically worked to keep hell monsters from taking over the city, it fit. We just didn't call them Cerberus to their faces.

Quad Two (us) and Quad Four (not us) were assigned to the goblin issue, even though what I really wanted to be doing was looking for a cure for the illness plaguing our vampire allies. But I was a soldier, not a general, so goblins it was. Our two quads were chosen because between the eight of us, we had the most experience dealing with goblins. Wyatt, Milo Gant, and I had all partaken in the massive nature preserve battle in May that pitted us against a shit-ton of goblin warriors—plus all of our combined Triad-related experience in hunting and killing the nasty beasts. The fourth member of our quad, Marcus Dane, made up for his lack of goblin slaughtering hours with his sharp senses, strength, and the two-hundred-pound black jaguar he shifted into.

Marcus and Milo were waiting at different places in the hospital, acting as lookouts so Wyatt and I didn't get caught by any of the hospital staff. Marcus hated playing lookout, though, so thinking of him standing in a corridor somewhere, bored out of his mind, made me grin.

"What?" Wyatt asked. He was still watching me, one gloved hand poised to pull down the zipper on the black bag.

"Nothing." I moved to stand on the opposite side of the tray. "Let's do this and get out of here."

"Good plan." He pulled the zipper tab, its teeth snicking open with an ominous staccato, then pushed the sides of the bag out of the way.

The police report we'd intercepted said the teenage boy had died of an animal attack—like so many of the others. Sooner or later the explanation wasn't going to fly anymore, because we lived in a big damned city, not the middle of the Everglades. Cities had rats, pigeons and alley cats, not carnivorous beasts who could rip a human to pieces half-a-block from a busy street without a single pedestrian hearing the fight.

Unless you lived in our city. Then there was a good chance your neighbor could shift into an animal, that the tall, pale-skinned woman with the white-blond hair was actually a vampire, and that a gremlin really did screw up your wireless internet last night.

The body in the bag definitely looked like it could have been ripped apart by a wild animal. Or in this particular case, a couple of goblins. The teen's face was mostly gone, torn to ribbons of flesh and muscle, some down to the bone. His throat was slashed in several places. The majority of his T-shirt was gone, exposing a torso that looked like cubed steak, and a slashed abdomen with hints of exposed intestine.

And it only got worse the further down Wyatt pulled the bag's zipper. The teen's groin was covered in bite marks—too small to be a dog, but just the right size to be goblin teeth, which was our first big clue. Except for the deep bruising and scrapes on his knees, the front of his legs were mostly unscathed. Wyatt checked the backs of his legs.

"Thighs are pretty cut up," he said. He glanced up higher and his eyes narrowed. "Dammit."

I knew his tones too well. A surprised "dammit" would have prompted me to ask what he saw. The resigned, almost sad way he'd said it told me what he'd seen. I didn't need him to say it.

In goblin society, females are both rare and revered, much like the queen ant of an ant colony. It means only the most elite goblin warriors get to mate. And human bodies are not designed to handle hooked appendages of any kind. It was the worst kind of agony any human being could endure before they died, and I could say that from my own goddamn experience.

I closed my eyes against the visual and mental assault. Six months ago, I'd have shrugged at the torture and gone about my job hunting and killing the goblins responsible. But I'd been through too much this summer, changed too much to be so unaffected by the violence that permeated my life. Empathy for this boy—someone I didn't know, but who'd died so horribly by the same monsters who'd tortured and killed me once—choked me.

Warm arms wrapped around me from behind and I leaned against Wyatt's chest, hands coming up to squeeze his where they clasped over my heart. A heart that was pounding too damned hard. He pressed his chin to my left shoulder, and I inhaled the familiar scent of him—coffee and cinnamon, and the new earthiness of his werewolf half.

"I can finish this up," he whispered.

"I'm fine, I just need a second."

I could hear all of the things he wasn't saying: *You shouldn't have come in here with me, I should have brought Milo, I hate that you're reliving this, goddamn fucking goblins.* It was all in the way his arms tightened, as though he could hug away all the painful memories. And I loved him for it. I loved him for a lot of reasons.

"There's more than enough proof that this was a goblin attack," I said, opening my eyes and straightening up.

Wyatt let go and shifted to stand next to me, the concern still plain on his face. "Agreed," he said. "The goblins are getting bolder. Estimated time of death was five o'clock this evening."

And considering it was late August, that meant broad daylight. Goblins used to only come out at night, preferring to spend the day down in the sewers. This was seriously bad news.

He reached for the zipper and started tugging it up. Just past the dead boy's knees he stopped. Leaned down to peer at something. "Evy, look at this."

I stepped around him and followed his gaze to a spot on the body's inner thigh. At first, all I saw were a bunch of deep cuts, like razor slices. But as I stared, they turned into letters. And then a word.

Kelsa.

"Fuck me," I said.

Kelsa was the goblin Queen who'd ordered me captured, tortured, raped and left to die, all at the orders of an elf whose grand plan included stealing Wyatt's free will. I killed her a few months ago, at the same time the rest of the goblins went underground. Seeing her name carved on the leg of a dead human said one clear thing to me: this was fucking personal.

***

After Wyatt took a few pictures of the carved name with his phone, we put the body back and then got the hell out of there. I texted Milo and Marcus that we were leaving, so they'd meet us at the arranged location.

They were already waiting when we arrived, leaning against the metal barrier that protected one side of the sidewalk from a steep drop into the Anjean River, as though they had every right to be loitering there at one-thirty in the morning. The rush of the river below us was the only real sound as Wyatt and I made our way toward them.

I was still a little shaky after our morgue trip and had broken a sweat the instant we stepped outside into the humid late-summer air. Usually I'm better at hiding my immediate need to vomit, but I must not have been doing a very good job on approach because Milo stood up straight as soon as he got a good look.

"Evy?" he said.

"I'm okay," I replied.

"That bad?"

"Worse, but it was definitely goblins."

"This behavior is extremely unusual," Marcus said. He hadn't moved from his casual lean against the rail, and the female in me appreciated the way he could make such a simple stance look sexy. Marcus was tall and muscular (but not muscle bound), with tan skin and long, black hair he liked to wear in a ponytail at the nape of his neck. A little bit of scruff on his chin—not quite a goatee, but more than a soul patch—gave him a look I could only describe as "pirate."

Contrast to Milo Gant, who was about my height of five-foot-seven, and lean enough to occasionally appear scrawny, despite his speed and strength. He had sandy brown hair and brown eyes that, once upon a time, I'd have described as kind. Nowadays they were mostly cold. Mostly, depending on the company he kept. Lately Marcus was one of the only people who could make Milo smile.

"There was more," Wyatt said and held out his phone. "They're making this personal for Evy."

Marcus studied the image, while Milo blanched and looked away—the photo did have an unfortunate angle of the dead man's mangled testicles. "What's your assessment?" Marcus asked.

"That whatever's happening isn't random," Wyatt replied. "We know the goblin warriors can't plan for shit, so at least one of the Queens has been cooking this up for a while. Maybe since Kelsa died."

"Could it be tied to the Fey?"

"Possibly. They followed orders from an elf once, so it isn't outside the realm of possibility for them to follow the orders of a sprite."

My temper began a slow burn, as it always did when I thought about Amalie and how the Fey Council had betrayed and lied to us since first contact more than ten years ago. The Triads had been duped and manipulated to serve their whims, and while the Fey were pacifists who couldn't attack us directly, they'd put a lot of other enemies directly into our path. Sending the goblins against us was not beneath them.

"It definitely gives them a more controllable way to hit us than with the Halfies," Milo said. "Even the Halfies that are still partly sane." He said the word "Halfies" like it was a vile taste in his mouth—the way he'd said it for the last five weeks. Since Felix died.

Instead of dropping off with the death of Walter Thackery and the loss of his Happy Serum—meant to make typically deranged half-Bloods act in a rational manner—the Halfie population had seemed to increase. It was as if the handful of sane Halfies we hadn't managed to execute had gone forth and multiplied, and created more sane Halfies.

You might think sane Halfies would be preferable to crazy ones, but not for me. Crazy means they don't plan ahead, and they almost always screw up in some way or another. Sane means higher thought and the ability to formulate a plan of action. Halfies with plans scared the hell out of me.

"I just wish they'd man up and come at us head on," I said, referring to the Fey. "All of this puppeteer bullshit is getting old."

"Agreed," Marcus said. "The Fey are irritating and cowardly. Therians fight for what they want. We don't have the luxury of living for millennia, as the Fey do."

Milo glanced at Marcus, and the pair shared a look I couldn't decipher. They'd become good friends in the last few weeks, and they spent a lot of their free time sparring in the Watchtower gym. Physically, Marcus looked like he was in his mid-thirties, but he was only ten calendar years old—which put him at the halfway point of his life. And even though I'd seen a were-osprey grow from newborn to toddler in only a few months, a twenty-year life expectancy wasn't an easy thing to remember daily.

"The Fey are cowards," Wyatt said in a deadly voice. "We'll find a way to make Amalie accountable for the things she's done and the suffering she's caused." Including his own suffering. Putting every betrayal of the Triads aside, Amalie had protected the Lupa pups who'd infected Wyatt, which made her responsible for his change. Every time I saw Wyatt struggling to control his wolf, to maintain his humanity when the animal seemed stronger, I renewed my vow to be there the day Amalie paid her dues.

Unless we all died before that happened, which was entirely possible.

"So we got what we needed on the body," Milo said after a moment of awkward silence. "Assignment complete?"

"Assignment complete," I said. "Can we hit a drive-thru on the way back? I need a burger."

"It's one-thirty in the morning."

"So?" After inheriting a new, untrained body and then suffering three weeks of hideous torture (and a fifteen pound weight loss) less than two months after that, I was now finally (finally!) at a healthy weight and had some pretty awesome muscle tone going on. I deserved a big, greasy burger once in a while.

"I could eat," Wyatt said. "We'll swing by that place on Tenth. It's open all night, I think."

We split up for the walk back to the car, making two potential targets instead of one. Wyatt and I went west up the block, toward the hospital, while Marcus and Milo went east. We'd all turn north at the next respective street, go up a block and double back to where we'd parked.

It was a short, quiet walk. Wyatt and I had gotten to a place in our evolving relationship where we didn't need to fill silences with idle chatter. He knew that if I wanted to talk about the body we'd seen tonight, I'd bring it up in my own time. Forcing me to do anything only made me kick back in the opposite direction. It was a fatal flaw that had gotten me in trouble almost as much as it had saved my life.

We reached the car first, which set off internal alarms immediately. Marcus and Milo should have at least been visible on this side street, with its random parked cars and overflowing trash cans waiting for an early morning dump.

Somewhere down the block a large cat snarled. Wyatt and I took off running.

CHAPTER TWO

1:55 a.m.

We were too late.

Or right on time, depending on who you asked. It must have been a brief battle, because when Wyatt and I raced around the corner and spotted our friends, the fight was over. Halfway down the block, three torn and bleeding bodies were scattered on the sidewalk, limbs askew (one of them separated from the rest of itself), and very much dead. Halfies from the look of them—and the way they were slowly starting to shrivel.

Milo was sitting against the bumper of a parked car, with a naked Marcus crouched in front of him. He slapped away Marcus's hands with a sharp, "I'm fine, okay?"

"You went headfirst into the car," Marcus replied.

"Not my first time, believe me. I'm fine." He spotted us, then rolled his eyes. At what or who, exactly, I wasn't sure.

"What happened?" I asked, even though it was pretty obvious.

"The half-Bloods were well-hidden," Marcus said. "We didn't realize we were being stalked until they attacked."

He hadn't turned to look at us, so I stared blankly at the back of his head. It wasn't like Marcus to be unaware of his surroundings, or to fall victim to a sneak attack. What the hell had them both so distracted that they hadn't seen the Halfies coming?

"One of them latched onto my back like a fucking tick," Milo said, rubbing at the side of his neck with one hand. "Tried to bite me, so I ran us both hard into the side of the car. Knocked myself silly for it, too." He sounded like he'd rather chew glass than admit such a thing.

"I shifted and took care of the problem," Marcus added. He finally turned his head and angled to look up at us, and I saw the blood streaking his chin and neck like grotesque war paint. "Will you tell him—"

"Oh, for Christ's sake." Milo pushed sideways and stood up with perfect ease. Not a single wobble. He stepped around Marcus and presented himself to me and Wyatt. "I'm fine, see?"

He looked fine. Pupils normal size for the darkness of the alley, no blood in his hair or on his face. Except for an expression stuck somewhere between anger and mortification, he seemed normal enough. "You got a knot?" I asked.

Milo touched the side of his head. "No, it's barely sore. I did not lose consciousness, either."

I pulled his other hand away from the side of his neck, where he'd been rubbing. The skin was red, but not broken. "What's that?"

"It's where the fucker tried to bite me."

As he said the words, I finally saw how hard Milo was working to keep it together. He'd been one good lunge away from getting infected and ending up a half-Blood—all because the pair of them hadn't been paying attention. Almost two months ago, he'd seen his best friend Felix bitten and infected, and two weeks later had witnessed Felix's final death. And even though he'd never revealed his feelings to Felix, Milo had been in love with him.

The loss had been devastating and had placed a near-permanent coldness in Milo's eyes.

I gave his hand a squeeze before letting go. "He didn't bite you."

"No." He squared his shoulders, then glanced at Marcus. "Thanks for the save."

"It was my error as well," Marcus replied. He walked a few feet away and grabbed his discarded jeans.

The more I worked with Therians, the less their frequent nudity bothered me. Not that most of them (especially the men) had anything to be modest about, but us humans still had some hang-ups about wandering around in our birthday suits. Not so much with shape-shifters.

"Did they say anything at all?" Wyatt asked, waving his hand to indicate the bodies.

"One of them had a few choice words when I ripped his arm off," Marcus said. "Other than that, no. Nothing of consequence."

"They were probably hungry and looking for dinner," Milo said.

I crouched next to one—a teenager, with a buzz cut and lots of silver rings in his left ear. Pulled back his upper lip to take a look at his teeth. "Young, too, or they would have smelled that Marcus wasn't human," I said. It took several weeks for a half-Blood's fangs to develop to full length, which made it easy to pick out the fresh ones. And this kid's teeth were barely pointed.

"Let's clean this up so we can get out of here," Milo said.

"Good idea." I stood up, then noticed Wyatt staring intently at the roof of a building down the block. "Wyatt?"

He didn't reply. I took a step closer and tracked his gaze, but didn't see anything amiss. Not that I had his werewolf vision, but still.

"Wyatt?"

"What?" He blinked hard, then looked at me.

"Did you see something?"

"I thought I did."

His confusion made me uneasy, and even more eager to get this scene clean and get back to the Watchtower. I didn't like the idea of being watched. None of us did.

It never led anywhere pleasant.

***

The burger joint, it turned out, closed at two, so we settled on invading the cafeteria as soon as we got back to the Watchtower. Wyatt made our report over the phone during the drive back, including the little Halfie skirmish. He rode shotgun, while Marcus drove. That left me and Milo in the backseat, him slumped against the passenger side door and me biting my tongue to keep from bugging him with questions. Milo had become my best friend in the last month or so, and the only thing that kept me quiet was knowing he wouldn't tell me anything with Wyatt and Marcus in the car.

So I kept my questions and my glances to myself until we were alone, glad to have something other than our most recent goblin victim to think about.

The Watchtower was a somewhat deceptive name, since our headquarters was built inside the skeleton of the old Capital City Mall. Shaped like a long, wide U with department stores on both ends and a magic glamour that kept straying eyes from noticing our activity there, the mall was the perfect place to house a hundred humans and Therians. Living quarters and bathrooms had been built inside old storefronts, as well as a gymnasium, a weapons locker, a refurbished jail (our first jail got blown up), and the sprawling Operations center.

Marcus drove into the canyon of the U and right through what looked like an old restaurant patio. The glamour tickled my skin, as it always did when we passed, and we drove into a wide parking area. The sense of awe I'd once felt at what they'd created here, out of the bones of an old structure, didn't come as often. But the whole thing was still damned impressive.

He parked, and we all tumbled out as a group. Like the city we tried to protect, the Watchtower never really slept. Even at almost three in the morning, the hum of activity buzzed in the corridors. Most of it seemed centered around Operations, which was the norm, as well as down the east branch of the corridor—the way to the cafeteria and living quarters.

We were halfway to the cafeteria when Marcus's cell phone rang. He pulled it out without breaking stride, glanced at the display, then replied with a quick, "Yep?" A few seconds passed before he stopped walking.

The rest of us paused, too.

"On my way." Marcus closed his phone. He didn't seem upset, only curious. "Astrid needs to see me. I'll catch up with you in a bit."

He pivoted neatly and marched back in the direction we'd come. We continued on. Only a handful of people were in the cafeteria, sitting in small clusters. The available food at this hour was mostly wrapped sandwiches or hot dogs off a little roller cooker that looked like it was stolen from a convenience store, so I grabbed two hot dogs and a bag of potato chips.

Wyatt took four hot dogs, plus a tuna fish sandwich, and two bags of chips. I smiled at the laden tray, still amused at how his appetite had increased since becoming half-Lupa. Contrasting both of us, Milo grabbed a soda and nothing else. Our trio invaded a table where Tybalt Monahan and Kyle Jane were seated and finishing their own snacks.

Both seemed agitated and not because of our arrival. "What's up?" I asked as I sat down across from Tybalt. Wyatt took the seat on my right, while Milo sat next to Tybalt.

Tybalt and Kyle shared a look. They worked together on Quad Four, and if their night had been anything like ours….

"Rough night," Tybalt said.

"Bullshit," Milo replied. He popped the soda tab, then glared at Tybalt. "Try again, pal." The pair had been friends for more than a year and a half, and had worked together in the defunct Triads. They knew each other well enough to spot the half-truths.

Tybalt frowned. He reached out with his prosthetic hand and turned Milo's head to the side, exposing the red mark on his neck. "What's that? Love bite?"

"Close encounter." Milo pulled away and gave Tybalt a hard look. "Don't change the subject."

"It's not our place to share this kind of news."

"It'll become common knowledge soon, anyway," Kyle said. "And Marcus is their quad-mate."

Milo's stare became more intense, and my own interest piqued exponentially. "What about Marcus?" he asked.

"Elder Dane is stepping down from the Assembly," Tybalt said. "He has the Shadow."

The Shadow is what Therians called the cancer that only affects their people. It kills quickly and is incurable. About five months ago, the same illness had killed Seamus Dane, the former Pride Alpha, and his son Keenan (Marcus and Astrid's cousin) had taken over the role of Alpha. Elder Marcellus Dane had been Seamus's uncle, and also Marcus and Astrid's grandfather.

From what I understood of most Clan politics, the role of Elder was passed from parent to child, in order to avoid a lengthy voting processes—and any sort of lengthy process was avoided by Therians, considering their average life spans.

"He's dying," Milo said.

"Yeah." Tybalt picked up his fork and poked at the remnants of something on his plate. He'd been raised by the Felia Pride, within the Dane family specifically (something I'd only learned from him recently), and then kicked out when he was sixteen. He found the Triads soon after and was taken in by another kind of family. The loss of another father figure had to hurt, after losing Seamus earlier in the year.

"Who's in line to take over as Elder?" Wyatt asked.

"That's the problem," Tybalt replied. "Elder Dane has no surviving children."

"So wouldn't the title of Elder pass to Marcus or Astrid?" I asked. "They're his grandchildren."

"It's supposed to."

"But?"

Tybalt pressed his lips together, and I saw a spark of anger in his eyes. "But Elder Dane wants to ensure the Elder title remains within the family line. Since Astrid and Marcus are both unmarried and childless, as well as at the half-point of their lives, Dane has named a younger cousin in their place. Keenan's brother, Riley."

"Hell," Milo said.

Keenan was the current Pride Alpha and Elder Dane's grand-nephew. Giving the title to Riley instead of one of Dane's own grandchildren was pretty harsh.

"Would either of them have even wanted the position?" I asked, pretty certain the answer was no.

"That's not the point," Tybalt said.

"No, I see the point, and I understand why you're upset. But my question still stands."

"I don't think either would have wanted to be Elder, no. But this is also a public announcement, and it's a public embarrassment. Astrid's choice to protect the Clan, rather than be a mother, was never a popular one. Female Felia who don't have children are considered second-class."

I bit back hard on a scorching comment on the status of feminism within the Clans. My opinion on women, Felia or not, as nothing more than baby incubators had no place in the current conversation. I'd vent it out in the gym later.

Kyle flinched. His girlfriend, Lynn Neil, was Felia as well, and the simple fact that she was dating a Cania (a were-dog, instead of a fellow were-cat) meant she had eschewed tradition and forgone having children—as long as she was with Kyle, anyway. The Therian Clans simply could not inter-breed; it wasn't genetically possible.

My respect for Lynn went way up.

"And Astrid doesn't want to be a mother," I said.

Tybalt made a scrunched face I couldn't readily decipher. "Astrid's past is complicated. At one time she was promised to Keenan, but she never wanted to be the Alpha's mate."

"Keenan is the current Alpha of the Felia."

"Yes."

"And her grandfather is Keenan's uncle?"

"Yes."

"So Keenan is her cousin."

Tybalt seemed to see where I was going with that, and he deferred the topic to Kyle. Kyle shrugged both shoulders, unconcerned. "Clans are small, enclosed societies compared to humans.

And before you judge, don't forget that it was once acceptable for humans to marry one's first cousin."

Yeah, like two hundred years ago, and maybe still in other countries. But I got his point, too, and who the hell was I to judge who other Felia married? "So she ditched her cousin for the single life," I said. "What about Marcus? He's handsome enough that I bet he could find a wife with no trouble and pop out a litter of kittens."

"That's not what Marcus wants," Milo said, surprising me by being the one to answer. Even Tybalt gave him an assessing look.

"How do you know?" I asked.

Milo held my gaze steadily and opened his mouth.

"Because I told him so," came the reply from the topic of conversation himself. And he wasn't alone.

Marcus and another man stopped behind Tybalt's chair. The stranger had the same black hair and strong, square face as Marcus, but he carried himself differently. Higher, more proudly. *I'll swallow my tongue if they aren't related.*

"This is Keenan Dane," Marcus said. "Our Pride Alpha." He introduced me, Wyatt, and Milo. I guessed Tybalt and Kyle knew him already.

"To what do we owe the pleasure of your visit, Alpha Dane?" Kyle asked with a heavy amount of respect in his voice.

"Family business," Keenan said. "Business of which you were just now discussing?"

No one denied it. Keenan took a seat on Kyle's left. Marcus circled around the table and plunked heavily into the empty chair next to Milo, weariness weighing him down. Tension from Keenan's unexpected arrival wafted over the table like a fog.

I picked up my hot dog and took a big bite. Wyatt had already polished off two hot dogs and one bag of chips, and he was starting in on the tuna fish sandwich. Even though he seemed to be concentrating on his food, I knew he was paying attention to everything said at the table.

"I'm sorry about your grandfather," Milo said in a gentle voice that made me look up from my food. To Keenan, he added, "And your great uncle."

"Thank you," Keenan said.

Marcus tilted his head in Milo's direction in an acknowledging nod. "It's his time. The Shadow seems to run particularly strong in our family, and Marcellus is twenty-one." Same age as Milo. And that was a truly bizarre observation. "Riley will make a strong Elder, if he manages to not get killed."

"Killed?" I said it at the same time as Milo and Tybalt, our three voices a squawk of protest that might have been funny if the word wasn't so serious.

"The Bengals," Tybalt said. "Have they challenged Riley?"

"Not formally, not yet," Keenan said. "That's why I'm here. I wanted to discuss the possibility with Astrid and Marcus. They were once elite guards in the Pride, and I value their tactical input."

"It's possible someone is picking up where Prentiss failed," Marcus said.

Prentiss? The name didn't ding any bells for me.

"So it seems."

"Hold on a minute," I said, knocking my knuckles on the table. "How about a little back story for the rest of us? Should I know about this? Who's Prentiss?"

"No," Tybalt said. "The thing with Prentiss went down while you were, uh, missing. Before you died. The first time."

Translation: while I was being tortured to death by goblins. Got it.

"Several months ago," Keenan said, "when it became known that my father Seamus was ill with the Shadow, his position as Alpha was challenged by a man named Prentiss. His true form is a Bengal tiger, and the entire family is quite…"

"Fanatical?" Tybalt said.

"A less polite word comes to mind, but yes. They don't like change, and they are quite rigid in their view of Pride roles. Our families have clashed often over the last few generations."

Pride roles. Just the way he said it made my eye twitch. "Such as Astrid choosing to not marry and be a mother?" I asked.

"Among other things," Tybalt said. "They weren't very fond of Seamus taking me in, either, and they let me know it as often as possible."

"But Prentiss obviously didn't win the position of Alpha from Seamus." I was staring right at the current Alpha. "What happened?"

"As the Alpha's son," Keenan said, "I was allowed to answer the challenge and fight in my father's stead, only I kidnapped by Prentiss's people."

With a nod from Keenan, Marcus took over the storytelling. "With Tybalt's help, and with a little covert assistance from Milo, we were able to locate and free Keenan. Prentiss was captured and executed by the Assembly for treason."

"Those who we could not prove were involved then are likely responsible for sowing the seeds of discontent among several other Felia families now."

Kyle made a frustrated snort. "That nonsense with Belle back in June didn't improve Felia unity, either."

That nonsense was the kidnapping of two Therians from my personal care, because Belle and a few of her friends decided that Therians protected Therians, and the personal freedoms of the kidnappees meant jack shit. Belle also tried to kill me and got shot for her trouble, then turned over to the Assembly of Clan Elders for punishment.

"Other Felia agreed with what Belle did?" Wyatt asked, finally taking part in the conversation.

"Not with her methods, but with her rhetoric, yes," Keenan said. "And Felia isn't the only Clan experiencing division on the topic of human-Therian relations, especially with the Fey threat looming over all of us."

"They blame humans for what the Fey are doing."

"Some, yes. Others are using Michael Jenner's murder as an excuse to pull support from the Watchtower. It's become extremely complicated."

The bit about Jenner didn't surprise me. He was the mouth-piece for the Assembly, the one who went into the field and issued directives on their behalf. We never got to be friends, exactly, but he let me recover in his apartment after I got caught in an explosion. He didn't deserve to die the way he did, at the mercy of a (very literal) mad scientist.

"What happens if Riley is challenged for Elder and loses?" Milo asked.

Marcus's expression turned thunderous. "Then the Watch-tower will lose Felia support."

Felia made up a good quarter of our Therian members. Never mind the fact that Astrid was one of our leaders, and I was kind of fond of Marcus, too. And from the identical look of outrage of Milo's face, I wasn't the only one.

"Let me guess," Wyatt said. "The loss of Felia support will cause a cascade effect within the Assembly, and very soon there will be a majority vote pulling all Therian support. Is that the general direction this is going?"

"In a nutshell, yes," Keenan said.

"Fuck," I said, torn between anger and fear over a potential outcome that meant tragedy for the city. "We can't do this without the Therians."

Wyatt took my right hand and squeezed it hard. I held on, ignoring the little smile tugging at the corners of his mouth. Yes, it was probably funny hearing me say that, considering six months ago the only Therian I trusted was a young were-falcon named Danika. But it was true. The Watchtower had been hatched by Therians and vampires, and humans were invited in later. The humans-only Triads had already failed.

We could *not* do this alone.

"Is Riley a good fighter?" Wyatt asked.

"He's an excellent fighter," Keenan replied. "I'd match him against the best in the Pride, myself included. But this is also the best chance for a change in leadership, and the challenger will make sure of a victory."

"You mean they'll cheat?"

"Yes. "

"Where is Riley now?"

"At our family compound with our great uncle. Until he has officially been granted the title of Elder, Riley is safest there. The home is well protected."

It was protected and then some. It was the only reason I agreed to allow Aurora, Ava and Joseph to live there. They were the last of the Coni Clan of shape-shifting birds-of-prey—except for Phineas, who was off who knows where, doing hell knows what. He'd been gone for five weeks, and I missed him.

"Are you supposed to be wandering around with all this going on?" I asked before I could wonder if the question was rude or not.

Keenan's lips twitched. "Trust me, I am well protected."

"So we're at a standstill on this," Tybalt said. "Even if the Bengals challenged Marcellus now for Elder, Riley would fight in his place, and he stands a high chance of winning. There's no benefit to an early challenge."

"No, there's not." Marcus drummed his fingers against the tabletop, his irritation coming out in that short, jerky motion. "We have no way of knowing when the challenge will be issued."

No way of knowing when the last protection force for the city might suddenly find itself without half its members, leaving all humans vulnerable to attacks from goblins and half-Bloods.

"Is there a way to identify the potential challengers and, you know, encourage them to back off?" I asked.

"Everything we know so far is hearsay," Marcus said. "There's no proof, only rumors. And without proof of wrong-doing, the Assembly will punish any action taken, even as a pre-emptive measure."

"I wasn't talking about busting kneecaps or leaving horse's heads in their beds."

Marcus bristled (almost literally), and I realized he didn't understand the film reference. He probably thought I was making some tasteless joke about Jenner's death (which I wasn't). Shit.

"Evy means talking to them, not bullying them," Wyatt said, stepping in to save me before I crammed my foot any further down my own throat. "Informing them of the consequences of any actions taken against Riley."

"Threats will only strengthen their resolve," Marcus said. "It's not a good idea."

"So we do what?" Milo asked. "Sit and wait and hope they don't cheat when they send someone to fight Riley?"

"Yes."

"That plan sucks ass."

Marcus's mouth twitched. "Regardless, it's our only course of action right now. Our people don't need more inner turmoil, so we'll wait for the challenge."

Milo snapped the tab off the top of his soda can, then flipped it between his knuckles a few times. "I fucking hate waiting," he said.

We all hated waiting, but on this we had no choice.

***

Our table broke up a while later. Keenan whisked himself away to parts unknown, probably his aforementioned family home. Tybalt and Kyle headed off to their respective rooms; Wyatt wanted to stop by Operations and talk to Astrid and Baylor about everything going on; Marcus shuffled off somewhere with an intense look on his face. I was too keyed up to sleep, so I wandered toward the opposite end of the mall and the exercise and training rooms down the far leg of the U. It took a few seconds to realize Milo had fallen into step next to me.

"How's your head?" I asked.

"Nothing a few hours sleep won't cure."

"So why aren't you heading toward the bunks?"

"Too much energy to sleep."

I know the feeling. "Spot you?"

"Sure."

The exercise area was two rooms. The first was full of weights and various stationary bikes and other machines. Almost anything you could want in a gym. The second room, at the rear of the first, had a dance barre on one wall for stretching and coordination techniques, and blue mats covered the floor. I'd spent almost a solid week in that room, mostly on my ass, while Phineas kicked it hard trying to get me back into fighting form after I'd been tortured for three weeks.

Ah, memories.

Two other people where there, riding the bikes, and I smiled through a strange sense of déjà vu. Shelby and Jackson had been working out in the gym the very first time Milo and I ever saw it, and there they were again. Shelby and Jackson were both Ursia (were-bears), and while I liked the latter a whole lot, the former still made my skin crawl sometimes. Like the polar bear in Shelby was always sizing me up as a meal.

We all exchanged friendly greetings. I'd worked with both Shelby and Jackson in the field, and they were among the dozen or so Therians working with us whom I mostly trusted. I don't give my trust easily. It has to be earned, and they were almost there. Shelby had a little more work to do than Jackson. Astrid, Marcus, and absentee-Phineas? Total trust. Everyone else was on a case-by-case. Most I trusted on a limited basis solely because Astrid vouched for them.

Milo and I used a freestanding folding screen as cover to change into sweats that always seemed to be on hand there. He adjusted the weights on one of the bars, settled himself on the bench, and I stood over him as he pressed himself into a sweat. We didn't talk, but I knew the look on his face.

He was angry about the Felia news, yes, but he was also punishing himself for earlier. For letting those Halfies get close enough to put that bruise on his forehead and mark on his neck.

When his face was red, sweat was trickling down his cheeks, and his reps had slowed too much for safety, I grabbed the bar and guided it back into the support. "Take a break, pal, before you hurt yourself."

He lay there a moment, arms dangling, staring up at the ceiling. I didn't bug him until he'd gotten his breathing back under control. I leaned down, dropping my voice until it was barely audible over the whirring noise of the bikes. "So you helped out the Felia Clan, huh?"

"Didn't know it at the time." Milo sat up and spun around on the bench to face me, hands on his knees. "It was actually the day before you were found at the train station, when Tybalt called and asked me to get some information for him. I didn't ask why, and he didn't tell me about it all until a few weeks ago when—" He stopped himself, then shrugged.

Now I was crazy curious. The train station referred to the place I was held captive and tortured by goblins, then left to die—my first death. That was months ago, though. Or technically, maybe a lifetime. "When what?" I asked.

He picked at a healing scab on his knee, courtesy of a hard tumble last week. "I asked him how he knew Marcus so well, and he finally told me the whole story."

It was a story I wouldn't mind having. I knew Tybalt had been raised by the Felia, and that he'd chosen his own name when he was eleven. I knew he'd been close with Marcus and Astrid before his banishment from the Pride, and that he hadn't had contact with them for six years prior to this spring. And rumor was he and Astrid once had a fling, back when they were both teenagers—which was a weird thought, given that Tybalt was going on twenty-three and Astrid looked like she was in her late thirties. But like the rest of us, Tybalt didn't like talking about himself.

Another little detail hadn't escaped my attention, and it created a funny little mix of hope and worry. "You were asking about Marcus?"

His eyes narrowed. "So?"

"Do you like him?"

"Sure, I do."

"I don't mean as a quad-mate, dumbass."

He stared at me with an expression I couldn't figure out, like he was thinking about denying it but was tired of not being honest. "I like him," he finally said in a tone that said the topic was over, so I let it go. But I couldn't help thinking back to earlier, when he said marriage and a litter of kittens wasn't what Marcus wanted.

I almost asked Milo about the specifics of this state of "like," considering how things had turned out with Felix. Or rather, hadn't turned out. Milo had allowed himself to fall in love with a man who couldn't love him back—not in the same, romantic way, at any rate. I didn't want Milo to fall into the same trap with Marcus. Therians lived incredibly short lives and procreation was expected of everyone in order to ensure the survival of the Clans; I'd never before heard of a gay Therian. Which really meant nothing, considering how little I collectively knew about Therians, anyway, and—

Speak of the devil.

Marcus rumbled into the gym like a thundercloud. He spotted us and seemed to relax just a little. I tilted my head. He came over, already dressed in sweats, his entire body coiled tight. "Couldn't sleep, either?" I said.

"No," Marcus replied. Milo twisted halfway around to see, and it was to Milo that Marcus added, "Astrid and I will be visiting Elder Dane in the morning to pay our respects, and to offer our support to Riley. How's your head?"

"Still attached," Milo replied.

Marcus quirked a slender eyebrow. "So I see. Pain?"

"Just one in my neck." *You* dangled at the end of the statement. "I'm serious."

"Well, stop already. There's enough seriousness to go around. My head's fine, so stop worrying about it, for fuck's sake."

I stayed quiet, too amused by the friendly bickering to distract them. I also noted that both Jackson and Shelby had abandoned their bikes and were taking their time wiping down with towels. Probably listening. Damned Therian hearing. I caught Jackson's eye, gave him a glare, and he hustled Shelby out of the gym.

"Then how about a few rounds on the mats?" Marcus asked.

Marcus liked to wrestle. He was really fucking good at it, too, and he'd handed me my ass twice while I was still in post-torture training. Now I could hold my own, but I couldn't pin the bastard. Yet. One day I'd get the chance to win, but it wouldn't be today. Because he'd asked Milo.

"You sure you want to, old man?" Milo asked in a perfectly reasonable voice. "Don't think I'll take it easy on you because you got bad news."

"I know you won't take it easy on me. I think I need the challenge."

"It's your ass on the mat."

I couldn't see Milo's face as he got up and followed Marcus into the other room, but I heard the note of pleasure in his tone. And from the smile that kept quirking the corners of Marcus's mouth, he was looking forward to the battle, too. The first time the two ever sparred, Milo had hustled Marcus beautifully, luring the larger, more muscular were-cat into a sense of overconfidence just broad enough to trip and pin him in the third round. And it had been a beautiful pin.

Feeling a bit like an intruder this time and not entirely sure why, I left them to their wrestling.

CHAPTER THREE

12:30 pm

With Marcus and Astrid out of the Watchtower for a while, our quad was given a day off from official business. This meant Wyatt and I had a few hours to spend on the unofficial business of finding three teenage boys in a city of half a million people—three teens who just happened to shape-shift into werewolves, and whose bites were highly infectious (and deadly) to humans. Wyatt found that out the hard way five weeks ago when he was bitten.

After several hours in a painful fever, he woke up…different. With silver-rimmed eyes, enhanced senses, and the ability to affect a partial-shift that was probably the scariest thing I've ever seen in my life. I've seen some scary shit, things that would give people nightmares, but nothing compared to seeing his handsome face at odd angles, chin and neck covered in black fur, upper and lower jaw extended and full of sharp, deadly teeth. His eyes had gone completely silver, with a tiny red pupil. His fingernails had turned black and hard, and he'd actually grown a few inches in height.

He tried to describe the shift experience once: "Imagine the worst Charlie horse ever, all over your body, until the shift completes. Then imagine pins and needles racing up and down your limbs until you let yourself go back to normal. Everything's louder, sharper, like someone's messing with the focus on your computer screen, but you can't get it back to normal. It's awful, but it's also…freeing."

I didn't understand the "freeing" part. I couldn't see what was freeing about having a monster prowling around in your subconscious, ready to fight and attack at a moment's notice. Always angry, always hungry, always aroused—the first two he was letting me help him with. It was the third that made me want to whack him in the head with a solid object on a very regular basis. Lupa were apparently very sexual creatures, and they also mated for life. For complex reasons, Wyatt had declared me his mate to the Assembly several months ago, around the same time that we finally had the best sex ever.

Long story short: he wanted me, I wanted him, but he was still worried about controlling himself. I've been abused by a lot of people in the last couple of months. I was raped by a goblin. My pinkie finger was chopped off in the name of science. I was strapped to a table and tortured for three weeks. And the very last thing he wanted to do, Wyatt said over and over again, was to be another person who hurt me. Which was why every time we seemed to inch past the kissing and light petting stage, he shut back down.

It was also why I had a plan for later today; it was about damned time he stopped being so careful and let me take some control of our relationship. Maybe the timing wasn't ideal, given everything we were currently dealing with, but our lives never slowed down. There was no such thing as the perfect moment. We didn't get breaks for romance. I had to make this happen.

But first, teenager hunting.

Not as easy as it might seem, since the only information we had to go on were general descriptions (appeared between fifteen and seventeen years old, red hair, pale skin, tall and lanky) and names: John, Mark and Peter. The good news was that in the last five weeks, there had been no reports of animal attacks linked back to the Lupa pups. The bad news was that we had no reports of animal attacks linked back to the Lupa pups—no reports meant no leads. Our usual informants had nothing for us. The pups simply have not been seen.

And the disappearing act made me nervous. The man who raised them was dead. Half of their brothers were dead. The fact that they were given to a human by the Fey suggested they'd gone back to the Fey (or were taken by the Fey), but we had no way to verify that. So we were stuck driving around Mercy's Lot and hoping Wyatt's mental werewolf detector went off—some sort of telepathic link that exists among the Lupa packs. So far, no dice.

I turned onto Cottage Place and slowed a bit as we passed the empty storefront that had once been Old World Teas. Last month we'd busted the mage who ran the shop and given him a non-choice about getting the hell out of town. Brutus was a freelance magic worker who did spells and enchanted crystals, and he'd taken work from Wyatt on occasion. He'd also taken work from Walter Thackery and the Fey, and we were sympathetic enough to his sense of capitalism and the need to make a living that we didn't kill him outright.

The shop has been empty ever since.

A few blocks down, I spotted the familiar shape of my old residence. The building housed a couple of businesses, including a kitschy jewelry store, as well as the walk-up apartments on the second and third floors. I'd lived in one for four years with my old Triad partners Jesse and Ash. We'd abandoned it for good several months ago, but I couldn't stop a pang of guilt as I thought of my dead partners. And grief, too.

"Ash's birthday is next week," Wyatt said suddenly.

"Is it?" I was never good at remembering things like that, and our random birthday celebrations usually involved cheap cake and cheaper liquor, followed by maudlin comments about being happy to have made it to another birthday.

"Yeah. She'd have been twenty-eight."

It was a good age, since few Triad Hunters ever lived past twenty-two—kind of ironic, since that's how old I was when I died my first death. My new body was twenty-seven, and I had no idea when her (my?) birthday was.

"What's that face for?" Wyatt asked.

"Huh?" Had I been pulling a face?

"You looked confused for a second."

"Just wondering which birthday is technically mine now. When Evy Stone was born, or when Chalice Frost was born."

"What about May twentieth? The day you came back to me?"

I gave him a smile. "I can go with that."

His face went blank. "Stop."

"Stop what?"

"Stop the car."

I was in the middle of traffic and not very good at parallel parking, so I went up to the next block and found a small lot. He was already out the door before I shut off the engine, so I had to scramble to catch up. Back down the block. He was practically jogging. The foot traffic was pretty thin for a Sunday afternoon, but I still had to dodge a few bodies and angry glares.

"What is it?" I asked when I finally caught up with him.

He'd stopped across the street from our old building. His nostril twitched and his eyes were dilated. "I smell them. It's faint, but it's here."

"Right here?"

"Over there." He pointed at my old building.

I wasn't even going to ask if he was kidding, because I knew he wasn't. I steered him through traffic so he didn't get splattered by both his inability to find the crosswalk and his inattention to anything except the scent of those pups. He led us inside the dank, cement stairway that reeked of urine and sweat and old things—disgusting and familiar. I'd trod these steps a thousand times before in my old life, and a few times in my new one.

Wyatt pushed through the fire door at the top of the stairs, and we exited into a cement block corridor. Industrial doors marked the apartments, and we walked down to my old unit. He tilted his head, listening. "Their scent is here, but it's not fresh. I don't hear anyone inside."

"How would they know to come here? It's not like we ever introduced ourselves."

"It's possible one of them followed Jaron or Token here."

True. A few months ago, a goblin-human hybrid named Token had tracked the dying sprite Jaron to our apartment, and a little tussle had ensued. We learned later that Token was only one of many hybrid experiments being used by Walter Thackery. "Too bad they didn't leave a note taped to the door," I said.

"Maybe they left one inside."

"Something tells me the super changed the locks."

He smiled, then held his hand out, palm up, fingers pointed toward the lock. The air hummed with magical energy as Wyatt harnessed his Gift. Metal grated. The mechanism from the inside of the lock appeared on his palm, summoned right to him. He could only summon solid objects, and his control had been off a little since his change, but he was getting the hang of it again.

I turned the knob and the door opened. "You do realize this is officially breaking and entering?"

"It's not the first time."

"Good point."

So we broke into my old apartment. Which turned out to be okay, because it didn't look like anyone was living there except some squatters. It was empty of furniture and the appliances were missing from the kitchenette. The cement floor was scrubbed and bare. The only signs of our squatters were the pile of blankets in the far corner of the living room, and the black garbage bag overflowing with what looked like takeout containers. The place smelled closed up and stale, but not overwhelmingly gross, even with the old food containers.

I checked the window, which looked out onto a rusty fire escape. It was unlatched and open just wide enough to slide something thin through, like a pocket knife. "This must be how they get in and out," I said.

He'd crouched next to the blankets and held one close to his nose. "It's the pups." His eyes had gone perfectly silver.

"They're living here?"

"Yes. Or crashing on occasion. The scent is old, so they haven't been here in at least a day or two."

Stopping by once out of morbid curiosity for their new Packmate made some sense, if I looked at it sideways. But living here? It was like—"Do you think they want to be caught?"

"It's possible." He dropped the blanket and stood. "They've lost their family, and they don't know where to go. They may be putting themselves in my path so that we can meet."

"Or so they can follow Amalie's orders to kill you."

He nodded. "Also possible."

"So what do you want to do? Hang out and hope they come back?"

"No," he said without hesitation. He closed his eyes and pinched the bridge of his nose. After a few beats, he opened them again. The silver had receded to a thin line around the iris. "No, they may not return today or at all."

"We could always come back later and bug the place."

"We could."

He didn't sound very on-board with that idea. He grabbed the bag of trash and started rifling through it, sending up stronger odors of old food and rot. I took a step back, curious, but trusting him. He produced a few squeeze packs of mustard. Ripped one open. Spent a good solid minute using that mustard to write his cell phone number on the wall above the blanket pile, very careful to not smear any of the characters.

I guess when you traveled without pen and paper, you left notes any way you could.

"Think they'll know who it's from?" I asked when he didn't sign his name.

"They'll smell me here."

Living around Therians for the last few months kept that from sounding as strange as it ought to. "We should go then."

He followed me out with no small amount of regret. He wanted to find those three Lupa boys before they hurt someone else, but he also wanted to find them for himself. They were blood now, whether they liked it or not. And Wyatt never turned his back on family. He'd lost his real family to violence eleven years ago, and now he clung to the few personal relationships he managed to create. He'd never forgive himself if they were killed by one of our many enemies.

Or by one of our few allies.

***

We didn't return to the Watchtower until around seven pm, having spent the rest of the afternoon wandering aimlessly around the city. We did manage a decent sit-down dinner at a tiny Italian bistro that had seven tables, a short bar, and a funky smell that was either old cheese or dirty socks. But the food was decent, not a single person besides our waiter bothered us, and it almost felt like a real date.

Almost.

Wyatt was distant the entire meal, and I knew it was because of the Lupa pups. And I didn't even mind it, because I'd texted Gina Kismet while he was in the bathroom. She was at the Watchtower preparing phase one of Operation: Trust Me. Phase two was my job, and I got to it as soon as we arrived by separating myself from Wyatt with the excuse that I wanted to check on Milo's head. He bought it and headed off to Operations.

Kismet met me inside the empty storefront that we'd chosen earlier in the week. It was down the corridor near the gym area, across the hall, tucked back in the corner near the under-construction department store which would one day become an obstacle course training center—if the Watchtower was around long enough for it to be finished. Our location had once been a bank branch center, so it had a fantastic little safety deposit box area in the back, complete with steel walls and a prison-bar door that we'd fashioned an exterior lock for.

It was empty of the old safety deposit box lockers, which gave us a space that was about ten feet by fifteen feet, with smooth walls and a solid cement floor. Kismet had put a small cot mattress inside, as well as a few folded blankets, and she'd sprayed the room down with lavender-scented air freshener. Lavender was, according to Astrid, something of a Therian aphrodisiac, so I figured what the hell?

"How was he today?" Kismet asked as I inspected her handiwork.

"Focused. We may have a way of getting the pups to contact him, so I think he's also hopeful."

"That's good. He'll take it insanely hard if they're killed or captured before he finds them."

"I know."

Kismet was Wyatt's oldest friend, nine years and counting, and they knew each other in and out. They'd also betrayed each other several times in the last few months, only to reconcile and become friends again. It was one of the oddest love-hate-love-even-more relationships I'd ever seen, and she was growing on me as well. She was the closest thing I'd ever had to a girlfriend, and the only person in my life who listened when I talked about my and Wyatt's sexual problems (Milo and Tybalt got that *look* on their faces and plugged their fingers in their ears). Operation: Trust Me was her idea.

Whenever we were alone like this, part of me wanted to ask for more details of her friendship with Wyatt. All I really knew was that Wyatt recruited Kismet into the Triads when the entire organization was still in its infancy. The rest of me—the part that didn't like to dwell on the past—kept silent. It wasn't my business, and like her confessions about falling in love with her own Hunter once upon a time, it was something she could tell me if she wanted to.

"You know he's going to be pissed about this," Kismet said. She waved her hand at the vault.

"I know. But he'll get over it. He needs this."

"He doesn't trust his wolf."

"I know that, but I trust Wyatt to keep his wolf in check and to stay in control. He's strong enough to do that. He's just afraid to take the risk with me."

"You've been through a lot, Evy."

"And I have no doubt I'll go through a lot more before my nine lives run out. But I cannot stand Wyatt handling me with kid gloves. He needs to stop being afraid of hurting me."

"Easier said than done."

"That's why you're my backup."

She rolled her eyes. "Yay, me."

"Listen, off topic, can I ask you something about Tybalt?"

"The last time you asked if you could ask me something about Milo, I told you to go ask Milo."

"Well, this is actually about you, too."

Her eyebrow quirked up. "Okay."

"Did you know he was involved with the whole Seamus/Prentiss kidnapping thing back in May?"

"Not while it was happening. Marcus approached Tybalt during the Triad's off-time. He didn't tell me until a few weeks later. Why?"

"Just curious. Tybalt has a pretty complex relationship with the Felia Pride, doesn't he?"

"Yes, he does. He was never very close to Marcellus, but he still cares about Astrid and Marcus. Marcellus's impending death is going to hurt all of them. And if Riley is challenged, Tybalt will do everything he can to make sure the Dane family remains in control of the Pride."

"The Pride kicked him out onto the streets, and he's still that loyal?"

"Funny, huh?"

"Yeah." And as interesting as the conversation was, I needed to get my mind on someone besides Tybalt. "Time for phase three."

"Good luck."

"Thanks."

While she went to fetch Wyatt, I stripped and threw my clothes into a pile in the corner of the vault. It was chilly and my nipples pebbled right away. I stretched out on the thin mattress, closed my eyes, and let my thoughts wander. Back to that morning so many months ago when we'd made love in a narrow twin bed—our first and only time since my resurrection. I pictured him naked in my arms, his toned body fitting so perfectly with mine, and felt a familiar warmth between my legs. I held onto those feelings and remembered his hands, his touches, his kisses all over.

I almost didn't hear the bank door open, or the sound of voices. Wyatt would be blindfolded (he trusted Kismet enough to allow that, we both knew), but very soon he'd smell my arousal and know something was up. I sat up on my elbows and watched her lead him to the vault. Inches away from the door, he dug in and stopped.

"What's going on?" he asked, danger in his tone.

"Therapy," Kismet said. She gave him a hard shove, then swung the barred door closed with a clang.

Wyatt yanked off the blindfold as he turned, so he didn't see me yet. He grabbed the bars and tugged, snarling, "What the fuck, Gina?"

She ignored him. Looked past him to me. "You know the safe word."

"Yep," I said.

He pivoted to face me, even as she pushed the vault door almost the entire way shut. Mostly to muffle noise—she didn't want to shut it completely and suffocate us. Wyatt's eyes blazed pure silver and his nostrils flared as he took me in, stretched wantonly on the mattress, completely naked. He backed up to the wall, but had nowhere to go.

"What the fuck is this?" The cold in his eyes had crept into his voice. It wasn't encouraging, but it also wasn't unexpected. We had tricked him, after all.

"Couples therapy," I said.

"Let me out."

"Not a chance."

"Gina!"

I stood up, a little weirded out by my complete lack of clothes. I didn't do vulnerable very well, and not only was I about to put my heart out there for him to take or stomp on, I was doing it while exposed. "Scream all you want, Wyatt. She won't open that door without my safe word, and good luck figuring it out."

"Why are you doing this?" Instead of angry, the question came out as a plea. I hated hearing him like that, but I held my ground.

"Because you need to take the muzzle off and start trusting yourself again. I'm your mate, and your wolf knows it. I'm your lover in every way except physically. I believe with my whole heart that neither you or the wolf will hurt me, and this is the only way I can think to prove it to you."

"Evy, I will not be—"

"Another person who abuses me, yeah, I got that memo. News flash, Truman. This distance between us hurts me every single day, because you're *not* touching me."

He flinched.

I took three long strides forward and was halfway to him. He didn't pull away, just watched me with hooded, angry eyes. "You know I'm better with actions than with words, but here goes anyway. I love you so much, Wyatt, and I want to be able to make love to you. And you need to show your fear who's boss. Every time you let what the goblins or Thackery did to me stop you from loving me, they win. And I don't want them to win anymore. Not with this.

"So take off your fucking clothes."

Something in Wyatt's demeanor changed, and I couldn't quite put my finger on it. His eyes stayed silver, yet they seemed to warm. His expression went from icy and angry to calm and collected. A muscle in his jaw twitched. It was the oddest switch. I rarely gave him any sort of direct command like that, so maybe he was just surprised—oh wait. Weeks ago, Phineas told me that the Lupa were a matriarchal society, their Packs led by Alpha females and her mate. Women were the boss.

And I'd just ordered Wyatt to take off his clothes.

Huh.

He reached up and tugged off his shirt, and the black cotton crumpled to the floor. I held still, even though I wanted to run my hands over his skin and feel every sharp line of the muscles on his arms and torso and back. He'd always been in amazing shape, but his Lupa change had increased his metabolism and melted him down to muscle and sinew and the results were jaw-dropping.

Even before he worked his belt and shoved both jeans and boxers down to his ankles, I knew he was hard. I kept my eyes directed right at his face, waited for him to step out of his shoes and the rest of his clothes, and caught his gaze. Bald desire smoldered in his eyes, as well as silent concern.

"I love you," he said. His voice was hoarse, tight.

"Hold still for me." It came out as a whispered request, rather than a command.

"I trust you, Evy."

"I know. But this is about you trusting yourself again."

He made a noise that was as much a plea as it was a warning. I moved to stand toe to toe with him. Our heights were nearly matched, so I could look him right in the nose (eyes would be too much of a direct challenge). His body radiated heat, and a fine sheen of sweat covered his forehead. I leaned in and pressed my left cheek to his, my nose near his ear, and inhaled deeply. Inviting him to do the same. Warm breath puffed against my neck as he accepted.

My hands came up to his shoulders. He tensed with that contact, and my stomach fluttered with nerves. I wasn't good at this seduction stuff; I was going with whatever felt right. Touching him definitely felt right, and the simple sensuousness of it was stoking my own arousal. I trailed my fingers down his arms, tracing muscles and bone and skin, down to his hands, which I lifted and put on my hips.

He did not move on his own.

I flattened my palms over his pecs, allowing my fingers to skate lightly over his nipples, and he growled. It was a human growl, though, and that shot a bolt of pleasure straight through my midsection. The hands on my bare hips squeezed a fraction harder. I took another step closer, obliterating the distance between us. My breasts pressed against his chest. His erection, hot and hard, was trapped against my belly.

"Fuck," he whispered.

I nuzzled his cheek with my nose. "Yes, please."

Fingers tangled in my hair and pulled my head back with a gentle tug, and then his mouth devoured me. Wyatt's kisses were always special, often intense, but this was different. This kiss was a declaration, a claiming, more so than any of the dozens of kisses we'd already shared. I opened for him willingly, wanting him in me in every way possible, and his tongue licked inside my mouth. I wrapped my arms around his shoulders to keep him there, hips moving on their own as the need for friction overwhelmed me.

My lips tingled faintly with a soft brush of otherness that had been there ever since Wyatt's infection. Unlike the full-blooded Lupa, his saliva wasn't dangerous to me or anyone else. His blood, on the other hand, could be, especially if it came into contact with an open wound. My handy healing powers would likely allow me to defeat any sort of infection, but Wyatt wasn't one to take unnecessary chances on things that might cause me pain.

So I wasn't surprised when he had the wits to break the kiss. His eyes were still black, with only a thin ring of silver, but more silver flashed deep within the iris. The wolf wanted out, to dominate, but Wyatt was fighting to stay in charge. "Evy, what about—?"

"I have condoms."

He blinked, and his face melted into something between awe and joy. Then a wicked grin made my knees wobble. "How many?"

"Let's find out."

I pulled, and he helped me walk backward to the mattress on the floor. It wasn't fancy, and it wasn't wine-and-roses, but nothing about our relationship had ever been those things—mythical things written in books about perfection and forever. It had always been real—messy, loving, hurtful, painful, and in the end, worth every hug and tear and moment simply spent holding each other.

Wyatt turned and laid down first, then pulled me on top of him. I laughed as I settled with my knees braced on either side of his hips. I caught him in another tingly kiss. Our hands roamed, relearning familiar swells and valleys and plains, teasing and touching. He relaxed beneath me, his initial fear and hesitation disappearing behind confidence and control. Mouths found intimate places, and he brought me through one orgasm and close to a second before we made good use of those condoms.

All three of them.

Chapter Four

Monday, September 1
5:45 am

I could have stayed on that thin mattress, tangled up with Wyatt's body, for the rest of my afterlife—if it wasn't for the sudden need to pee. The pressure in my bladder pulled me out of a very comforting slumber, and clued me into the fact that the world was waiting for us outside this bank vault.

Damned world. Go away.

"How long have you been planning this?" Wyatt asked in a sleep raspy voice.

I raised my head from its pillow on his chest and met his gaze—all pleased man, with no sign of the wolf. "Couple of days."

"With Gina's help?"

"Mostly. I think sometimes she still feels bad about trying to blow me up."

"I think she's just getting better at making and holding onto friends. She's really good at putting up walls."

I didn't know all of Kismet's losses, but I did know some of them. Her Hunters were her family, and losing Felix had hurt her terribly. Nearly losing Tybalt a few weeks before that to a Halfie bite (his life saved when Milo cut half his arm off to stop the infection). Losing Lucas two years ago, who'd been not just her Hunter but also her lover. The devastation of the Triads, which was an organization she'd helped build in its earliest days. And there was an entire back story I was missing that had to do with her changing her name—something I'd learned thanks to a nosy PI named James Reilly, who was now on our payroll.

"Most of us are good at putting up those walls," I said.

"Just means those of us who love them have to work harder to break them back down."

"Are you talking about me or Gina?"

"Among others." He crooked a finger beneath my chin, and I slid up higher so I could kiss him. A gentle, good-morning kiss that made my angry bladder feel a little less important. I pressed my face into his throat and kissed the faint scars left behind from the Lupa's attack.

"You're remarkable, Evy."

I looked up and quirked an eyebrow at him. "Keep that in mind next time you're pissed at me for doing something stupid and reckless."

"You always act with good intentions, no matter the danger to yourself, and that makes me crazy."

"I know."

"Thank you for this. For being brave enough to get in my face and make me stop treating you like…" He pulled a face.

"Like a victim? Like brittle glass? Like I thought for one minute you'd do anything to intentionally harm me, when all you've ever done is protect me?"

"All of the above?" His smile was sad, but hopeful.

I planted another hard kiss on his mouth, then levered up on my elbows. "You're welcome. And I don't know about you, Truman, but I have to pee really bad."

He laughed long and loud—a truly beautiful sound. "I didn't want to be the first to say something…"

#

In the bathroom mirror, I studied a faint hickey on my collarbone. My T-shirt would hide it, but I kind of liked knowing it was there. Possession wasn't a concept I ever thought I'd be comfortable with, and on some levels I still wasn't, but I kind of liked having Wyatt's mark on me. In Therian circles, it was a sign of belonging to another, and it would serve to reinforce the fact that we were declared mates.

Even if most humans would point at the hickey and snicker.

At the next sink, Wyatt was washing his face with vigor and a smile that always seemed to be playing with his mouth. More than anything, seeing him smiling so much told me that Operation: Trust Me had been a good idea, as well as a rousing success.

"I think I need a shower," I said to my own reflection. My bath stuff and robe were in a locker in the next room, closer to the dormitory style showers. It wasn't that I particularly wanted to rid myself of Wyatt's scent, but it could be distracting to the other Therians we worked with. And if the position of Elder was challenged—or had been while we were getting busy last night—we'd be working around a whole lot of them very soon.

A computerized tone filled the room, signaling the start of an intercom announcement. "Quad Two, report to Ops immediately. Quad Two, report to Ops," said Rufus's disembodied voice.

I groaned. So much for my shower.

"Do you think this is about the Pride?" I asked.

"We'll know soon enough," Wyatt said.

We left the bathrooms, both of us dressed in yesterday's clothes (not incredibly unusual) and smelling of sex (less usual). It was still early, so we didn't see many people in the corridor. Marcus came down the hall from the opposite direction, dressed in workout sweats, a towel draped over one shoulder.

Milo, dressed in sweat-shorts and a T-shirt, was already in Ops when we got there, learning against the desk where Rufus sat in his motorized chair. They weren't talking, but there was a strange air of tension around both men. Astrid strode over from another computer station, and the look she cast said this wasn't going to be a happy conversation.

"What's going on?" Wyatt asked. "The Bengals?"

"I'd like to tell you we saw this coming, but I'd be lying," Astrid replied. "And it's an additional complication that we do not need right now."

"Thank you for the dramatic preface," I said. "Care to get to the problem so we can go about dealing with it?"

She pointed at the computer. We all shifted so we were standing in a semi-circle facing the monitor. A video player was frozen on an image of three people—a man and woman sitting on a sofa, and a second man on a chair opposite them. It looked like an interview setup, and the ticker at the bottom of the screen said "Parents Worst Nightmare."

I studied the woman. Her heart-shaped face and thick, brown hair, and somehow I knew she had freckles on her nose. Just like I did. *Holy fucking hell.*

Rufus hit Play on the video.

"…been six months since the Frosts have had contact with their daughter, Chalice," the single man said.

My heart nearly stopped. Beside me, Wyatt put an arm around my waist, and I clung to it as the full weight of the video hit me like a gargoyle's stone fist. On May 20 of this year, Chalice Frost committed suicide in her apartment bathtub. She was found by her best friend Alex, who called the police. Chalice was taken to the morgue at St. Eustachius Hospital. A few hours later, an elf performed a magic spell that brought me, the murdered Evangeline Stone, back to life—in Chalice's formerly dead body. While small threads of who Chalice had once been lingered in my mind, she was gone. Dead and mourned and technically nonexistent in this city thanks to some gremlins running computer interference.

In all of the incredible drama of my afterlife, it never consciously occurred to me that her parents were still out there somewhere, wondering what happened to their daughter.

The camera angle switched to a close-up of the parents, and their names appeared on screen: Stephen and Lori Frost. I had only the vaguest sense of familiarity. They might have been the parents of the body I was in, but they weren't *my* parents. I never knew my loser father, and my mother died when I was ten. But the pain these two people were in still felt important. Real.

"Our daughter Chalice moved here three years ago," Stephen said, straight to the camera. "I remember the day she left home. But no one in this city can find a record of her ever being here. She took classes part time, but the university has no file on her. She had an apartment, but her name isn't on the lease and her roommate died on May twenty-second. Her old employer remembers her, but says the computer has no information on her employment. It's as if someone made our daughter disappear."

Next to him, Lori was doing a poor job of holding herself together. She clung to her husband's arm as tears rolled down her cheeks. The resemblance to me was uncanny, from hair to eyes to cheekbones.

Stephen squeezed his wife's arm, then continued. "Six months ago, we got our last phone call. It wasn't about anything in particular, but she sounded so sad. I know Chalice struggled with depression, and local police keep telling us to prepare for the idea that she took her own life, but I can't believe that."

I let out a grunt. Showed what he knew about his own kid.

"My wife and I aren't rich people, but we are willing to pay a monetary reward for any information that helps us find our daughter. We just want to know the truth, so that we can bring her home"—he wiped his eyes—"or put her to rest. Please."

Lori broke down and fell into Stephen's arms. The camera cut to a close-up of the interviewer. I didn't recognize him or his news show. "If anyone has information on the disappearance or whereabouts of Chalice Ann Frost, please contact the Metro Police Department Major Crimes at—"

He rattled off a phone number as the screen changed. To my face. Or rather, what looked like a school ID photo of Chalice, taken maybe a year or two ago. She wasn't smiling, her hair was pulled back in a messy bun, and her eyes were haunted. It was a face I'd seen in the mirror every day for almost four months, but it was also the face of a stranger. And it was being broadcast all over the city and the fucking internet.

Rufus hit the Pause button on the video.

One by one, everybody turned their head to look at me, but I couldn't stop staring at my photo on the computer. This was going to make my life way more complicated than it needed to be right now—just like Astrid had said.

"Well, shit," I said.

"Your parents are still alive?" Milo asked.

"They're not my parents. They're her parents." I pointed at the screen.

"And that's your face, Stone," Astrid said. "The last thing this operation needs is a lot of tips going to the police, and them coming looking for you. You don't have police protection anymore."

Too true. Back when the Triads were active and effective, we had three moles in the police department who made files disappear, reassigned cases, and kept the cops off our asses while we did our jobs. Up until the Triads were wrecked and those supposed moles all killed themselves in a group suicide. We found out too late that they were all sprite avatars—fully controlled by three sprites who reported back to Amalie, the queen bitch who'd betrayed us all.

The closest thing we had to an "in" with the police was James Reilly. A former West Coast cop, he became a private investigator after his own partner was killed by a vampire, and his investigations led him here. We managed to snare his loyalty by providing him with answers to a lot of burning questions, and he in turn was able to work his police contacts in our favor. To an extent. Even he couldn't do anything about this shit-tastic problem.

"There's no way to halt the broadcast?" Milo asked.

"It's been showing since last night," Rufus replied. "Even if we could get it off the internet, it's been seen. And it doesn't sound like the Frosts are going away."

"They want to know the truth about what happened to their daughter," Wyatt said.

Rufus turned his head away, but I saw the flinch. He was keeping a very large secret of his own from Wyatt, and sooner or later he'd have to spill.

"This is going to be a major problem for us," Astrid said.

"No kidding," I replied. "What would you like me to do? Resurrect myself into somebody else?"

"Hardly."

"And don't even say you want to bench me, because there's too much going on right now—"

"May I speak?" A slight feline growl came out at the end of that, so I shut up and let Astrid talk. "I was going to say exercise extreme caution when you're in the field. I can't afford to bench anyone right now, but you've been racing around the city for months wearing this girl's face. People are bound to remember they saw you, and others will be flat out looking for you."

She was right. And what if the Frosts managed to track down Leo Forrester, father of Chalice's dead roommate Alex? He was a kind man, but he was a recovering alcoholic and not a very good liar. He couldn't tell them that he didn't know who I was. I'd given him a condensed version of the truth about myself and his son's death before running him back out of town for his own safety.

"You could always dye your hair," Milo said. "And cut it. Make it harder for people to recognize you."

I nodded, even though the idea didn't appeal to me. Before I died, my hair had been short, thin and blond. Now it was long, thick and wavy brown, and it had taken some getting used to. But I was used to it. Not that it wasn't a pain to take care of on occasion, especially when I got blood in it. Maybe it was time to try a new look.

"Is hiding her truly the best option?" Marcus asked.

Milo frowned. "As opposed to what?"

"Having Stone contact the parents and put their minds at ease about their daughter's well-being."

Marcus's suggestion didn't surprise me; it also wasn't something I was comfortable with for a whole slew of reasons.

"Their daughter's dead," Milo retorted. There was a level of anger in his tone that caught my attention. He seemed genuinely annoyed, but I suspected it had more to do with Marcus himself, than with his words. The unusual tension between the pair was suddenly unmistakable.

"And yet her body is wandering the city still."

"So she should pretend to be their dead daughter? For how long? A day? A month? Ten years?"

"It was an alternative to hiding, Milo, that's all."

"Okay, so I've got options," I said. "Great, I'll consider them all while I keep my head down and try to not be noticed. Meanwhile, are there any developments with Riley and the challenge?"

"Not so far," Marcus replied.

Good news so far. "Are there any new goblin sightings we should know about?"

"None that have been reported," Astrid replied. Her cell phone rang. She glanced at the display, then put it to her ear. "Dane." Her eyes slid in my direction. "Yeah, hold on."

She held the phone out to me. "It's James Reilly. Said he's been trying to get you on your cell."

I tried to remember where I'd left—back pocket. I'd turned it off so it didn't interrupt my night with Wyatt. I took Astrid's phone. "This is Stone."

"You're a hard woman to reach sometimes," Reilly said. His normally even, conversational tone was tinged with annoyance. Had everyone woken up cranky today?

"Sorry about that. Extenuating circumstances."

Wyatt squeezed my hip.

"Indeed. Some information has fallen into my lap, Ms. Stone, and I thought it would be of some use to you and your colleagues."

"Depends on the info."

"It isn't about the Frost girl's parents, if that's what you're thinking. Although I imagine that's a complication you didn't expect."

I rolled my eyes. "Something tells me you expected it?"

"It had crossed my mind a few times when I was first looking for her and Alex Forrester. But no, I'm not calling about that. This has to do with some very sick, former allies of yours."

The vampires. I knew without him saying it. We'd been trying for weeks to get information on the condition of the vampires infected by an unknown virus that was slowly killing them. Isleen, Eleri, Quince, and others had been carted off by their Families and not seen since. I needed whatever he had.

Downside of working with Reilly: he hated giving information over the phone. "When and where?" I asked.

"Usual place. Be there in an hour."

"I can be there in half that."

"Terrific. I'll see you in an hour."

I handed the phone back to Astrid, then held up a hand before Wyatt could say anything. "You're not coming with me."

He lifted an eyebrow. "Why not?"

"Because you scare the hell out of him, and I really like him on my side."

"You're not going alone."

"I'll take Milo." No one objected. "Excellent. Let's go."

***

Fifteen minutes later, Milo eased our borrowed car out of the parking area and through the mall corridor that led outside. He'd beaten me to the car, so I didn't much care that he wanted to drive. It was more important that I take a few minutes to change into fresh clothes, twist my hair up, and hide it under a light blue bandana. It wasn't much of a disguise, but it was something. He'd likewise traded his sweat-shorts for a pair of jeans and looked less like he'd just rolled out of bed.

The usual meeting place was Sally's Coffee Shop. It was open twenty-four hours, was in the middle of Mercy's Lot, and Milo, Tybalt, and Felix had frequented it back during their Triad days. Reilly had an unhealthy obsession with the pancakes there—he was eating them every time I met him. But the coffee was good, and it was a difficult location to ambush.

It would take about fifteen minutes to get there, give or take traffic congestion, and I spent half the time silently staring at Milo from the corner of my eye. He looked pissed, wearing that same cloud of anger that had followed him around for a good month or so after Felix's infection. I hadn't requested his company so I could pick his brain, but the opportunity was just too good.

"Do me a favor today?" I said.

"What?"

"Whatever you're mad at Marcus about? Don't take it out on Reilly."

He glanced over at me, eyebrows furrowed and lips pressed tight, then back to the road. His hands tightened around the wheel. "I won't."

The fact that he hadn't denied he was pissed at Marcus startled me into a momentary silence. I'd never seen the pair not getting along, even from the first day they met on the Boot Camp battlefield. "Milo, you know I'm going to ask."

"I don't want to talk about it."

"If it's affecting quad dynamics, we need to talk about it. The four of us have to be able to work together."

"We can work together."

"Uh huh."

"Can you leave it alone for now?"

I stared out the window and left it alone for the time it took him to park two blocks down from Sally's in the first open space he could find. One he turned off the engine and palmed the keys, I asked, "What did you do?"

He shifted around in his seat, eyes wide, caught somewhere between stunned and angry. "What did *I* do? What the hell makes you think it was something I did?"

"It was something you did or he did, so I had a fifty-fifty shot of being right. Am I wrong, then?"

"Yes."

Now I was really confused. For all of his growling and bluster and bulk, Marcus had a gentle soul. He loved his sister Astrid, and he was fiercely loyal to both his Pride and his friends at the Watchtower. He was the kind of guy I wanted on my side, so what could he have—fuck. "Did he give you shit about being gay?"

Milo's eyebrows rose into his hairline. "Hell no. He didn't give me shit."

"But he knows?"

"Of course he knows."

Okay, that wasn't it, and good thing or I'd have knocked Marcus on his furry ass. I didn't know much about Milo's pre-Triad years, but I'd seen the scars on his back—they were the kind of scars you got from repeated beatings. I had seen them on my old Triad partner Jesse, and he'd once drunkenly admitted they were gifted to him by his stepfather's leather belt. Milo's heart had been broken when Felix died, and I was protective as hell of the friendship Milo and I had built since then.

Even if it was a friendship built solely on the present, with little visitation of the past, or pondering of the future.

"So what's with the hostility before?" I asked. "You looked like you didn't want Marcus within twenty feet of you."

"It wasn't hostility, exactly.

"It looked hostile."

"It was frustration and confusion."

"About?"

Milo let out a long breath. "Marcus he kissed me."

Before I could even process that bomb, much less respond to it, Milo sprang from the car and slammed the door shut. He was halfway down the block before I caught up with him, and I still couldn't get control of my whirlwind thoughts. Thoughts that shifted from confusion (over Milo's frustration), to joy (over Milo finding someone who seemed interested in him, too), to concern (over all of Marcus's current troubles and the possible backlash over a human/Therian pairing during so much Pride upheaval).

It was too much to talk about on a public street, and Milo gave me a quelling glare when I fell into step next to him. We walked to Sally's in silence. I kept my gaze moving, wandering over the faces of strangers, feeling truly exposed for the first time since my resurrection. Any one of these people could have seen my face on the news. Hair covered up or not, I was still recognizable, and I didn't like it.

And even though this city was pretty big, with my luck I'd run right into Chalice Frost's parents and have no idea what to say to them.

Sally's was nearly full with the seven a.m. breakfast crowd. A harried waitress pointed us toward an empty booth near the back. We sat across from each other, mostly to mess with Reilly's head. I freaked him out a little because I'd been resurrected into a dead girl, and he'd only met Milo once before. The waitress swooped by to pour our coffee. Milo and I stared at each other from opposite sides of a grimy Formica table that had seen better days. He seemed to be daring me to bring up Marcus, but I had enough self-control and respect for Milo to not bring it up here.

Reilly's shadow fell across the table a few minutes later. In his mid-forties, with curly gray and brown hair, he looked more like an accountant than a former cop and current private investigator. He eyed his choices of seating, then gingerly slid into the booth next to me.

"Why do I feel like I just interrupted an argument?" he asked.

"You didn't," I replied. "Milo's always grumpy this time of morning."

Milo made a face at me, but said nothing. The waitress zipped by and poured more coffee. "The usual for you, hon?" she asked.

"Yes." Reilly glanced at us. "Anything for you two?"

I hadn't realized I was hungry until he asked. "Scrambled eggs and toast."

"Wheat or white?" the waitress said, committing it all to memory.

"White."

"Sausage or bacon?"

"Bacon."

"For you?" she said to Milo.

"Uh, the same."

She nodded, then walked off with her coffee pot.

"What is it with you and pancakes?" I asked Reilly.

"They're really good here," he replied. "And they remind me of happier times."

"Times when certain things were only characters in books?"

"Precisely." He measured out sugar and stirred it into his coffee.

"So are you going to make us wait for the food before you tell us why we're here?" Milo asked.

Reilly stared across the table, his sharp gaze cataloguing Milo in seconds. Something seemed to stop on the tip of his tongue, then he shook his head. "No, I won't make you wait." He pulled a business card out of his shirt pocket and handed it to me.

Alucard Communications & Development.

The logo was a simple circle around what looked like an old-fashioned pair of radio headphones. Of course, if I looked at it sideways, it could have been a smiley face with fangs. The address was south of Uptown, near the outskirts of the city. I'd never heard of it, and there was no other writing on the card except a telephone number.

"Okay," I said and slid the card over to Milo. "Am I supposed to know who these guys are?"

Reilly blew across the top of his steaming coffee. "Look harder."

Milo squinted at the text, then blinked hard. "Oh, I get it. Alucard. It's Dracula spelled backward."

"It is?" I plucked the card out of his fingers. Oh. It was. But what did that have to do with—shit. "You found the vampires."

"I did," Reilly said, then leaned against the booth with a self-satisfied smirk.

I had to admit (not out loud) that I was impressed. The vampire Families moved around the city like ghosts, appearing and disappearing with ease. Considering the artillery they were packing during the battle at Olsmill, they had money and access to some serious technology, but no one knew exactly where they came from or where they lived.

There were five ruling Families, each governed by a Father. It was the Fathers who'd joined forces with the Watchtower, then pulled their people out last month after the infection. While the occasional Blood was spotted around the city now and again, the vast majority had disappeared from the streets. And we may have just found their hiding place.

"It's a very clever front," Reilly said. "The company does actual communication consulting work, as well as running half a dozen call centers through its switchboard. From what I can tell, the company is located on three of the building's ten floors. The other seven, plus a few basement levels, house the rest of the vampires."

"How do you know all this?" Milo asked.

"Ah, but a magician never reveals his secrets, nor a PI his sources."

"And you're sure it's legit? You aren't being fed information that'll lead us into a trap?"

Reilly's jaw twitched; he actually looked annoyed. "I'd never pass along information that I suspected to be wrong. And what you choose to do with that card is, of course, your own business."

"Thank you," I said. "I'll make sure Astrid processes your claim." Code talk for she'd make sure he was paid.

"Much appreciated, Ms. Stone. Can I be of service in any other way?"

I fiddled with a creamer cup. "Personal favor?"

"Perhaps."

"If anyone comes to you asking about Chalice Frost, your personal investigation ended with the apartment in Parkside East. We've never had any of these conversations."

He shifted in the booth. "Well, technically I've never met

Chalice Frost, have I?"

"No, you haven't." Something felt off all of the sudden, and I couldn't figure out why. He was being too careful with his words, and that made me nervous. "But you have met someone who looks a hell of a lot like her."

Milo stiffened. "Mentioned that fact to anyone lately?"

Reilly didn't reply, and a cold wash of dread raised goose bumps on my arms and shoulders. He didn't look guilty, exactly, just way too serious. And he hadn't denied Milo's question.

"When I was sixteen, my older sister Linda disappeared," Reilly finally said, about two seconds before I was apt to hit him. "She was a sophomore in college, smart and popular, but also prone to depression. There was no sign of a struggle, no suicide note, she simply left her dorm one night and was never seen again. Our parents went crazy with grief."

I gripped the edge of the table, afraid I'd lash out physically at him as my sense of dread and anger grew. I saw the ending to this story coming, but could do nothing to change it. The activity of the diner dimmed into the background as his words became my whole world.

"We never knew what happened to her," he continued. "To this day. Our parents died not knowing. Linda's the reason I became a cop, and she's the reason I find the answers other people can't."

Mouth dry, I swallowed hard before my tongue worked. "You sympathize with the Frosts," I said.

"Very much."

"Have you spoken to them in the last twenty-four hours?"

"I have."

I shoved the business card into my pocket. "Move. Milo and

I are leaving."

"Ms. Stone—"

"Now."

"Evy," Milo said. He was looking over his shoulder, toward the front door of the diner.

My mouth fell open. A few steps inside the door, Stephen and Lori Frost were clutching each other and glancing around with eager expressions.

CHAPTER FIVE

7:15 am

I sank down in the booth until the Frosts were out of my view, hopefully putting me out of theirs, and I resisted the urge to punch Reilly in the face for this little ambush. "Son of a bitch," I whispered. All the trust we'd been building between us these last few weeks crumbled.

"I didn't tell them about you," Reilly said, lips barely moving. "I asked them to meet me here."

I had to get out of there, but Reilly was in my way and slithering under the table like a child wasn't in my repertoire of tricks. I could use my Gift and teleport, but there was nowhere to go. No hiding places inside the coffee shop itself, and teleporting into the street was too dangerous. I could end up half inside someone's car. And Reilly didn't seem keen on providing a useful distraction.

Shit!

"What do you want to do?" Milo asked.

"Chalice!"

My stomach flopped to the floor. I remained hunched in the booth, at a complete loss as to what to say to the distraught parents bearing down on our table. In person, Lori Frost was an older, lighter-haired copy of her daughter, right down to a dark smattering of freckles on her nose and cheekbones. Next to her, Stephen was a thundercloud of anger and disbelief, and I had the oddest little-girl urge to hide under the table from his temper.

Some small parts of Chalice had remained behind when I took full possession of her body—images and physical memories of her life. Most of it had faded in the last few months until only vague traces surfaced in my dreams. But looking at them here, standing front of me, I felt a strange warmth in my chest. A tug that I didn't understand.

Lori hovered at the edge of the table like she was contemplating her ability to climb over Reilly and hug me, which made me extremely grateful to have Reilly as a buffer. She stared at me with leaking eyes, from my face down to—

I shoved my hands into my lap, heart thudding against my ribs, hoping she hadn't noticed the fact that my left hand was missing its pinkie finger. I so did not need her flipping out over nine digits when she had plenty of other things to freak out about. Words were burbling up in Lori's throat, but nothing came out that made sense.

"Where the hell have you been?" Stephen asked.

His tone tweaked my temper, and I sat up straighter in the booth. Grief and fear were hiding behind his anger, that much was obvious, but I didn't do well with people who bullied when they were afraid. "Here," I said. "Where have you been?"

He reeled. Okay, so maybe Chalice wasn't so lippy. "We've been trying to find you for months, Chal. You haven't called, you moved out of your apartment. You didn't even tell us Alex died."

My heart hurt a little at that one. In the first few days of my resurrection, Alex had been a good friend. He'd died trying to help me. I'd been able to give Alex's father some closure on his son's death, but I didn't know how to do that for these people. The obvious and true excuse of "I've been busy" seemed lame. Very rarely in my life had I been rendered completely speechless, but this was one of those moments.

"Stephen, please," Lori said. The words were choked with tears, and the noise was attracting attention from other diners. "You promised."

Milo slid out of the booth and stood up, facing Stephen, who he actually had an inch or two on, even though Stephen was far bulkier. "Is there something I can help you folks with?" he asked in a voice older than his age, and with far less patience than usual.

Stephen gave him a hard look. "You can allow us to speak with our daughter, is what you can do."

"Can I?" Milo folded his arms over his chest. "Don't you think the fact that she hasn't contacted either of you in six months speaks for itself?"

Lori gaped at Milo like he'd just slapped her, and I kind of felt sorry for her.

"What about school?" Stephen asked. "The apartment? Her job? How does a person just disappear off the grid like that?" He stopped glaring at Milo to look at me. "Are you in some kind of trouble, Chal?"

It was all I could do to not laugh. These days I was always in some kind of trouble, but it wasn't the kind he'd believe without a lot of therapy. And for fuck's sake, why couldn't I defend myself to these people? Had Chalice always felt so defenseless around them? So much like a child that all she could do was hang her head and nod along with whatever her father said?

"I'm beginning to see that this was a mistake," Reilly said.

"Of course it wasn't," Lori said. "She's our child. We've been worried sick."

"I didn't mean to worry you," I said, pulling the words out of nowhere. "But I've had a lot going on, and I just couldn't call."

"Oh, baby." Lori reached out a hand, but was too far away to touch me. "You always used to say you felt invisible to the world, and I'm so sorry I didn't see you better. Please don't push us away again. We love you so much."

My eyes burned. I wanted to say it back, to give them that much. A little sliver of the daughter they'd lost. I simply couldn't get the words out of my throat. It was a lie, and I didn't want to lie to them.

Milo's cell rang. He yanked it out of his pocket. "Yeah?" Listened a few seconds while the rest of us exchanged serious stares. "We're on our way." He hung up and turned to me. "We have to go."

He didn't look surprised or upset—only determined to get us both out of there, and I sent him a mental "thank you" for it. Reilly slid out of the booth without prompting, and I followed him out, careful to shield my left hand from the eyes of not-my-parents.

"Where are you going?" Stephen asked.

"Work," I replied. "I'm sorry, but I can't do this right now."

"Chalice—"

"I'm alive. I'm doing okay. A lot better, in fact, than the last time we talked. Please trust me about this."

"Have dinner with us tonight." It wasn't a question so much as a command.

"I can't."

"We're not leaving town until you sit down and talk to us."

"In that case, find a comfy hotel."

Lori's face scrunched up like she was about to burst into hysterical sobs. I angled around her and past her husband, and Milo came up behind me. We walked to the door like that, him a physical barrier between me and the Frosts. Reilly stayed quiet and stayed behind—good thing, too. I was angry enough at him to break his nose and not think twice.

Halfway back to the car, Milo moved up to keep in step next to me. I took a few deep breaths before I asked, "So what was the phone call about?"

"Nothing. When I saw who was at the door, I texted Gina to call me in exactly three minutes. Figured you'd want a retreat plan."

"Thank you."

"No problem. You okay?"

"Pissed as hell at Reilly for ambushing me like that."

"That stands to reason. I mean about seeing the Frosts."

"It was weird. I'm not their kid, not really, but feeling them bearing down on me like that made me feel like their child, you know?"

"You looked like you were going to cry at one point."

"Yeah, well, the last time my own mother told me she loved me I think I was five years old."

He made a soft grunting sound. "She did say it, though."

"I guess." I slipped my left arm through his as we walked. "So, you up for visiting a communications company on the other side of town?"

"Can't think of a better way to spend a Monday morning."

"Glad to hear it."

***

We had a long drive to the other side of town, which gave us plenty of time to call Kismet and explain the meeting at Sally's. She had a few choice curse words of her own for Reilly's ambush. Then she gave us directions to Alucard Communications, which had us going Uptown in morning rush hour traffic, so what should have been a fifteen-minute trek across town took nearly an hour.

I tried to not bring up Milo's earlier confession about Marcus. He didn't seem eager to talk about it, and my bringing up something personal made my own current Frost family drama fair game to his questions. But the longer we sat in traffic, not talking, barely listening to a pop hits radio station, the more my curiosity got the better of me. I needed to know something, but I also had to phrase it in a way that didn't make it sound like I thought that, a) Marcus was some sort of forceful asshole, or b) Milo couldn't defend himself.

Got it. "Milo, can I ask you one question?"

He flexed his right hand around the steering wheel, then sighed. "Yes. One."

"Did you kiss him back?"

"No. I was a little too surprised at the time."

"Do you wish you had?"

He gave me a sideways look. "That's two questions, Evy."

"I know."

His attention went back to the road, which left my second question hanging there. And something about his silence made me think the answer was yes.

Alucard Comm was north of Uptown, on the outskirts of where most of the city's higher end businesses and restaurants were located. The place reminded me of a military compound, with its electric perimeter fence and rolling front gate. The building itself was an experiment in modern art, with strange angles and architecture I couldn't hope to understand the aesthetics of. The exterior was mirrored to reflect the city around it and the sky above, giving no hint as to which parts were actually windows and which were walls. Seductive and scary, just like the Bloods.

I didn't have much of a plan in mind when Milo pulled up in front of the guard hut. An older woman with gray hair and a boring blue uniform stepped out of the hut, then crouched down to peer in through Milo's open window.

"Do you have an appointment?" she asked.

"Not as such," Milo said.

"My name is Evangeline Stone," I said, leaning closer to his window. "This is Milo Gant. We're friends of Isleen."

None of the names earned so much as an eyebrow twitch from the lady guard. She eyeballed me, then Milo. "One moment." She disappeared into the hut.

"You wanna lay odds on whether or not she's calling security to have us escorted off the premises?" Milo asked.

"I've been surprised too many times today to lay odds on anything."

We waited, engine idling, until the guard stepped back outside. "You're cleared to go in. An escort will meet you in the lobby."

"Thank you," Milo said.

The gate rolled back. He drove down a short road that opened into a small, twenty-car lot marked Visitor's Parking. A secondary road continued past the lot, probably to private underground parking. I was crazy curious where they kept their helicopters, too. Three other cars were in the lot—for show as likely as anything, since it was Monday morning when most people were going to work.

Unless they already lived in their building of employment. My own commute was a short walk down a mall corridor.

I sent a quick text to Wyatt, telling him where we were and what we were about to do. You couldn't be too careful before walking into a completely unknown situation, and I had too much to live for now to take stupid risks.

The main entrance to Alucard surprised me with its simplicity. For some reason, I expected higher security, or something akin to a prison visitation setup with iron doors and keycards. The revolving door could be found at any business center, and the lobby had a high, domed ceiling with modern chrome fixtures and two large, black leather couches. Behind the couches was a single elevator door, which dinged at almost the exact moment we walked inside.

The elevator opened. A tall, willowy man with short, white hair and piercing lavender eyes strode toward us. He walked with such grace he practically floated, and he wore a red robe reminiscent of one I'd seen Isleen's father wear once, only this one was far less ornate. He stopped just out of arm's reach, then bent slightly at the waist, as if bowing.

"Welcome," he said. "My name is Eulan, of the house of Noro."

"Evangeline Stone," I replied. "My associate, Milo Gant. We represent the interests of the Watchtower Initiative."

"I know. I have heard of you, Ms. Stone."

My reputation had a habit of preceding me pretty much everywhere. "Forgive my bluntness, but I've never heard of you."

He smiled, which only sharpened the angles of his face—and showed off his fangs. "That does not surprise me. Although I imagine you do not know very many of my kin on a first name basis. Aside from those who briefly partook in your Watchtower, of course."

"Speaking of whom, may I inquire about Isleen's condition?"

"Your inquiry is not unexpected, and it is why I volunteered to meet with you."

"So you can politely tell me to mind my own business?"

Eulan's mouth twitched. "Not quite. Isleen spoke of you more than once to me. She respects you, Ms. Stone, and she values your friendship. Few humans have ever made the same impression."

"She was the first vampire I ever trusted." It might have sounded like a small thing, but given my previous personal point-of-view on anything not human, it was huge. Once someone fully gained my trust, I'd fight hard for them. "I also valued her friendship. But she never spoke to me of you."

"She would have no reason. Vampires are not as...chatty as humans, when it comes to our personal relationships. Isleen and I are promised in our equivalent of marriage."

Are promised—present tense. It gave me hope. "So she's alive?"

"She is...not yet dead."

"What does that mean?"

Eulan directed us to the two black sofas. I sat with him, while Milo stood nearby and listened. "It means that we are still seeking a cure for our brethren who were infected by Thackery's virus. It is fast-moving and devastating, and the only way to halt the virus's progress is to subject it to extreme cold."

I stared. "You froze them?"

"They are being carefully monitored by our physicians as their bodies maintain temperatures well below that required for cognitive function."

"In English?"

"They froze them," Milo said.

Eulan raised a single white eyebrow in Milo's general direction. "The process is more complicated than that, but yes. Many of those infected have led long lives. We will not give up on them."

I appreciated the sense of loyalty the vampires had for each other, and it gave me a fresh perspective on the Fathers' decision to pull support out of the Watchtower. They had their own people—sick and well—to worry about.

"What about the Watchtower volunteers who were not infected?" Milo asked.

"Until we understand the virus better," Eulan said, "they remain quarantined. We cannot guarantee that they will not inadvertently infect others. Such results would be disastrous to our people."

"So they stay locked up indefinitely?"

"Correct."

I thought of Quince, a relatively young vampire I'd worked with for several weeks. He was a natural actor and eager to make a difference through the Watchtower. He hadn't been infected. The virus had been linked to a sunscreen that allowed vampires to walk around in sunlight, and Quince had never used it. But he was still locked up, a prisoner among his own people, for something that wasn't his fault.

"I am sorry I do not have better news for you," Eulan said.

"It's more news than I've had in a month," I said. "For all of our differences, I consider Isleen, Quince, and Eleri to be my friends. I care about what happens to them."

"Then allow us to do our work as we see fit. Humans have an uncanny need to control the uncontrollable, and in this we will not be moved."

"We won't interfere. That isn't why I came today. But please, if you need anything, you can ask."

"Appreciated, Ms. Stone. However, as I understand, you have your hands full with other obligations."

"You mean our old, sewer-dwelling enemies who are coming out of hiding?"

"The very same. We despise the goblins as much as you do. I am sorry that we cannot offer our assistance this time."

"So am I, but you have to see to your people."

Good Lord, who was I, and when did I get so understanding? A few months ago I would have called him selfish for being unable to see past his own problems and focus on the bigger picture. Now? I can totally see where he's coming from.

"If our situation changes, or if we acquire information that is useful to your cause, you will be contacted."

"I appreciate that."

Eulan nodded. "I assume that I do not need to ask for your discretion in regard to this facility."

"You don't," I said for myself and Milo. "And I'll make sure the person who gave us this location knows better than to open his mouth."

"Thank you. Shall I walk you out?"

"No, we're fine."

"Then be well, Ms. Stone. Mr. Gant. It is said that even the darkest chapters of our past may hold the key to the brightness of our futures."

"Said by whom?" Milo asked.

Eulan only smiled and walked away. The cryptic message didn't make me feel any better about anything. One of the darkest parts of my personal past was coming back to haunt me in the form of "Kelsa" scratched into dead people's legs. Vampires weren't known to be psychic, so I didn't read too much into it.

My cell rang on our way back to the car. I fished it out of my pocket. "Stone."

"It's Baylor. I need you to meet me under the Lincoln Street Bridge. Someone left you a note."

***

The Lincoln Street Bridge extended over the southernmost leg of the Anjean River, right before it fed into the larger Black River that bisected the western side of the city. The pedestrian and vehicular bridge ran parallel to a train bridge, and it was the only way to cross from Mercy's Lot and Downtown into the East Side. Since we were Uptown, on the other side of the city, we had a trek to get to the location.

I didn't have to ask Baylor on which side of the river I needed to go. I knew exactly where to meet him. On the northwest bank, the first exit off the bridge wrapped around to a narrow one-way street that ran along the bank of the river. The road was barely wide enough for a single car to pass, and two other cars were already parked on the thin shoulder near our location. Milo pulled up behind the last car.

"Yes," he said, as though we'd been in the middle of a conversation.

Hand on the door pull, I stared at him blankly for several seconds until I realized he was answering my second question from earlier. He wished he'd kissed Marcus back. I grinned. "Okay."

He gave me a shy smile—so unlike him—then climbed out of the car.

I followed him along the shoulder with the constant thunder of cars passing overhead a head-splitting soundtrack to the afternoon. The ripe odors of the river mixed with motor oil and tar to create a toxic stink that made my eyes water. Wyatt, Marcus, and Adrian Baylor stood on the other side of the chain link fence that protected the underside of the bridge from trespassers like us, and the dozens of graffiti artists who'd already visited. Milo and I slipped through the same hole in the fence.

Once upon a time, I'd come here to talk to a bridge troll named Smedge. He wasn't a friend, exactly, but we were friendly. He gave me information when he had it, on almost anything I asked pertaining to the supernatural races of the city. I hadn't spoken to him in months. The last time I'd come here, someone had poured tar all over the cement to prevent Smedge from rising.

Trolls are made from the very earth themselves, and they can move through any natural dirt or stone material. Things like tar and metal, though, stopped them cold. Trolls were also part of the Fey, who were now our enemies, and even though Smedge couldn't rise through the layer of tar still clinging to the ground, being here again made me nervous.

"You've had a busy morning," Wyatt said as he came to join me.

"No kidding," I replied. "I owe Reilly a black eye for that stunt he pulled with Chalice's parents, but I may forgive him for the tip on the vampires."

"Anything useful?"

"Just that the Bloods are keeping to themselves until they find a cure for those Thackery infected."

"They're still alive?" Baylor asked. Another ex-Triad Handler and long-time friend of both Wyatt and Kismet, Adrian Baylor had an easygoing personality that contrasted sharply with his fierce fighting skills. He was the kind of guy you wanted to have leading you into battle—or helping you figure out random, cryptic messages.

"Kind of. From what we were told, they're in some sort of frozen stasis for the undetermined future."

"That's something."

"Yeah. So where's this message that couldn't be left on my cell phone?"

Baylor pointed at the underside of the bridge. I moved closer, studying the spray-paint splattered concrete that angled up in steep slabs, all the way to the steel bottom of the bridge. In glittering silver paint someone had written "Stony" with an arrow pointing to the right. Curious now, I walked in that direction, until I found a spot on the ground where the tar had been scraped away. Not a large spot, maybe the size of a manhole cover, but it was there. In that same glittering paint "knock three times" was written on the stone.

"Why do I feel like I just fell into the plot of a horror movie?" I said to no one in particular.

My backup had fanned out into a wide circle. Baylor produced his sidearm and held it pointed at the ground, his finger braced on the trigger guard. Milo stood next to Wyatt, whose eyes had gone silver. Opposite them, Marcus's hands hovered near the waist of his jeans, just in case he had to strip and do a fast shift. No one gave me advice.

"Let's see who's home," I said.

Knocking your fist against solid rock hurts like hell. Doing it three times was just plain cruel. I stepped back from the circle, heart kicking a little harder, both excited and scared to see what came out of the ground.

A deep rumbling rose up from below my feet almost immediately. I tensed, but didn't move. The stone inside of the circle fell in on itself, like someone had let the bottom out. It swirled down like water into a drain, the opposite of what I usually saw, which was a big fist or face growing up out of the ground. A rabbit hole of some kind had formed, deep and too dark to see down.

"You are not going in there, are you?" Milo asked.

"Not a chance in hell," I replied. I'd jumped into Smedge's mouth once before and ended up in the middle of the Fey's underground city, and I had no idea where this particular troll's gullet stopped.

Disappointment over not actually seeing Smedge again was quickly brushed away by the appearance of a tiny bald head with tufts of white hair fluffing up from the perimeter. More hair poked out of his pointed ears, framing his whole wrinkled, ancient face like a cotton cloud. Small, sparkling eyes peered at me from beneath bushy white eyebrows, and he leaned forward on a spiraled wood cane. He kept rising up until the he was completely above ground, the earth beneath him solid like it had never moved.

"Horzt," I said, recognizing the old gnome immediately.

He nodded, but did not smile. His sharp eyes took in his audience, and he didn't speak until he seemed satisfied that he was among friends. "Greetings from the Apothi, Evangeline," he said.

"Greetings." I knelt down to get eye-level with him, curiosity beating against the inside of my skull like a hammer. "I never expected to see you again."

"Nor I you, child."

This was the creature I had to thank for even being alive today—the one who'd gifted (or cursed) me with my healing powers. The powers Thackery never believed were magical. So much pain because this little gnome had been tricked by an elf. And so much joy, I realized, with a quick glance at Wyatt.

Wyatt watched us with a wary expression, and I understood. This could easily be a trap from the Fey.

"Sorry to be blunt, but why are you here?" I asked.

"A war is coming," Horzt replied. "The Fey are quiet now, but Amalie is cunning and she is planning. Always planning. You confound her, Evangeline, but not for much longer."

"Can you tell me anything?"

"I can't. The Apothi are no longer welcome among the Fey Council members. Our people are divided, thanks to Amalie's reign. Not all agree with her end game goal."

"Which is what?"

His deeply wrinkled face squished down into something horribly sad. "A return to a time before man ruled this earth. She means to see you destroy yourselves, and she will use every tool available to do so."

"Without lifting a finger of her own?"

"Correct."

We'd learned, to our utter shock and amusement, that despite Amalie's apparently bloodthirsty nature, sprites and the rest of the Fey were actually pacifists. They couldn't make a physical move in a fight to hurt me. However, Amalie had no problem sending a horde of goblins in my general direction. Or taking over the bodies of three police officers and using their influence over the Triads to have me set up for murder. She was the ultimate manipulator.

"She will attack you sideways," Horzt said. "By any means necessary to accomplish her goal."

"Yeah, we've noticed. Is she behind the upswing in goblin violence?"

He nodded. "The loss of Walter Thackery and his machinations have left a void in her reach. She's going to fill it with whatever will hurt you most. Your allies are thinning out, but I can offer you two small gifts."

Horzt reached into the folds of his robe and removed a long, narrow leather pouch. I took it, the material impossibly smooth, and unfolded the top. Wyatt came forward a few steps to watch me pull out a roll of thin, yellowed paper with a white, bone-like pole at each end. A scroll of some kind, tied together with a piece of silky thread.

"This is a written history of the elves," Horzt said. "We keep very little written down, as our languages are oral and not transcribed."

I gentle unrolled part of the scroll. The tiny lines of black ink were written in characters I didn't recognize. "What language is this?"

"Aramaic. The scroll was written by humans as a favor many, many millennia ago. We came into possession of it when the elves were all but destroyed."

"So we need an Aramaic expert."

"Or a really smart internet translator," Milo said behind me.

Horzt frowned. He probably had no idea what the internet was.

"Thank you for this." I handed the scroll to Wyatt, then tipped the tube over for the second object weighing down the bottom. Another leather pouch, about the size of a grapefruit, dropped into my palm. The pouch was cinched tight, but whatever was inside wasn't solid.

"You needn't open that," Horzt said. "Not yet."

"What is it?" I asked.

"The cure for your infected friends."

My heart slammed against my ribs. "For the vampires? You found a cure for Thackery's virus?"

"I did. A teaspoon dissolved in a cup of warm human blood. Split the dosage among six. You should have enough for them all."

Relief flooded my chest, and sharp tears stung the corners of my eyes. "Thank you so much for this. But won't Amalie be pissed at you for helping us?"

"She no longer cares for the future of the Apothi, no matter our actual worth. So we will follow our gargoyle brothers to the north and leave the city for the mountains."

"I thought the Fey needed to be near First Break." First Break was the underground home of the Fey, built to protect a gateway to another plane of existence that housed the worst sort of monsters and demons.

"We need to be close to a Break, to our source of power. And this city does not house all of them."

"We could offer your people sanctuary at the Watchtower," I said without thinking—or discussing it with the people actually in charge of those decisions.

"A generous offer, but I must decline. Amalie will not chase us if we leave. Her wrath is far reaching and her memory long. I cannot risk my people becoming nearly extinct like the elves."

Like the Coni and Stri—two Clans of shape-shifting birds of prey that Amalie had helped destroy. My thoughts turned to Phin, and I missed him more than ever. "I understand," I said. "So this is good-bye, right?"

"For now. Perhaps we will meet again in a brighter future." Horzt turned around and gazed up at Wyatt. "I'm sorry I can't do anything to fix you, but your infection is beyond my ability to heal."

"You've already given us so much," Wyatt said. And he wasn't just talking about today's information and gifts.

"Be well and good journey to you all."

"Good journey," Wyatt said, and I echoed him.

The ground beneath Horzt rumbled, and he slowly lowered back into the ground the same way he'd come up. As the concrete swirled into place, shapes began to form. Shapes that became words: Good Bye Stony.

"Good-bye, Smedge," I said. "Horzt, too."

The words disappeared, and the rumbling ground was lost to the thunder of traffic overhead.

I studied the medicine pouch, shocked that I had the answer to one of our biggest problems sitting in the palm of my hand. It seemed too damned easy. Nothing fell into my lap like this, and yet I had no reason to doubt Horzt's sincerity.

"Something tells me Eulan will be surprised to see us twice in one day," Milo said.

"No kidding." I dropped the pouch back into the larger leather holder, then put the scroll inside with it. No sense in damaging either one of them.

"Do you think we'll find anything useful on that scroll?" Baylor asked as our group headed back for the hole in the fence.

"Hard to tell until someone translates it," Wyatt said. "But I doubt Horzt would have risked giving it to us if it was useless."

"Agreed," I said.

Marcus held up the piece of fence while the rest of us ducked through. We stopped as a group next to the first car.

"I want to get the cure back to the vampires," I said before anyone else could.

"Right," Baylor said. "If this works, we can certainly use their help again. Take Milo and Marcus with you. Truman and

I will take the scroll back to the Watchtower and get started on translating it."

Across the circle from me, Marcus tensed at almost the exact same moment that Wyatt did. The hairs on the back of my neck stood up. Marcus growled. Wyatt grunted, then collapsed face-first to the pavement. A splash of red feathers poked out of his back, right between his shoulder blades.

"Get dow—!" Marcus couldn't even finish his thought before a dart hit him in the throat, and he dropped like a rock.

Milo lunged for Marcus. I grabbed Milo and yanked us both behind the parked car. Baylor skidded to a stop at our feet, a dart in his thigh, and he fell unconscious a split-second later.

"Where the fuck are they?" I asked, clutching the case to my chest. We were facing the road and the water, with no hiding places for snipers. They had to be under the bridge.

"No idea," Milo said. He grabbed Baylor's gun from his hand. "Call it in."

I fumbled into my back pocket for my phone. Something small bounced off the roof of the car, then hit the pavement in front of us. A round object that made my chest tighten. I didn't have time to reach for my emotional trigger, to attempt to teleport us out of there.

Milo tackled me to the ground right as the flash bomb exploded.

Chapter Six

Later

Some serious discomfort in my left arm helped wake me up from total blackness. I blinked a cement block wall into focus. The ground beneath me was hard and cold. I wiggled my left arm, which was bent beneath my body and numb from the pressure. My head hurt from the concussion blast and I tasted blood in my mouth.

"Evy?"

Marcus's voice somewhere nearby. It echoed, though, hinting at close quarters. I grunted in response. Got my arm out from beneath me, then tried to sit up. Something heavy weighed against my neck—a metal collar of some kind. A collar attached to a length of chain. The chain was threaded up to the ceiling, connected to some sort of pulley, and it went out the front of my cage.

Shit. I knew exactly where I was. I'd been here before.

Five-by-eight jail cell. Iron bars in front of me and to my left. Four cells, and I was in the last one. I'd been jailed here once before, months ago, by a bunch of idiot teenage Halfies working for Tovin the Crazy Elf.

I yanked at the thick metal collar and couldn't get it off. Reached for the Break, intent on teleporting my ass out of that cell—only the Break wasn't there. Just like the first time, something was blocking its magic from me. "Fuck," I said. To compound the badness of the situation, I'd been stripped out of my damned clothes. Right down to my bra and panties.

And I wasn't the only one half-naked. In the cell next to mine, Baylor lay unconscious, modesty protected only by his boxer-briefs. Marcus was next to him, already on his feet and prowling his cage. Unlike Baylor, he was totally naked—he'd told me once clothes made shifting take longer, so he wore as few layers as necessary, which meant commando. The skin beneath his collar was bright red.

Silver. Damn.

In the far cage, the same one where I'd watched my friend Alex die only to come back as an infected half-Blood, lay Milo, also skinned down to his boxers. He was starting to wake up, though, and Marcus squatted close to the bars on his side.

"Milo?" Marcus said. "Milo, wake up."

"Working on it," came the pained reply.

Baylor grunted and twitched, and soon all four of us were awake.

Four of us. "Where's Wyatt?" I asked.

Marcus lifted his face and sniffed. "Truman hasn't been down here." His lips curled back into a snarl. "Bengals."

"Seriously?" Milo asked. "The Bengals kidnapped us? Why?"

"We will assuredly find out."

"Evy," Baylor said. "Can you teleport?"

"No, I'm being blocked." The first time I'd been here, a magically infused orange crystal had been blocking my access to the Break. I didn't see another crystal, but that didn't mean it wasn't there somewhere. And how the hell had a Bengal gotten his paws on one, anyhow?

Our clothes lay in a heap near the basement door—a door that wouldn't open to anything good. Strange to think that I'd been here before, and I still had no idea where "here" was. Wyatt and I had gotten out the first time thanks to Smedge. And Smedge wouldn't be coming to the rescue today. I had no idea if Wyatt was still alive, and my heart ached with the uncertainty.

We didn't have to wait long for answers to our burning questions. Marcus began growling seconds before the door swung open. A tall, muscular man with dark auburn hair walked in. His shining copper eyes gave him away as Felia. Marcus snarled louder. The stranger ignored him and stepped over to a pulley system with several levers—our chains and collars.

Not good.

He flipped a switch and turned a crank. Instantly, the tension in my chain tightened as the slack was pulled upward into the pulley. The chain went taut, the stiff collar pressing against my throat, tight enough to pull me nearly to my tiptoes. He stopped and locked the chain in, leaving me with nowhere to go. My hands and feet were still free—thank God—but I was one solid yank from being choked to death.

The man went down the row until all four of us were strung up in a similar way, never saying a single word.

Marcus broke the silence first. "What do you want, Vale?" he asked.

The fact that Marcus knew the bad guy surprised me more than it should have. There weren't that many Felia in the city, and being part of the ruling family meant Marcus probably knew most of them. Still, everything about this felt personal, and that made me very, very nervous.

"I have a simple request, Marcus," Vale replied. "I want the security codes to the Dane mansion."

Marcus made a noise that was part-laugh and part-snort. "You know that will never happen."

"Never say never."

This wasn't going to end well. The Dane mansion was a small fortress, and it housed not only Marcus's family, but also the last members of the Coni Clan. Marcus would never betray the people there like this, no matter what Vale dealt out.

"So this is how your family will see Riley defeated?" Marcus asked with a disgusted snarl. "You fear a fair fight just as your brother did, so you'll sneak up from behind and stab him in the back?"

"Actually, I was planning to stab him in the face."

The coldness in Vale's voice gave me chills. Not simply because of the lack of emotion as he spoke of murder, but that he'd said it in front of all of us. We were dead in his eyes, no matter what. *Please, Wyatt, please be alive.*

"You're a fool, Vale, as is your entire family," Marcus said.

I wanted to tell him to shut up and not antagonize the bad guy, only he was doing exactly what I usually did. Bluster and bray in order to buy time for help to arrive. Only we hadn't managed to call anyone in time. No one at the Watchtower knew where we were. They might not even realize we were missing.

"We'll see who's the fool," Vale replied.

He snapped his fingers, and a second Felia came inside. He was shorter than Vale, but had the same auburn hair and muscular build. The Goon walked to my cell, unlocked the door with a set of keys, then pushed the door to the side with a metallic clank. My stomach tightened. Every instinct in my body screamed.

Goon got close enough. I grabbed the chain over my head with both hands, held tight, and kicked out hard with my feet. My heels slammed into Goon's mouth and snapped his head back. He yelped and stumbled right out of the cell until he hit the far wall. Blood dripped from his split lip. His copper eyes flashed with fury.

Vale chuckled. "I see she lives up to her reputation."

"Take the collar off and you'll see what I can do, Fuzz Face," I snapped. I'd been sparring with Marcus for weeks just for the practice, and I had no doubts I could deliver a solid beat-down to Vale's ass. Especially with so much extra motivation hanging by their necks.

Vale came to my cell door, but stayed out of reach of my kicks. His nose wrinkled. I really hated it when Therians—Felia, Cania, or otherwise—sniffed me. It made me want to apologize for having not showered recently, even if I had. Athough in this case, I hadn't.

"You reek of the half-breed," Vale said with obvious disgust in his voice. "What sort of person would lie down with an animal like that?"

"You got a wife I can ask the same question to?"

His eyes narrowed. "This one belongs to another. His smell is all over her. She won't be useful."

Crap. Yes, I'd seen my fair share of torture recently, but of the four of us here, I was the fastest healer. I needed to keep this asshole's attention on me as long as possible. "Where's Wyatt?"

"Who?"

"The half-breed, where is he?"

Malice pulled the corners of Vale's mouth into a twisted smile. "Don't concern yourself with him any longer, woman. Enjoy your final few hours alive."

"Like I haven't heard that before."

Vale's gaze wandered from me up to the chain keeping me dangling from the ceiling. "Suffocation is a slow, painful way to die."

My guts twisted. "I've been tortured before."

"Indeed."

Vale and Goon left my cage door open—which didn't help me any, because I couldn't get out of that damned collar—and walked down the row. Past Baylor—whose intimidation face was on full-force and looked as easy to persuade as a brick wall—and past Marcus, who looked pissed enough to pop a few blood vessels. Vale opened Milo's cell door and took a single step inside.

Shit.

I had to angle a bit to see them through the bars and the two bodies in my line of sight. Milo seemed relaxed, but I'd seen him fight. I knew his poker face and how quickly he reacted to threats.

"How about you, boy?" Vale asked. "Have you been tortured before?"

Milo didn't answer. Didn't seem to react at all, and I wanted to know what he was thinking. He'd been beaten as a child, and he'd been wounded as a Triad Hunter. But torture was another animal altogether, something not really understood until it was experienced. Milo had suffered so much these last two months already.

"I'm the only one with the information you want," Marcus said.

"You're right," Vale replied. "But you know as I do that some things hurt much more than physical pain. And this human smells like you, Marcus. Why is that, I wonder?"

Milo's shoulders flexed. Marcus moved toward the bars, only to be jerked back by the collar around his neck.

Good God, that must have been some kiss, if Vale still smelled it.

Vale snapped his fingers. Goon turned the crank, and the chain yanked Milo right off his feet by the neck. Milo gasped and grabbed the chain with both hands. The collar lifted from behind, putting the curve of metal directly over his windpipe. Vale lunged forward and punched Milo in his unprotected midsection—the perfect blow to make his lungs seize up and knock the wind out. Milo's face flushed bright red. He coughed and sputtered and couldn't seem to keep his grip on the chain.

Marcus roared—a terrible sound more animal than man. I wanted to scream and yell, too, to make them stop hurting my friend. To make them hurt me instead. I'd heal. I always did. Milo didn't have my healing powers, and I'd already lost so many friends.

All I could was watch, and somehow that hurt more than any physical blows that Vale could have landed.

The moment seemed to last for hours, though in truth was probably only a minute or two. But when you can't breathe—when you're watching a friend who can't breathe and you can't do anything to help—even a minute is an excruciating eternity. Vale finally gestured at Goon, who released the slack on Milo's chain. Milo hit the floor hard and rolled onto his side, away from us, coughing and gasping.

Vale stepped out and closed the cell door. "Think about it a while, Marcus," he said. "You're quite alone here, and I can make his death last for days."

"I will kill you with my bare hands, Vale," Marcus said in a voice so deadly it sent chills down my spine.

"Who's the one in a cage, Jaguar?"

Vale and his goon exited without loosening our chains, leaving Marcus, Baylor and I no choice but to stand there.

"Milo?" I said.

His reply was a fierce grunt. He raised his right hand and gave a thumbs-up, but didn't turn to face us. He just laid there, panting.

"I'm so sorry," Marcus said. His voice was a whisper, but sounded incredibly loud in the silence of the prison. I'd never heard him so unsure of himself.

"Not your fault," Milo rasped out. He rolled onto his back, then sat up. His face was still red and he looked like he wanted to vomit. "I know you won't tell them anything. You can't."

"He'll kill you."

"Maybe." Something sad passed across Milo's face. Sad and determined. "But the future of your people is more important than me. More important than any of us."

Marcus's hands clenched into fists. He looked like he wanted to disagree. He didn't, though, because Milo was right.

"Can you tell how many Felia are in the building?" Baylor asked. Leave it to Cerberus to get us back on point.

"I can detect three distinct scents, including Vale and Peck." Peck must equal Goon. "Both have been in contact with Truman recently too, because I caught his scent on them."

Which really meant nothing—they could have killed Wyatt as easily as locked him up somewhere in the building.

"Anything useful about our location?" Baylor asked.

"Not much," Marcus said. "No traffic sounds, so we aren't near a highway. There are odors of rot and disuse, but nothing distinctive."

"This is some kind of lockup area," I said. "Wyatt and I were held here once before."

"You were?"

I explained it for Marcus's benefit, as much as Milo and Baylor, who had some idea of this part of my past. I'd been on the run from the Triads at the time, during what seemed like a different life altogether. "Are there any old jails or precincts that this could be?" I asked Baylor.

"Several, actually," he replied. "Depends on what part of town we're in. I'm surprised you never went looking for this place."

"It never seemed important, what with everything else going on." Vale's earlier animosity toward Marcus came back. "Marcus, why does Vale hate you so much? It seemed more personal than Riley."

Marcus growled, low and deep. "It is personal. Prentiss? The Bengal who kidnapped Keenan?"

"And was executed by the Assembly. Yeah, I remember him."

"Prentiss was Vale's brother."

Fantastic. A whole family full of crazy, treasonous tigers.

"So this is revenge?" Baylor asked.

"In all likelihood. Vale's personal revenge is tangled up with his fanatical need to unseat my family from our position of power within the Pride."

"That's comforting." Even Baylor could be sarcastic once in a while.

"Sooner or later, our absences will be noticed. Our friends will search for us."

"Who else knew about the message under the bridge?" I asked.

"Gina and Astrid knew," Baylor replied. "But Vale isn't completely stupid. He won't leave any clues behind, and scents are difficult to detect there with the river and highway so close."

"But they'll start looking."

"For five people in a city of half a million?"

I didn't answer. I had to stay optimistic about our chances of escaping alive, and Marcus beating down each argument wasn't going to help. Let him be Mr. Negativity. I had to find Wyatt and make sure he was okay. I had to know what Vale did with the elf scroll and the medicine pouch. Most importantly, I had to get that cure to the vampires as soon as possible. None of that could be accomplished while dead.

Somehow we all had to stay alive.

***

With no way to measure the passage of time, I could only guess at how many hours I stood at the end of my taut chain while Milo was tortured. I couldn't do anything but remain present—checking out or turning away felt like abandoning him. I wouldn't do it. Baylor and Marcus didn't either, even though the silver collar around his neck was making Marcus feverish and unsteady.

The first time Vale and Peck came back, they cuffed Milo's hands behind his back and then choked him unconscious. Before they left, Vale asked Marcus for the security codes. Marcus told him to fuck off. Not long after Milo woke up, they were back with a wooden cane.

Each sharp thwack of the wood against the backs of Milo's legs echoed in my brain like shrill whistles—harsh and painful. Stretched by his neck onto his tiptoes, Milo couldn't avoid the blows. Couldn't do anything except take them until his legs gave out. Fat tears rolled down my cheeks as I cried silently for his agony—agony I knew too well and desperately wanted to take away from him.

"Your family is so smug," Vale said during his fourth go at Milo. "The Danes think themselves kings of the Felia when you're anything but."

"We've always been fair," Marcus replied. "You came at us first when you kidnapped Keenan."

"Perhaps, but you drew first blood the day you killed my brother."

"He was judged by the Assembly and executed according to our laws."

"You turned him over. You and Astrid and that human fool. You're all responsible."

The name Prentiss rang in my head from last night's conversation in the cafeteria. This wasn't only about leading the Pride. This was personal for Vale, which meant he was being ruled by his emotions. Emotional people made mistakes.

Milo's chain had been loosened enough to allow him to kneel. His back, legs and arms were a mosaic of welts and blossoming bruises, with the occasional stripe of drying blood. Sweat trickled down his face and chest. He didn't seem quite aware of what was happening, as if he'd gone deep inside of his own head where the pain couldn't touch him.

Rage for his agony and hatred for Vale built up in me like a shaken soda bottle, the pressure too damned much. Desperate to explode somewhere. To make someone pay for Milo's suffering. And for Marcus's suffering as he watched someone he obviously cared for tortured because of those feelings. Even the normally cool-under-all-kinds-of-pressure Baylor was getting twitchy as one hour turned into two, and then more.

Vale stopped for a while to take a phone call. Peck followed him out. The only sound in the prison was Milo's ragged, shallow breathing. His entire body was shaking. I tugged at the chain around my own neck, desperate to get loose and help him. I sought the Break and couldn't find it. I couldn't do anything, and I did not wear helpless well.

"Talk to me," Milo said in a broken voice. "Anyone, please, just something." He hadn't cried out once during the beatings, but he was close to the shattering point. It was in his voice, his shivering body, the harshness of his breathing.

"The obstacle course is coming along well," Baylor said, his voice clear and steady. "Gina's brilliant when it comes to physical training."

"Army Rangers," Milo said.

"Yes, because she was a Ranger. Construction will take a little time, but the plans are fantastic. Better than what we had at Boot Camp."

Milo made a snorting sound. "Anything's better than Boot Camp."

"That is the fucking truth," I said. "But it had some good ideas, and Gina will help design a fantastic obstacle course for training. It'll keep all of our asses in fighting shape, especially yours, Gant."

"Don't think I'll be running it for a while."

"Bullshit. You'll be the first to show me up, and you know it."

He angled his head sideways and gave me what seemed like a grateful smile. Distance made it hard to know for sure. "Can't do this much longer," he whispered.

Fresh tears stung my eyes and closed my throat, making words impossible.

"You'll do this as long as you have to," Marcus said. "Until we get out of this. But you must be awake and aware when we do. Please, Milo."

"I'm trying."

The door swung open. Peck waited there while Vale came into the room again. Sauntered was probably a better word and it made me hate him even more.

"Word on the street is the Watch has sent out several of their little squads to look for you," Vale said. "This is, as you can imagine, excellent news."

"How's that?" Baylor asked.

"Because it gives my people more moving targets. We can't touch you when you're holed up in your Watchtower. In the city, you're vulnerable. You idiots proved that this morning."

"More targets also means more eyes looking for us."

"They won't find you here. Although I may plant a few breadcrumbs. I'd love a chance for a go at the human traitor Tybalt. It's certainly a shame he wasn't with you today, Marcus. Maybe your little toy wouldn't be taking the brunt of my attention."

"Leave Tybalt alone," Milo said. He had a strength in his voice that surprised me and shouldn't have—Tybalt and Milo were as close as any blood-related brothers.

Vale laughed and walked over to the chain levers. "You, boy, won't be around to see me kill your friend. But I promise you I will kill him for his betrayal. You can take that promise to your grave." Vale turned the lever.

The chain yanked Milo to his feet. He cried out as he was lifted up to the tips of his toes. Then Vale lifted him a fraction higher, until he could no longer touch the ground. Milo didn't kick, didn't scream. He just…dangled there.

"You're going to kill him!" I screamed. I couldn't help it. The building wave of hatred was rising up and right out of my mouth. "You fucking asshole, let him down!"

"No," Vale said.

"Marcus won't tell you anything. It's pointless."

"Hardly. I find it entertaining to see the unflappable, badass Marcus Dane coming undone over the death of a scrawny human male."

Marcus snarled. He had murder in his fevered eyes.

Vale stepped into my open cell door. He made a point of looking me over, which made me want to gouge his eyeballs out with my thumbs.

"Like I said, take off the collar and let's go at it, Fuzz Face," I said.

"I'm tired of you," Vale said. "And let's face it, you have a habit of not dying when you're supposed to." He reached beneath his un-tucked shirt and produced a handgun, which he pointed right at me. Finger on the trigger, safety off.

I stood up straighter, stomach tightening. I could survive a lot of things, but not a point blank bullet to the head *Stall. Stall. Stall.* "The goblins, Halfies and Fey are your enemies, Vale, not the humans. And certainly not your own Pride members."

"Pride politics are not your business, human."

"They are when my friends are involved."

"Those so-called friends have divided loyalties. They made their choices."

"We've all made our choices, and I have some pretty well-placed friends. Not just Therians, but vampires and gremlins and a few other species." Maybe I was stretching it with the gremlin thing, but Vale didn't know any differently. "You kill me and you'll be making the Pride some serious fucking enemies. You gonna take on that responsibility, *Alpha*?"

Vale hesitated. He stared at me, his expression neutral, long enough to freak me out a little bit. Milo was slowly strangling to death, and I was having a stare-down with a pissed-off Bengal. Finally, Vale blinked. He tucked his gun away, then stepped over to our pile of clothes. Selected a blue shirt—Baylor's, I thought, but I honestly hadn't been paying attention to what anyone was wearing earlier—and then reached for the pulley controls. My collar lifted me just past my tiptoes, then right off the ground. My throat constricted. I grabbed the chain and held on tight before it choked me.

Baylor said something I didn't catch, then something was touching my belly. I kicked out instinctively, but Vale was already out of reach. What the hell had he done? Rubbed Baylor's shirt on me?

"You're right, I think," Vale said. "There's no sense in me killing you when someone else can do it for me."

With my arms above my head and my whole body stretched out, breathing became a minor challenge. Pain was also an issue, in both my shoulders and hands. Vale stood outside my cell door, waiting. I figured out what he was waiting for when Peck came through the prison door, dragging something with him on one of those poles that animal catchers used on wild creatures.

My heart nearly stopped when I saw Wyatt on the other end of that pole. His face was half-shifted—jaw elongated, cheekbones broken, black fur sprouting all along his throat. His eyes were pure silver, his teeth sporting a pair of wicked fangs. I'd seen this face only twice before, and it scared the hell out of me both times. He was also shirtless, his torso and face bruised, showing evidence of his own abuse at Vale's hands.

Wyatt snarled at Marcus when Peck pushed him closer to the bars. Marcus hissed right back.

"Bring him here," Vale said.

Peck changed his angle, putting Wyatt between him and Vale. I knew Wyatt, could see the fear and confusion in his eyes. Saw how hard he was battling the wolf and trying to keep it together. They'd done this to him, forced the wolf out.

Putting Baylor's scent on me made chillingly perfect sense.

"I told you, half-breed, that she would break your trust," Vale said, as though he and Wyatt had been in the middle of a conversation. "I can smell the human male on her. He tried to rid her of your mark."

Wyatt bared his teeth at Vale, then took a step toward my cage. Peck stepped in first, keeping a distance from me by putting his back to the cement block wall. He stopped with Wyatt right in front of me, close enough to touch.

Vale stayed nearby. "You can smell him on your mate," he said.

"Wyatt, you know better," I said. Talking wasn't easy hanging like this. "I love you."

"How could the unfaithful bitch love a half-breed like you? You're a monster. Embrace your beast."

Wyatt's eyes flashed with pure fury, and for an instant, I thought he was lost to me. Lost to the animal that was a part of him. Lost to jealousy and rage. He raised his right hand, fingers longer, the nails hooked into black claws. One swipe and I'd be dead. For good.

Shit.

CHAPTER SEVEN

Monday Afternoon

"Wyatt," I said. Talking wasn't easy with that collar pressing into my throat, but I had to get him to listen to me. To focus. "Wyatt?"

He snarled, a sound that sent ice through my veins. Behind him, Vale laughed.

"Truman, stand down," Baylor yelled.

Wyatt growled at him. So not helpful. Wyatt moved closer to me, enough to feel his heat, his breath, to see the sweat beading on his forehead and chest. To smell him. My arms ached from holding on so tightly to the chain. Next to me, Peck slipped the noose off Wyatt's neck, then moved behind me, out of sight.

"Kill her," Vale said. "Now!"

Wyatt bared his teeth at me—and then he winked. He fucking winked at me.

Son of a bitch. Big faker.

He lunged. Instead of at me, he pounced on Peck. Peck yelped and gurgled something, which was lost to the horrific sounds of ripping flesh. Vale yelled vague obscenities and reached behind himself.

"Gun!" I shouted.

Wyatt was a blur as he slammed into Vale, knocking the gun out of his hand. It clattered to the floor. Vale fought back with surprising strength, and the pair of them rolled into the bars of Baylor's cage, snapping and trying to land solid punches. Wyatt was fighting with emotion, though, not with his head. Vale struck Wyatt's temple, which knocked Wyatt sideways and into the opposite wall. Vale didn't stay to fight, the coward. He bolted right out the door.

"Keys," Baylor yelled.

Wyatt grabbed the keys off the floor where they'd fallen and tossed them at my feet. Not exactly the smartest plan ever—only he hit the release lever on the chains as he chased after Vale.

I hit the floor with a pained thud, my arms tingling from the strain. The keys were somewhere underneath me. As I shifted around, I came face to face with Peck's throat-less corpse. I scooted away from the expanding blood pool and scooped up the keys. Fitted the smallest key into the hole in the front of my collar. It snapped open. I yanked the fucking thing off. My skin was clammy and raw, and I was glad to be free of it. I rubbed at my throat with one hand while I used the other to grab the bars and haul ass to my feet.

"Stone, he's not breathing!" Marcus's shout propelled me out of my cage and down the line to Milo's.

All of our chains had been released, and Milo was crumpled on the floor, face down, hands still bound behind his back. I found the key for his door and yanked it open. Dropped down by his head and unlocked the collar. His throat was a study in bruise patterns from that fucking collar, and Marcus was right—he wasn't breathing.

"Dammit, Milo." I couldn't roll him over because his hands. Fear started to creep in and turn to panic. I tested the keys on his handcuffs—not standard cop cuffs, either, but shackles reminiscent of old prison movies. The last key finally opened them.

I tossed the keys at Marcus's outstretched hand and let him release himself. I got Milo arranged on his back, then pressed my ear to his chest. The stutter of a heartbeat gave me enough hope to tilt Milo's head back and begin CPR. I wasn't good at it, but I knew how to do it, and he was not dying on me, goddammit.

"Come on, breathe," I said.

Marcus's cell door slammed open. The keys jangled, changing hands to Baylor, because Marcus was suddenly crouching opposite me, his face a twisted mask of misery. He reached out, like he wanted to touch Milo, then drew back. I ignored him and focused on breathing for Milo, and getting him to breathe for himself.

"Breathe, damn you, you are not dying today. " More reps. "Breathe!"

Milo sputtered, then drew in a deep, ragged gulp of air. His eyelids fluttered, but stayed shut. His hands flailed out.

Marcus caught them. "It's okay, Milo, you're going to be fine," he said.

Milo made a noise that broke my heart with its pained helplessness. Marcus scooped him up and held him against his chest, somehow finding a way to hold him close that didn't aggravate his bruised and bloodied back. Milo pressed his face into Marcus's shoulder and clung to him as he gasped and coughed.

I felt like I'd interrupted something very private, so I scooted away and stood. Baylor was gone, probably after Wyatt. The gun was gone, too. I dashed up the three small stairs and out into a dark, dirty hallway. Dim light came from further down, where the hallway opened up into a wider office area of some kind.

Cubicle walls remained, but desks and furniture had long since been removed.

The sound of furious growling caught my attention. Wyatt. I followed the noise past a row of cubicles and spotted Baylor standing next to a boarded up door. Wyatt was sitting on the floor, holding his head, bleeding from his left temple. The half-shift was gone, but his eyes remained pure silver.

"What happened?" I asked.

"Vale got away," Wyatt replied. He admitted it like he'd tasted pig shit—with utter disgust.

"There's another dead body back there," Baylor said, pointing to our right. "Looks like another Bengal. Milo?"

"Alive," I said as I squatted in front of Wyatt. "How are you?"

"In control," he said. "Barely."

"Adrian, can you give us a minute?"

Baylor moved away. I reached for Wyatt's chin. He jerked his head away from me with a soft snarl. I grabbed his chin anyway and made Wyatt look at me. "Are you okay?"

"I almost lost it, Evy, when I smelled him on you." Fear crept into his silver eyes, the same fear he'd carried since his infection. The fear of hurting me.

"But you didn't. You stayed in control, Wyatt, and you saved our lives. Whatever Vale did to you, you stayed in control."

"He wanted me to kill you."

"Yes, he did."

"Why?"

"Because I was irritating him. He wants the security codes for the Dane mansion. Marcus wouldn't give them up. We need to regroup and get the hell out of here before Vale returns with backup."

"Is he likely to?"

"I don't know, but we know who he is and what he wants to do. Shutting us up will probably become a priority for him, and I don't want to be here if he does come back."

"Me, either." Wyatt brushed gentle fingertips over my throat. "They hurt you."

"Barely. I've had worse."

Emotion flickered in his eyes. "I hate that."

"Me, too." I pressed a quick kiss to his mouth, wishing we had time for more. "Come on."

We went back down to the cells. Baylor and Marcus were both dressed. They'd ripped Milo's t-shirt down the back and managed to get each arm through a sleeve, giving him some protection. That seemed about as much as he could manage. Milo's face was horribly pale, his whole body shiny with sweat, and shivering like he was cold. The individual bruises on his back and legs were darkening into one large, horrific splotch of color, and the skin was starting to swell.

Wyatt and I dressed fast. Our weapons and phones were missing, and the scroll satchel wasn't with our things. Fucking Vale. Marcus carried Milo up into the outer offices. Wyatt, Baylor, and I did a quick search, just in case, and turned up nothing. Vale had either disposed of everything else or taken it with him.

"Vale's scent goes this way," Marcus said, inclining his head toward another hallway.

Wyatt led, using his nose to follow the scent. Baylor backed him up with Vale's dropped gun, while I took the rear. The short hallway ended at what looked like an emergency door. The exit sign above wasn't lit, the entire hall barely illuminated by a crack of light from beneath the door.

"He must have gone out here," Wyatt said. He listened a moment. "No obvious voices or sounds."

"Doesn't mean there's no ambush waiting," Baylor said. He felt along the door's frame, testing for wires or trips.

I checked for the Break and found its power waiting. Whatever Vale had used to block my access, he'd apparently taken it with him. I nearly offered to teleport out, but it was a stupid idea. I had no clue what was outside that door and fusing my legs with a car fender was not on today's agenda.

Baylor and Wyatt shooed us back a few paces, and I took a defensive position in front of Marcus and Milo. Wyatt stood to the left of the door, Baylor to the right. Wyatt pressed the emergency bar down. Nothing squealed. Pushed the door open a few inches. Sunlight streamed inside. Wyatt sniffed the air.

So far, so good.

He pushed a little more.

Baylor inched forward and peeked outside. "Looks like a parking lot, small one, back end of an alley type," he said. "No cars. Older buildings, too, unkempt."

"Any ideas on location?" I asked.

"Nothing I recognize, but I'd lay good money we're close to Mercy's Lot." He nodded at Wyatt, who let the door shut. "Okay, there's a plank fence straight ahead, about twenty feet, but no cover. Wyatt and I will go out first and make sure we aren't being watched. When we're sure it's clear, the three of you follow on my signal."

I glanced behind me at Marcus, who nodded his agreement. Milo ignored all of us, swallowed whole by the pain that was his entire world. "Understood," I said to Baylor.

Our trio backed deeper into the hallway. Wyatt and Baylor shared a look. Wyatt shoved the door open wide. Its hinges squealed. Sunlight flashed in my eyes, and I blinked hard. Heard an odd popping sound, and then the door slammed shut again. A second thud.

As the orange dots disappeared from my vision, two things became clear: Wyatt still stood to the left of the closed emergency door, and Baylor was down.

Flat on his back on the ground. Eyes wide open. A red hole centered perfectly in his forehead. Blood pooling around his head.

"Adrian?" Wyatt asked.

Oh God, no.

Chapter Eight

I didn't have to check his pulse to know Adrian Baylor was dead, but I did anyway. Knelt down and pressed my fingertips to his throat. Nothing. A perfect storm of shock and grief formed in my throat and slowly choked me, preventing any real tears. I closed his eyelids, the skin still so warm.

This can't be happening.

"It was a fucking sniper," Wyatt said.

The thick rasp of his voice made me look at him. He'd slumped to the floor next to the door, as devastated as I'd ever seen him. He'd worked with Baylor in the Triads for years, him and Kismet. I wanted to comfort Wyatt, to pull him into my arms and hold him until the shock went away. But Baylor would still be dead, Milo needed a doctor, and Vale was getting further away.

Action first, grief later.

"Stay here, I'll be right back," I said.

No one argued with me. I ran back down the short hallway and poked around until I found some stairs. Up to the next level. More offices, just as empty and dusty. The thickness of the closed up air made my eyes itch and my nose tingle with the need to sneeze. I navigated my way back to where I guessed the emergency exit to be and found a boarded up window.

The boards had enough cracks for me to peek through. To see the empty alley parking lot below and the buildings around us. We were downtown, somewhere near the train tracks and Black River, if my guess was right. The back of this building faced a long, empty alley, and at the end of it was another brick building and a nice flat roof. Perfect place for a sniper to lay in wait and pick us off one by one. I studied the rooftop a section at a time until a small flash of light caught my attention. The kind of flash a scope makes when the sun hits the lens just right.

"Bingo, you fucker," I said.

Downstairs, Wyatt hadn't moved. Marcus had settled himself and Milo on the floor, and Marcus gave me an expectant look.

"I know where the sniper is," I said, scooping Baylor's gun off the floor. "I'm going to go kill him, then I'll be back for you guys."

My announcement broke through Wyatt's haze of shock. "What?" he asked.

"Just hang tight, please."

"Be careful."

"You know me."

"Be careful anyway."

I smiled, then closed my eyes. My emotional tap into the Break was loneliness. I imagined if it was Wyatt on the ground dead, a hole between his eyes, lost to me. Grief and loneliness clutched my heart and real tears stung my eyes. I latched onto the emotions and let them build. Pictured the alley beneath the other building, the empty pavement and shadows. Let the Break suck me in and rip me apart.

Teleporting hurt every single time I did it, and today was no exception. I hurtled through the magic of the Break and focused on that spot. Pulled out of the Break and came back in one piece. Tiny hammers pounded the inside of my skull. Acid bubbled up in my stomach. I doubled over, clutching my abdomen, and managed to not barf. As my mind and my eyes cleared, I took in the alley. The building two hundred feet away where my friends were waiting.

I circled what looked like a cheap apartment building until I found the fire escape. Climbed up and slowly, quietly ascended. Each squeal of rusty metal made my nerves fray a little bit more. Every step upward came with the expectation of another shot, this one blasting through my own skull. Four stories up to the roof.

The sniper was too confident in his hiding place, because he never heard me coming. I peeked over the edge and spotted him about twenty feet away from me. The barrel of his rifle was resting on the roof ledge, and his attention was fixed on the scope. I thumbed the safety off my borrowed gun, aimed, and fired.

The idiot was so surprised when I shot him in the calf that he let his rifle fall over the edge of the building. I kept my gun trained on his chest as I climbed over onto the roof. He stared at me with wide copper eyes. God, he was young. Looked about sixteen human years, which meant maybe four Therian years. Only a kid and still a murderer.

"Where's Vale?" I asked as I approached.

The teenage Felia started shaking.

"You just murdered a friend of mine, asshole, so don't think for a second I won't kill you, too."

"I don't know," he replied. "I swear, I don't. He told me to guard the door and to shoot anyone who wasn't one of ours."

"Do you know who I am?"

He shook his head so hard I thought he'd snap a vertebrae.

"So you do what Vale tells you without asking questions?"

"He's my cousin."

"And he's my enemy. I gotta tell you, kid, my enemies have a bad habit of dying."

He started crying. Actually fucking crying, and I almost felt sorry for the kid. Almost.

I loomed over him. "Your cousin is an idiot. I know he wants to murder Riley Dane, and I won't let that happen. So if you don't want every other surviving member of your family to die while I'm hunting Vale, you give me something useful."

"There's a house in Mercy's Lot," he replied through choking sobs. "452 Ashmont Road. We've met there a few times."

"Who lives there?"

"It's bank-owned now."

"Fine. Take the laces out of your shoes."

"Huh?"

"Now!"

He acquiesced. I used one lace to bind his wrists behind his back so tight his hands started turning red before I was done. The second I looped around his ankles. It wasn't ideal, especially for a Felia's strength, and I couldn't have him getting away. So for good measure, I shot him in the other calf. He screamed. I slammed the butt of my gun into the back of his head, and he slumped to the roof, unconscious.

I checked him for a cell phone and didn't find one. Teleporting back with him was going to hurt like hell, and I didn't have the energy for it. I'd have to hope he was still there later, after I got backup. I tapped into loneliness, into the Break, and teleported to the parking lot two hundred feet away. After the dizziness went away, I knocked hard on the exit door.

"Wyatt, it's me," I said.

The door opened, and I slipped inside. Right into Wyatt's arms. I hugged him back, breathing in the familiar scent of him.

Feeling the heavy thud of his heartbeat against my chest, the warmth of his breath on my neck. I hugged him, not because I needed it but because he did.

I pressed my lips to the stubble-rough skin near his ear, then whispered, "I'm so sorry about Adrian. So sorry."

He held me tighter, shaking ever so slightly. His Lupa infection had heightened all of his emotions to extremes, and he was feeling his grief more strongly than he'd usually show. Wyatt didn't break down in front of others. He broke down in private where no one could see.

"The sniper's unconscious and tied up," I said, as much for Wyatt as for Marcus. "No cell phone, but gave me an address in Mercy's Lot."

"Do you trust his information?" Marcus asked.

"Not a hell of a lot, but it's all we have." I pulled back from Wyatt's embrace so I could look him in the eyes. He'd calmed considerably, the silver returning to thin rings around his irises instead of overtaking his entire eye. "I need to find a phone and get some backup, okay?"

Wyatt started to speak, probably to say he was coming with me, then stopped. He saw the answer to that request in my face. "Do you know where we are?"

"I have an idea, yeah. Protect them for me?"

He nodded. "Watch your back."

"I love you."

"Love you, too. So much."

I handed him the gun, which he only took under protest, then I slipped back outside.

Judging by the shadows on the ground, it was late afternoon, closing in on dinnertime. My empty stomach concurred with the assessment. That late night snack in the cafeteria felt like weeks ago. Thanks to Reilly's little surprise, I hadn't eaten any of the breakfast I'd ordered. A stack of those greasy pancakes he loved sounded like heaven.

I slipped around the side of the building and headed for the street. A cold wash of familiarity hit me. Corcoran Street. It ran parallel to the railroad tracks, along an alley dotted with abandoned businesses and construction sites, and less than two blocks from here was the Corcoran train bridge. The place where my old Triad partners, Jesse and Ash, had died back in May. Only days before I died the first time, too.

The street was cracked and dotted with potholes, a testament to its lack of use or repair. No cars drove past. The sounds of the city seemed so far away. The air was thick with the ripe odors of the nearby Black River, as well as soot and ash from the train tracks. Freight trains still occasionally ran through the city, and we hadn't heard one all afternoon.

When I looked back at the building we'd been trapped in, I spotted a partial wood sign still hanging over the boarded-up front doors: lice Depar. We'd been in some sort of police station after all.

I started jogging down the street toward the train bridge, eyes open for any signs of life or modern technology. Even a pay phone would be useful. None presented themselves, and then I was standing under the bridge, its metal pylons stretching high above my head.

I hadn't been back here since the night my partners died. We'd been set up, called here individually and them ambushed by half-Bloods. We fought well, like we always had. We'd been a unit for four years, had each other's backs, and made a lot of kills. Until that final fight. Jesse slipped up and got infected. He turned so fast, so horribly, and then he killed Ash right in front of me. So I'd killed him.

Memories of another lifetime tried to come back and I pushed them away. I had other people I cared about depending on me, waiting for me to bring help. I didn't have time for a trip down Memory Lane. The jail's proximity to the bridge, though, did help explain the ambush from that long ago night. Everything had been connected, orchestrated by a pissed-off elf with a grudge against the other Fey.

If I'd known then what I know now, things would have turned out so differently for everyone.

The hair on the back of my neck prickled. I stopped in the middle of the street and turned a slow circle. Something wasn't right—I'd learned long ago to trust myself when I got that weird sensation of being watched. It had kept me alive for four years as a Hunter, and it needed to keep me alive a good while longer.

Nothing presented itself as out of place, until the shadows near the pylons shifted. Glittering red eyes blinked at me. Multiple sets of eyes. My insides went watery and bile rose into my throat.

Goblins.

In the fucking daylight.

The eyes didn't move, but somehow the shapes of the goblins became more distinct. Their oily black skin, their oddly shaped heads and pear-shaped bodies. My fingers itched to reach for a knife and to start slashing throats. Only I didn't have a weapon on me. There were at least six goblins in the shadows, possibly armed with daggers and definitely armed with sharp teeth and claws. They were watching, not moving.

What were they waiting for?

I'd read once that discretion was the better part of valor, and I hadn't understood it at the time. Now that I was older and wiser, the saying told me it wasn't always cowardly to run from a fight—especially a fight I would definitely lose. And I had already lost enough today.

I ran.

Ran full-tilt out of there, down Corcoran Street, away from the jail and my friends. The thunder of feet behind me made my adrenaline spike. They were chasing me. I'd hunted in this part of the city dozens of times and I knew these streets, but they looked so different during the day. I knew darkness and shadows, not sunlight and reflections. I ducked through an unfinished construction site which was little more than a hole in the ground surrounded by plank fencing. I scanned for weapons along the way, hoping for a crow bar or even a solid piece of two-by-four.

Nothing.

The goblins kept pace, their huffing and snarls growing louder. Fear chilled me to the bone, and I ran harder, faster. Ducked through a hole in the fence and came out on another side street. More empty lots. I kept running north, aiming for a bigger population that might scare the little bastards off.

Something slammed into me sideways, and I tumbled to the pavement in a pained heap, scraping skin off my elbows. I threw a fist at the goblin that had knocked me down. Hit it right in the eye. It screeched and backed off. I rolled sideways and lurched up to my knees. Another goblin leapt on my back and knocked me flat onto my stomach.

I twisted sharply and mashed the smaller creature beneath me, using my shoulder blades to slam its head into the pavement with a solid crunch. Its hold on my back loosened. I lunged away and came face to face with another goblin. It bared jagged teeth at me, practically smiling, while its three companions circled us.

I am in so much trouble.

"Who sent you?" I asked.

They started giggling, which was a truly horrific sound, like manic, phlegmy coughing mixed with nails screeching down a chalkboard. I wanted cover my ears, but didn't dare move. If they all attacked at once, I was dead. I'd been killed by goblins once, and I'd be damned if I was going out that way again.

The goblin nearest me licked his lips with a thick purple tongue. "Nessa," it snarled.

"Nessa," the others repeated like a Greek chorus. Truly fucking creepy.

A distant rumbling caught my attention, like a train coming down the tracks. Only it was closer than the railroad, which was two blocks to the west. *Please, God, be a car.*

The goblins tensed, their pointed ears twitching and swiveling like a dog's. The rumbling grew closer. And then the head of the goblin farthest to my left exploded with the simultaneous report of a gunshot. Relief hit me hard, and I channeled it into hitting the goblin nearest me in the face. It tumbled sideways from the unexpected blow, and I tucked and rolled in the opposite direction.

More gunshots broke, followed by the squealing of tires. I came up on my knees a few feet from my old position. The six goblins lay in an odd pattern of fuchsia blood and gore splatters. One twitched as it died.

"Stone?"

Tybalt jogged over to me and reached out his natural hand. I took it, as grateful for the help up as for the unexpected save. Behind him, Kyle was holstering his gun and poking at a dead goblin with his shoe.

"You have incredible timing," I said.

"Where have you been? We've been trying to reach you guys for hours."

"Long story. Where are Gina and Shelby?"

"Searching a few blocks from here. Astrid put three quads out when you'd been out of contact for four hours after Baylor called in the meet up at Lincoln Street. Where's everyone else?"

"Not far."

"Wounded?"

"Yeah." Baylor's death and Milo's injuries stuck in my throat. I couldn't make my tongue form the words.

"Let's go, then," Kyle said. "We can clean up this trash later."

Leaving six goblin corpses in the middle of the street, untraveled or not, wasn't good policy, but I didn't have the mental focus to argue the point. Kyle drove, while I rode shotgun and gave directions. Tybalt called Kismet, who knew where the old police precinct was.

Kyle navigated the narrow alley that led into the rear parking lot, and Shelby pulled in right behind us. Even though Kyle and Shelby were both on the list of Therians I mostly trusted, their proximity after the events of the last few hours had my hackles up. They weren't the enemy, though, and I had to stop from giving Shelby a hairy eyeball he didn't deserve.

"Christ, Stone, what's going on?" Kismet asked as she climbed out of her Jeep. She made a gesture at her throat. "What happened?"

Mine was probably bruised from that stupid collar. Wyatt had to have heard the vehicles, but he hadn't opened the door yet. Explanation time was now or never.

"We were ambushed on Lincoln Street," I said.

Kismet's eyes went wide. "The message for you was a set up?"

"No, that part was actually kind of helpful." I explained Horzt and his gifts, the ambush, waking up in our cells, and Vale's demands. Cold fury swept over Kismet when I told them about

Milo; I couldn't even look at Tybalt. I glossed over our escape, Vale's escape and skipped straight to cold-cocking the sniper and my quest for help. "Tybalt and Kyle saved my life."

"Sounds like," Kismet said. She narrowed her eyes. "What aren't you telling me?"

I swallowed.

The door swung open. Wyatt stepped out into the sunlight, and I was grateful for his appearance. She shouldn't have to hear this from me.

"Adrian's dead, Gina," Wyatt said.

She spun to face him. "What?"

"He was shot by the sniper. None of us saw it coming."

"But…" The single word made her sound so small, so unlike her blustery, powerful self.

Wyatt came down the steps and folded Kismet into a hug. I turned away from the sight before their joint grief unleashed my own. I didn't have time to grieve for Baylor right now. Too many things were left undone.

"Where's Milo?" Tybalt asked me.

"Inside with Marcus," I replied.

Proving himself to once again be a man of impeccable timing, Marcus appeared in the doorway with Milo in his arms. Despite the fact that Milo was five-foot-seven and weighed at least a buck-fifty, Marcus held his weight he might a child half his size. Marcus turned a fierce scowl on the new arrivals, a protectiveness in his face and stance I'd never seen before.

"And still in need of medical attention," Marcus snapped, as though he'd been part of our conversation.

Milo's shirt hid the majority of the bruises on his back, but his legs were nearly solid purple and definitely swollen. Tybalt let out a string of impressive cuss words that cut through Kismet's grief and got her attention. She pulled away from Wyatt with a gasp.

"Put him in the back seat," Shelby said. He opened the rear passenger door of his SUV.

"We need to update Astrid and Rufus," Wyatt said. "The Danes have to be warned."

"Vale made a grave error by not killing us all when had the chance," Marcus said as he walked past.

"Agreed," I said. "but he also has two things that we need. The scroll and the cure. If he realizes they're valuable to us, he'll try to bargain."

"The only thing I'll trade him for is a quick death versus a slow one," Wyatt said.

"Once word of Vale's treachery is out to the Clans, he'll have few places to hide," Shelby said. "The Elders do not suffer fools, nor will they sympathize with Vale's attempts to cheat in the course of Riley's succession to Elder."

"Good," I said. "Vale gambled on Marcus giving up the mansion security codes and he lost. He's overconfident, and he rabbits at the first sign of real trouble. Now that we know his game, we know what to expect."

"So what's our next move?" Tybalt asked.

I thought of the sniper on the roof nearby, and of the address he'd given me. "I've got one place to start looking. Who's up for a trip into Mercy's Lot?"

CHAPTER NINE

5:50 pm

A quick phone call to Astrid divided our rather large group into three neat little units. Wyatt and Kismet were heading straight back to the Watchtower with Milo, Baylor's body, and the trussed up Bengal sniper. Marcus, Tybalt and I were going across town to check out 452 Ashmont Road. Shelby and Kyle got stuck with goblin cleanup duty.

Ashmont wasn't very far from my old neighborhood in Mercy's Lot, a narrow north-south street that eventually connected to Cottage Place about three blocks from where I once lived with my Triad partners. Number 452 was eight blocks north, in a cluster of dilapidated row homes that hadn't been new in about seventy years. Our target was one house from the end of the block. Tybalt drove past and parked halfway up the street.

"What's our play?" Tybalt asked.

"Vale isn't foolish enough to still be here," Marcus said.

I scooted forward between the two front seats. "He was smart enough to leave a sniper behind at the last location."

"You're right. However, it's likely that this house was abandoned before he enacted today's scheme."

"So front door?"

"Front door."

The neighborhood was annoyingly busy, which made sense, since we were inching into the post-rush hour evening. Residents were parking their cars or walking home from the nearby bus stop. Marcus agreed to swing around to the access alley that ran down the middle of the block, between the postage stamp backyards on our side of the block and the identical homes on the opposite street. He'd go in from behind, just in case someone was still home.

We kind of blended, since only Tybalt was wearing his typical Watch uniform. I tucked my hair around my throat to try and hide the bruise that was slowly repairing itself, thanks to my handy healing abilities. Therians healed pretty fast, too, which was the only reason Astrid had allowed Marcus to come with us. His exposure to the silver collar had left behind a low fever and blistered skin that looked only slightly less painful than it had half an hour ago.

Tybalt's earlier anger had settled into an intense precision that fueled every movement he made. We walked up the cracked stone path to the sagging front porch. The screen door squealed on its hinges. Since we weren't alone, I made a show of checking my pockets for keys, while Tybalt used an attachment on his mechanical left hand to jimmy the locks.

He went inside first. I don't know what I expected to find—rogue jungle cats brought to mind images of caves and vines—but it wasn't this clean little home full of Victorian furniture. I didn't know much about antiques, but I'd bet that the silk chaise in the living room cost more than I made in a month. Despite the exterior, the house was nicely kept and kind of…regal.

"You sure this is the right address?" Tybalt asked.

"Yes." I gaped at a stained glass lamp that sparkled with shades of red, purple and green. "Maybe the sniper got the address wrong."

"He didn't," Marcus said as he came through the kitchen and out into the living room. "Vale was here. I can smell him, as well as several others. The scents are old, though."

We split up to search all three floors of the house, from ground level up to the cob-webby attic. Not a single personal item had been left behind, but we found evidence that at least four Felia had lived here until recently. The trash cans outside were stuffed full of takeout containers and frozen pizza boxes.

"Well, this was a bust," I said, frustrated by our lack of evidence. Vale might be a total coward, but he wasn't completely stupid.

"We should leave a bug, anyway," Tybalt said. "On the off chance someone does come back."

"If nothing else, we need to check the county assessor's office and find out who owns this place. The sniper said it was bank owned, but I want to make sure there isn't a corpse out there who didn't willingly let Vale squat here."

"Agreed."

"Great." No one else was volunteering, so—"I'll go get a bug from the car."

Tybalt handed me the keys without a word.

Each official Watchtower car came complete with an emergency kit that contained basic first aid, extra guns, rope, flares, walkie talkies, and two microphones that synched up to our computer systems at the Watchtower. I fetched the small box with the mikes and hoofed it back to the house.

An angry voice made me stop on the porch, hand on the screen door handle.

"….never meant for him to get hurt." Marcus.

I wasn't generally a fan of eavesdropping, but something kept me from interrupting the conversation.

"Yeah, well, plan unsuccessful," Tybalt snapped back, as furious as I'd ever heard him sound. "Vale nearly killed him, and not because he's part of the Watch, but because of you."

"I care for him, Tybalt."

"I know you do, but he's been hurt enough, Marcus."

"Hurting him has never been my intention. You know that. I would never purposely cause him more pain."

"Not on purpose, no."

"What would you have me do, then? Push him away after what just happened?"

"No! Just…make sure you know what you're risking before you pursue this."

"I know what I risk. My entire family could turn their backs on me."

A jolt of surprise shot through me. Intellectually, I understood that Milo and Marcus had grown closer, had even flirted a little. There was also the kiss. Now everything was starting to fall into place and I could see the shaky ground their fledging relationship stood upon. And how Milo's life had already been put in serious danger because of it. Hearing that Marcus could lose the support of his family surprised me—Felia were intensely loyal to their blood.

Love made us do insane things sometimes, though. I'd have taken on the entire Clan Assembly last month if they'd ordered Wyatt killed because of his Lupa infection.

"Do not let your experience with Astrid cloud your judgment of my feelings for Milo," Marcus said. "The two things are not the same."

"No? A Felia and a human in love? My feelings for Astrid nearly destroyed the both of us six years ago."

"And she's never stopped loving you."

Oh boy. I was really overstepping by not announcing my presence, but I was mesmerized by the information being fed to me about my friends. I started to reach for the screen door handle.

"It doesn't matter how Astrid and I feel about each other anymore," Tybalt said in a cold voice. "The Watchtower is more important than us. The city needs this, and we need to focus on the problems at hand, not our personal relationships."

"I'm sorry, Tybalt, but I won't do that. You know how short a Therian's life span is."

"Yeah, I do. You've got ten years left if you're lucky."

"We all have ten years left, if we're lucky. How many of your Hunter friends have died in the last four years?"

Footsteps slammed in my direction, and I barely got out of the way before Tybalt shoved through the screen door. He didn't look at me as he stalked down the walkway to the sidewalk. In an odd way, I saw both sides of their argument. I'd already died (twice), and so had Wyatt. So many of us had come close to death, and multiple times. We didn't know if we had ten days, ten months, or fifty years left to live. And as much as my job gave me a sense of purpose each day, my love for Wyatt fueled me when things seemed impossible.

I fought for the tiniest chance that we'd have a happy ending one day. Hope was an extremely powerful thing. Without it, my life was too damned bleak.

When had Tybalt lost all hope for the future?

***

The conversation I'd overheard stayed with me on the drive back to the Watchtower. Marcus's comment about all of us maybe having ten years stuck with me, and it returned my thoughts to Phineas. We hadn't heard a word from him since his disappearance five weeks ago. He'd gone off to find out if any other Coni or Stri existed in the wider world, or if he, Aurora, Ava, and Joseph were truly alone.

A simple text saying "I'm still alive" would be nice, just to alleviate the fear that he'd gotten in over his head. While he'd saved my life several times, I'd also returned the favor and saved his. I missed him and his no-bullshit way of framing things so I could better understand them. Phineas was one of my very best friends, and he only had ten years left.

No, thinking that way did none of us any good. Especially not considering the high-risk job we did, protecting the city and keeping the dark races in line. Adrian Baylor's death today had only proved that no one knew when their time would be up—I'd never expected to outlive Baylor. Like Wyatt, Kismet, and Rufus, he'd always been around, steadfast and strong.

Now he was dead.

The mood at the Watchtower was somber. A third of Cerberus was dead, and the Felia who killed him was locked up in our jail waiting for the Clan Assembly to make a decision on his fate—which I found out when I walked into Ops that evening.

All of the remaining Triad Handlers—Wyatt, Gina, Nevada, Morgan, and Rufus—were in one corner of Ops, talking and quietly mourning their collective loss. Wyatt caught my eye when I entered. I shook my head so he knew we hadn't found anything.

"The house was a bust," I told Astrid. "We left a bug, though, in case someone comes back."

"They aren't likely to," Astrid replied. She looked ready to explode into a fury. "The house belonged to Evan Tuck, the sniper you shot twice. His parents died of the Shadow two years ago and left it in his name. He couldn't make the mortgage payments and the bank foreclosed last month."

"He kept a neat house for an orphan." I also felt absolutely no guilt about having shot him in the leg. Both of them.

He hadn't gotten away, had he?

"Vale is Evan's first cousin, and they're all Bengals. So was the man Wyatt killed back at the police precinct."

"Peck." I blinked. "Wait, that guy's name was Peck Tuck?"

Astrid's eyebrow quirked. "Yes."

"That sucks."

"Evan also has a younger sister named Starr. She may be the other Therian scent from the precinct, and she's been reported by her employer as having not shown up for the last week."

"Do you think other Felia will shelter them, knowing what's happening with Elder Dane and Riley?"

"I honestly don't know. Vale is acting rashly and in blatant violation of both Assembly and Pride laws. I worry for the precedent he's setting among the Pride members."

"What precedent?"

She gazed around the people working in Ops, and I could almost see the ghosts of the vampire allies whose support we'd lost. "They may incite other Clans to challenge their Assembly representatives, and it could force the Assembly to pull all Therian support from the Watchtower."

I shuddered. "Worst case scenario?"

"No." She made a sour face. "The worst case scenario here is that Vale's open challenge could lead to civil war among all Therians."

"Yeah, that's definitely worse. Has that happened before?"

"According to legend, the last time we came close was when the Assembly ordered the decimation of the Lupa. Not all Clans agreed that genocide was the way to end their reign of terror."

"So Vale has himself a kind of win-win scenario here," I said as I puzzled it out in my head. "He wants the Danes out of power, and he also wants the Assembly out of the Watchtower."

"The trouble is, his methods will ensure the Tucks never regain power within the Pride. He has directly attacked Pride members and kidnapped the grandson of the Elder. He will likely focus his energies on the other Clans now, sowing discord from within."

"It only takes one match to start a forest fire."

"Exactly."

Hell, this just kept getting worse and worse. "Did Vale actually expect Marcus to give him the security codes to the Dane mansion?"

Astrid shook her head. "Doubtful, but he did succeed in putting Marcus in an untenable situation. If Marcus gave in, he failed both his Pride and his family. However, by resisting, he can be painted as heartless by allowing a loved one to be physically harmed."

Loved one. I should have chosen my next question with more tact, but it slipped. "It sort of outs him to the Pride, too, doesn't it?"

"It certainly verifies years of speculation. As reckless as today's kidnapping seems, Vale will absolutely benefit. Marcus will suffer the most."

"And Vale has it in for Marcus because Marcus helped capture Prentiss?"

"Yes."

I exhaled hard. "No one in this town ever does anything half-assed, do they?"

Astrid's mouth quirked. "No, they don't. Present company included."

"Does that mean you have a plan?"

"We find Vale, and we continue to deal with the goblin threat. The newest Queen targeting you is named Nessa?"

"Yeah." I'd given her a brief overview of my goblin encounter earlier. I retold it with more details, including a fun fact that had only now sunk in. "They were toying with me on the street. I had no chance against the six of them, not without better weapons. All they had to do was attack me en masse."

"Agreed."

"I want to go out hunting tonight, no mercy, like the old days."

Astrid only hesitated a few seconds before saying, "Who do you want to take?"

"Tybalt, Paul, Kyle, and Autumn for sure," I said without hesitation. Her help last month hunting down the Lupa pups had put her on the Mostly Trust list with Kyle. "And anyone else who wants to go. We used to hunt in threes, I'm thinking pairs will be more manageable. One human, one Therian."

"All right. I'll get that into the works."

"Thank you, Astrid."

At first, I hadn't known what to make of Astrid Dane. She was a small, powerful woman who looked to be in her mid-thirties, with the black hair and dark eyes of a Roman goddess and the personality of a rattlesnake. But she was incredibly smart, insanely loyal, and had a good heart when it mattered most. I could see what had drawn a teenage Tybalt to her—and what probably still drew the older versions of each to the other, even if they both seemed to actively deny it.

Before I left Ops, I got a new cell phone. One of the nice things about our financial setup was a ready supply of cheap phones, as well as the ability to transfer numbers with efficiency. Made it less of a problem when we lost or broke them.

Cell phone in hand, I reluctantly gave Reilly a call. I hadn't forgiven him for the scene in the diner,, and couldn't say for sure I still trusted the man, but we needed all of our allies on this. I did take a small measure of satisfaction in his timid greeting before filling him in on the latest drama with the Felia. He promised to keep an eye out for Vale and Starr Tuck, and to report any rumblings about the Assembly.

"I want to apologize again for this morning's ambush," he said before I could end the conversation.

I glared at the corridor tiles spread out in front of me as I walked toward the sleeping quarters. "Don't ever do that to me again, Reilly."

"I won't. As I said, they contacted me before—"

"Whatever. I don't want to talk about the Frosts."

"They aren't going anywhere, Evangeline. They've called me twice today, begging me to contact you on their behalf."

"They know their daughter is kind of alive. What more do they want?"

"A relationship."

"I'm not their kid."

"Do you plan on explaining how that's possible?"

"Not a chance."

"Then you need to talk to them. Convince them that Chalice is fine, so they can go home with a clear conscience."

"I can't lie to them."

He sighed long and loud. "They're parents. Ignoring them won't make them go away."

I hated so much that he was right. "Look, I have too much on my plate to make nice with Chalice's parents, okay? Maybe after we find Vale, prevent Therian civil war, save the vampires who are dying, and stop the latest goblin Queen who wants me dead. Maybe then I can make nice with the Frosts."

"That's some To Do list."

"Welcome to my life."

"If I hear anything useful, I'll be in touch."

"Thank you."

I hung up. Reilly was a somewhat- seful, occasionally frustrating, ally. The call also reminded me of a very important fact: I was a lot less anonymous now than I used to be. Running around the city in daylight would be a new challenge. Good thing the sun was setting in a couple of hours.

I had some goblin hunting to do.

CHAPTER TEN

7:20 p.m.

After a long shower and a change of clothes, I went down to the infirmary and was immediately denied visitation rights with Milo.

"He needs rest, not visitors," Dr. Reid Vansis said. He was an intimidating doctor, not because of his physical appearance—which was actually kind of bland, almost meek—but because of his gruff manner and the fact that he shifted into an enormous grizzly bear. We were alone in the infirmary's outer office, and I wasn't getting any farther.

"But he's okay?" I asked.

"The boy has serious contusions on his back and ribs, and some deep bone bruising on both legs. He's being kept sedated for now, while I try to reduce the swelling. He'll be in a great deal of pain when he wakes up."

"Nothing's broken?"

"No, no broken bones, but he's still looking at a minimum of several weeks before he's fully mobile again."

"Because of his legs."

"Correct. Now if you'll excuse me?"

He didn't have to ask twice. Milo's condition could have been much worse, but he was still in bad shape, and I hated that. Hated seeing any of my friends suffer, like so many were suffering over Baylor's death. My chest seized, and more tears threatened to show themselves. I tamped down on the unwanted emotion as I sought out the one person I really wanted to talk to about all of this.

I found him at the other end of the Watchtower, past the gym, in the old department store we were renovating into a training obstacle course. A frozen escalator took up space directly ahead—one of the few internal structures that hadn't been torn down yet—and Wyatt was sitting on the bottom step. He didn't say anything when I sat next to him. He simply turned and folded me into his arms. I pressed my cheek against his shoulder and slipped my arms around his waist, absorbing his warmth, breathing in his scent. Enjoying the beat of his heart so close to mine.

We didn't say anything for a while; there was no need.

"I'm sorry we lost the vampires' cure," he said.

"So am I." I'd been so excited to present Horzt's gift to Eulan, and now it was missing, along with the ancient elf scroll. Five minutes in my possession, and I lost a Fey artifact. That had to be some kind of record. "Reilly says the Frosts are still up his butt about talking to me."

Wyatt snickered. "Serves him right."

"Yeah. Astrid's putting together some hunting teams for tonight."

"Goblins?"

"Yes, among other things."

He pulled back enough that he could look me in the eye. "Don't make this personal, Evy."

"How can I not, when Nessa's making it personal? We need to get out there and fight back before more innocent people are mutilated and murdered."

"You're right, but we need to be smart about it."

"I know, and we will. That's why you'll be with me, so I don't do something impulsively stupid."

Wyatt smiled. I loved seeing him smile, because he did it so rarely, and he was so handsome when he did. I kissed him, just a gentle press of lips. Should have known better, because he angled his head to deepen the kiss. My tongue flicked out to meet his in a quiet, intense dance that filled my mouth with the flavor of him. It had been less than twenty-four hours since our lockup in the bank vault, but it could have been months for how my body responded to his touch.

His cell phone rang, and I laughed as we pulled apart. "Your phone hates me," I said.

"Hates me, too," he said with a huff. Wyatt held up the offending object. Unknown Number. He answered it anyway. "Truman."

A voice squawked over the other end, and Wyatt's eyebrows shot into his hairline. "Yes, this is Wyatt Truman. Who is this?" He mouthed the word Lupa at me.

Well, I'll be damned. The pups called.

"Hello, Peter." He listened, and I really wished he'd put the phone on speaker. "All right, I can be there in thirty minutes. I'll have one person with me, and that's not negotiable. I trust her with my life."

Road trip.

"The same goes for you boys. I'm coming in good faith, so no tricks." After he hung up, he didn't wait for me to ask. "They want to meet at Sunset Terrace."

That made sense, since Sunset Terrace is where we'd first seen the Lupa pups and where Wyatt had been infected. It was also once an apartment complex that housed the Coni and Stri Clans, before the whole thing was razed by the Triads and the Clan murdered to near-extinction. So many bad memories there.

"And I'm going with you, right?" I asked.

"Of course."

"Are we telling Astrid first?"

"Maybe after we're on the road...."

Snagging a Jeep and getting on our way took less than five minutes, and it was twilight by the time we parked next to the vacant lot that had been Sunset Terrace. Unlike yesterday, we weren't alone as we walked toward the center of the cement and asphalt lake that took up the entire block.

Three teenage boys with identical red hair stood in a cluster in almost the same spot where I'd confronted one of their brothers five weeks ago. A surge of hatred for these boys hit me with gut-wrenching force. They'd nearly killed Wyatt, and they'd willingly worked for my greatest enemy. But on the heels of that hatred was a cold splash of pity. They'd been raised by a madman and taught to do wrong. I couldn't heap all of the blame for their actions upon their own shoulders. The Fey had given the Lupa pups to Thackery, and he'd manipulated them. Thackery had made them into monsters.

The tallest of the three broke away and came a few steps forward. His clothes were filthy, his eyes sunken. He looked like he hadn't had a decent meal in a month—which was very likely, since the boys had been fending for themselves for a while. I doubted Thackery had taken the time to teach them basic life skills, like getting a job and managing money. They were relying on instinct, and instinct had pushed them to contact an older, more experienced Lupa.

"Peter?" Wyatt asked.

"Yes," Peter replied in the squeaky voice of someone who hadn't quite finished puberty.

"I'm Wyatt. This is Evy."

"I know."

"Are any of you sick or injured?"

"Not really." His wide, silver eyes shifted from me to him. "Do you have any food?"

"Not with me," Wyatt said gently, "but we can get some. When was the last time you ate?"

"A while. We eat what we can find."

Like mustard packets. *My God.* Despite my better sense, I started feeling sorry for them.

"And you live in the apartment on Cottage Place?"

Peter shrugged a bony shoulder. "Sometimes." He looked over at his brothers, who hadn't stopped surveying the lot. They were a twitchy bunch.

"What do you want besides food?" Wyatt asked.

"Help." He seemed one sharp word from bursting into tears. "I'm the oldest now. I have to protect them but I can't by myself. Because of our father… humans fear us." He gave me a nasty glare. "They want us dead."

"I don't want you dead," I said, and I meant it. "I want to know you won't bite and infect anyone else."

Peter gave Wyatt a guilty look. "We didn't know that would happen. Father told us after, and it was too late."

"I believe you," Wyatt said. "Have you or your brothers infected anyone else besides me?"

The Lupa pup shook his head so hard I thought it would snap off his skinny neck. "No, never. We've been very careful."

"Good, that's important. None of you have attacked humans, but you did participate in the kidnapping and detention of other Therians. That's a serious crime."

Peter hunched his shoulders. "Are you going to kill us?"

"Of course not. And I won't allow the Assembly of Clan Elders to kill you, either."

Oh, Wyatt, I don't know if you can keep that promise.

These boys had been complicit in so many crimes, and they'd kept Aurora and Ava captive in silver cages. The Assembly had barely granted Wyatt leniency, and that was because of his value to the Watchtower, half-Lupa or not. The three teenagers in front of me were an endangered species, sure, but the Clans had ordered them murdered once before.

Centuries ago, maybe, but did fear like that ever really die?

Wyatt must have seen something in my expression, because his own face went utterly blank—not good. "Evy, I need to ask you for a favor," he said.

"No good conversation ever started like that, Wyatt."

"I want to talk to them alone for a while, and I don't want to put you in an awkward position with Astrid."

I opened my mouth to argue, but his expression stopped me. He could be as stubborn about things as me, and he wasn't going to budge. Letting him have his way (this time) was a better move. "Fine."

"There's a coffee shop two blocks from here. I'll drop you off—"

"I can walk." The exercise would help burn off some of my temper.

"Thank you. I'll call you in an hour."

"Okay. Just be careful? Please?"

"I promise."

***

My trek to Carter Street Bakery only took a few minutes. It burned up some of my concern over leaving Wyatt behind. The pups were scared and starving, but I didn't trust them one bit. I did trust Wyatt, though—to know what he was doing, to talk to them in a way that got them on our side, and to be careful when I wasn't there to watch his back. Mostly I hated being out of the loop.

I bought a cup of coffee and a Panini sandwich to try and alleviate some of my persistent hunger, then settled at a sidewalk table to wait. Halfway through my sandwich, Tybalt called with an update.

"We took Brett Lewis out to the building where you guys were held," he said without wasting breath on a greeting. Or asking where I was.

Brett had never been a Hunter, but he was a Gifted human whose specialty was post-cognitive psychometric readings. He could walk around a space and "see" events that had occurred. Sometimes he could sense strong emotions around an object, too. Brett at the jail was a good call.

"What did he find?" I asked.

"He mostly poked around upstairs. He saw some of what they did to Wyatt to get him to turn. Besides the four Felia, there was a fifth person present."

"Who?"

"Brett couldn't see him or her. Said the mystery visitor was blocking any kind of psychic signals, or whatever, but it basically screwed with Brett's reception. They were all fuzzed out, like something censored on television."

A nugget of worry settled cold and hard in my stomach, and the sandwich no longer seemed appetizing. Two other tables near me were occupied, including one with a young, Hispanic boy who kept glancing at me—exactly what I needed. Someone checking me out while I was having a private conversation.

I lowered my voice before asking, "So are we thinking someone is pulling Vale's strings?"

"It wouldn't be the first time the person we're looking for isn't actually the one in charge."

"Tell me about it. Anything else useful?"

"No."

"Thanks for the update."

"You up to anything exciting?"

"Just having dinner."

"Uh huh."

"Bye, Tybalt."

I didn't put the phone away, in case Wyatt called before his hour was up. I sipped at my coffee and watched traffic flow by for a while, until the little hairs on the back of my neck told me I was being watched. The young man three tables away was still there, observing me poorly over an unfolded newspaper. He wasn't a Halfie, that was for sure, and I didn't get a Therian vibe. He was interested, though, and doing a bad job of hiding it. But was he interested in me as a semi-attractive woman out alone? Or as someone who saw my photo on television and wanted the Frosts' reward money?

Damn them for making my life more complicated than it needs to be.

Time to test the level of this guy's interest.

I dumped the rest of my sandwich, took my coffee with me, and headed for the sidewalk. Strolled in the opposite direction of where I'd left Wyatt. A glance in the reflective windows of the businesses across the street told me Stalker Guy was following me. Too closely, too, which also told me he was an amateur at this. Should be easy enough to scare him into staying the hell away from me.

At the end of the block, I turned left, then quickly ducked into a pay-by-the-day parking lot that was only half-full of cars. Even over the sounds of traffic on the other street, I heard his footsteps approaching. As soon as his shadow fell on the sidewalk, I moved.

I grabbed his arm and shoulder, and then spun him face-first into the brick wall that bordered the parking lot. He hit with a pained noise that got louder when I twisted his trapped arm up high against his back. He quit fighting when he figured out that only made me twist his arm harder.

"Why the fuck are you following me?" I asked.

"I'm sorry," he replied in a softly accented voice.

"That wasn't an answer to my question."

"Please…please…."

Another twist on his arm. "Still not an answer, junior."

"Please, stop. I was a trainee at Boot Camp."

I froze as his words registered. When Boot Camp was destroyed several months ago, not every surviving trainee had agreed to join the Watchtower. Most had, but not all. Junior here could very well have been one of the deserters. Not that I was taking him on his word.

"I don't know what you're talking about," I said.

"Sure you do. You're Evy Stone, right? I saw you fighting there. You killed that beast in the Pit."

"Who was your Weapons instructor?"

"Lena Donaldson. She died."

He had good information, but I didn't quite believe him. "Who recruited you into Boot Camp?"

"Bastian. He died too, later that day."

I loosened my grip, then spun Junior around so his back was to the wall. He gaped at me with wide eyes. He seemed younger than eighteen, barely an adult, but I saw the truth of the horrors he'd witnessed in the hardness behind his eyes. I knew those kinds of eyes too well. "What's your name?"

"Alejandro Gomez."

"Why were you following me, Alejandro?"

He had the good sense to look embarrassed as he said, "I remembered you when I saw the Frosts on TV this morning. I thought I could get them information. I need the money."

"The Frosts have seen and spoken to me, so good luck with getting reward money."

"Oh."

"Yeah, oh. Why don't you do us both a favor? Forget you ever knew me, forget you were ever at Boot Camp, and go start your life over somewhere else."

"Could you forget the things you saw and did at Boot Camp?"

Hot damn, Alejandro found a spine. I liked that. "No, I can't, but I've been at this a few more years than you. You can still get out."

"To do what? I have no money, no real skills other than what I was taught at Boot Camp. Please, may I join your Watchtower?"

"That's not my call."

"You can recommend me." He seemed ready to drop down to his knees and beg, and my heart went out to him. Life wasn't easy when you had no one to help you out, nobody to turn to when times got rough.

I thought of the three Lupa pups, finally desperate enough to ask for help. "Look, Alejandro, I can't—"

"I have information!"

I flinched at his sound level. "Information on what?"

"I've been tracking a female goblin for the last four days. I can show you where she went yesterday."

A female goblin moving around the city. It could be Nessa, or one of half a dozen others. Goblin females were not only very rare, they were also able to pass as humans—with a little makeup and help from their clothes. They didn't tend to pass for fun, though. Goblins only showed up in the city for business reasons. Alejandro could be bluffing, but I didn't think so.

"You can show me right now?"

"Yes. In exchange for a job."

"I can't guarantee a job, but good information will go a long way toward pleading your case with the people who can." I thought back to my half-eaten sandwich and the desperate, hungry look in Peter's eyes. Might as well try to help Alejandro out. "We do pay our informants, though. In cash, not in employment."

"It's a start."

He showed signs of a good Hunter and he probably would have made a passable one someday, had Boot Camp survived. I finally let him go, stepped back, and dug out my phone.

"Who are you calling?" he asked.

"Backup. We're not going goblin hunting alone, Junior."

"Ale."

"Fine, Ale." The Spanish pronunciation didn't exactly roll off my tongue, but I did my best.

The other line only rang twice between Tybalt picked up with a grumpy, "Monahan."

"It's Stone. You busy?"

"Not at the moment. What's going on?"

"Grab some people and meet me at the Carter Street Bakery. I've got a lead on a goblin."

CHAPTER ELEVEN

8:50 p.m.

In the twenty or so minutes it took for our ride to arrive, Wyatt called briefly to tell me he was all right, to not worry, and that he'd contact me soon. Only my absolute confidence in his ability to handle himself, even around three flighty teenage Lupa who'd hurt him once already, allowed me to hang up without insisting he provide more details. I trusted him to know what he was doing.

I still didn't totally trust my new BFF Alejandro—only time would gain him that—but I did buy him a sandwich at the coffee shop while we waited. He inhaled that sucker like he hadn't eaten in days. So many of the Hunters I'd trained with, the Hunters I'd known through the Triads, could have easily been him if Bastian hadn't found us—lost, starving, with no real hope for the future.

Not that being a Hunter had promised us much of a future, but we never went hungry or wanted for a place to sleep.

Tybalt's Explorer pulled up, already full of Kyle, Shelby, and Marcus. After a little rearranging of seats, I took the front passenger seat, while Alejandro kicked Shelby all the way into the rear compartment. The kid looked terrified to be surrounded by

Therians—a feeling I might have shared once upon a time and kind of sympathized with.

I gave everyone the bullet points.

"A goblin Queen, huh?" Tybalt said. "Impressive."

"Not if you know what to look for," Alejandro said. He even managed a little bravado through his fear. "I was two weeks from finishing at Boot Camp. I haven't forgotten a thing they taught me there."

Tybalt glanced at me, as if to verify the claim. I shrugged. We had no way to check up on Alejandro. All Boot Camp records had been destroyed the day we tore it all down. The last thing we needed was all of that information falling into the wrong hands. Giving it up voluntarily was the lesser of two evils.

"Where to, Junior?" I asked.

He scowled at me in the rearview. "Head west, toward the Black River docks."

As we headed out of the center of Mercy's Lot, the streetlights became fewer and farther between. The area between it and the river was mostly made up of factories and industrial centers, some functioning and most not. It was quiet out there this time of night, with the daytime shifts gone home and the nighttime shifts firmly entrenched in their duties. Nearer to the docks, a sense of wicked familiarity washed over me and not just because I'd been here five dozen times in the past.

I knew where we were going, and it hit me with a sickening kind of clarity.

The last time I came to this area to see the gremlins, I'd been with Baylor, and the memory sent a shot of grief right to my heart. We'd been looking for information on Thackery and his menagerie of Lupa pups. Ironic because the Lupa were now in Wyatt's custody, and I hadn't brought any sort of snack to feed the gremlins' collective sweet tooth. If a goblin Queen had been in the area, they wouldn't tell without a treat.

My instincts proved me right when Alejandro's directions landed us in front of the gremlin factory—a long, narrow building with four stories of papered-over windows. A chain-link fence surrounded it, the only entrance an old guard hut that still worked. They'd let us inside that way before.

Something about the place felt off, though, and I couldn't put my finger on it.

"You tracked the goblin to an old factory?" Marcus asked.

"Yes," Alejandro said. "She went into that hut, and then a few seconds later the fence rolled back a little bit. It closed again before I could slip inside."

"Did you see her leave again?"

"No."

"How long was she inside?"

Alejandro squirmed, and I almost felt sorry for him. Marcus had his full-on intimidation face going, and he could be a scary interrogator. "I'm not sure."

I twisted around in my seat to face them. "Let me guess. You didn't hang around to see what she was doing or how long she stayed, because you didn't know if an entire horde of goblins was inside waiting to eat you, right?"

He blushed, then nodded.

"Good instinct. Death by goblin is not a nice way to go, trust me. But you were wrong."

"What?" he asked. "How do you know?"

"Because a couple thousand gremlins live in there, not goblins. The only things gremlins like to eat are sugar and junk food."

"Oh." Alejandro glanced at Tybalt. "How does she know this stuff?"

Tybalt chuckled.

"So should we try the gate?" Marcus asked. "Or idle here and discuss it further?"

Tybalt drove up to the guard hut. I climbed out and went inside. The controls seemed simple enough, and I hit a red button that said Call. I expected a buzzer or beep, something to indicate the call went through. I held it down and said, "Ballengee be blessed," which is the traditional gremlin greeting.

Nothing.

I tried it again to more silence, which unnerved me. I hit a few other buttons, but nothing seemed to be working. The hut was free of electricity, and then I realized that's what bothered me about the place. It was nighttime and dark outside, and there wasn't a single indication of light or power about the place. It felt abandoned.

Had the gremlins packed up and left town, too?

I went outside and manually tugged on the gate. It surprised me by rolling back on its track. Definitely not good. Tybalt drove inside, picked me up, and we trekked across a narrow strip of parking lot. Last time a garage door on the south side of the building had opened automatically. Nothing happened tonight.

"This isn't right," I said. "Stay on your toes, boys."

Tybalt parked near a side door that had once said Authorized Personnel Only and had faded to only every other letter. We piled out of the SUV. Marcus, Kyle and Shelby immediately turned toward the building and sniffed the air. All I smelled was oil, rubber, and the far away odor of the river. Beneath it all was the familiar, cloying stink of gremlin piss—like whiskey, only more eye-watering and less enjoyable to drink.

"I smell death," Marcus said.

Terrific.

I pulled a knife from my ankle sheath, while Tybalt fixed a wicked double-blade attachment to his prosthetic hand. Marcus stripped and shifted into his jaguar form, while Kyle and Shelby stayed in their clothes. We gave Alejandro a hunting knife from the weapons stash in the back so the kid wasn't completely helpless. The three of us humans, with our poorer eyesight, also grabbed flashlights.

The door wasn't locked, and it opened with a groan when Tybalt pushed. A gust of hot, stale air stole outside, carrying the stink of gremlin piss and rot. My nose tingled with it, and I held back a sneeze.

This isn't going to be good.

I went in first, alert for anything. My yellow beam of light flashed down an empty corridor, its concrete walls and floor stained here and there with indescribable colors. The air became more ripe, more suffocating the deeper into the factory we went. Twenty feet of corridor ended at a large metal door that said Floor. I stopped to listen.

Normally this close to the gremlins' nests, I'd hear the scratchy scampering of thousands of small clawed feet, the chattering of their guttural language. That many gremlins in an enclosed chamber created a hell of a lot of noise.

Marcus nudged his big furry body up to the front, then crouched down, ready to leap at anything that might be on the other side of the door. Kyle pushed Alejandro into the rear. I grabbed the door handle and pulled.

The nightmare we found inside was unimaginable.

The gremlins hadn't just been slaughtered, they'd been destroyed. A layer of blood had congealed on the factory floor like gelatin, its surface roughly dotted with arms, legs, pointed ears, bit of hair, and other meaty, disgusting things. Nothing inside moved. The smell nearly made me double over. My eyes watered, and I told myself it was the stink and not actual tears.

I made it five steps inside, my sneakers squishing on the blood, before I froze and couldn't go any farther. There was no point. All we'd find were more filleted gremlins, more blood and gore.

"Jesus Christ," Tybalt said. "All of them?"

"A lot of them," I said. It was impossible to know if they'd all been killed or if some had managed to escape.

"One goblin couldn't do all this."

"No, but one goblin is all it takes to open up sewer access and allow a horde inside."

"Stone," Kyle said. He pointed at the high wall of a metal vat that was probably full of gremlin piss. "There."

I shined my flashlight in that direction. Written in gremlin blood was the word Kelsa. "Well, shit," I said.

The goblins were definitely making a statement. I took a few pictures with my phone.

Marcus backed out of the factory floor. Kyle and Shelby were both looking a little green. I recalled the way Phineas had reacted to the gremlins several months ago—an instinctual revulsion, he'd said. He'd run outside and vomited in the grass. Looked like all Therians had a similar allergic reaction to goblin piss.

"Take a breather," I told them. "Tybalt, Ale, and I will check for an entry point."

"We will?" Alejandro said.

"Suck it up, Junior, this is part of the job."

We didn't find an entry or exit point, for all of our searching. The closest we came was a trail of bloody footprints leading into a basement room full of metal pipes of all shapes and sizes. More blood had been splashed around the floor and walls, making it impossible to track the footprints into any single pipe.

Alejandro and I sat on those pipes while Tybalt retrieved something from the car. He set the explosives to go off in that room, then put the timer on five minutes. We were a block away from the factory when we felt the ground shake. Tybalt pulled off into an empty parking lot and we watched the flames rise high into the night sky.

The fire probably wouldn't go far enough into the sewers to touch the goblins, but we couldn't leave that sort of mess around for the human authorities. We may have very well wiped away all proof that gremlins had ever existed in the world, but I couldn't think about that. I wanted to imagine some had escaped and were searching for a new place to live—or better yet, had fled to another city altogether.

Thanks to their affiliation with me, another species of creature was facing total extinction.

"This wasn't your fault," Tybalt said, as if he could read my thoughts.

"Something tells me the gremlins wouldn't agree with you," I replied, unable to mask the bitterness in my voice. "And that little love note the goblins left behind tells another story."

He quit trying to change my mind, and since we still had the matter of Alejandro to deal with, I called Astrid. Explained who Alejandro was, the information he'd given us, and the results.

"Do you trust him?" Astrid asked.

"He hasn't given me a reason not to." I turned to give Alejandro a pointed look, and he went a little wide-eyed.

"Blindfold him and bring him in."

"All right."

"Have you heard from Truman recently?"

"Not in the last hour or so. He's made some progress on that, uh, pet project of his."

She didn't have to be so cryptic on her end. "The Lupa?"

"Yeah."

"He has them?"

"Made contact."

"Stone—"

"That's all I know. He didn't want me directly involved."

She made an all-too-familiar noise of frustration. "Fine. Bring the newbie to Ops when you get back. I want the others to stay out in the field."

"Will do."

I gave Alejandro the good news and relayed Astrid's orders. My next call was to Wyatt, who didn't pick up. I left a terse message to call me or else. Alejandro didn't protest being blindfolded. We didn't talk on the drive back across town to the Watchtower. Tybalt dropped us off inside the parking area.

Marcus didn't seem particularly pleased with having to leave right away. As I climbed out of the SUV, I met his worried copper eyes and mouthed "I'll check on him."

He nodded.

After the SUV left, I yanked off Alejandro's blindfold. He stared all around us as I led him down the old mall's corridor to Ops. If he recognized the place—and no reason he should, since he'd have been a toddler when it was last a functioning retail site—he didn't say so. People stared as we passed, suspicion in their eyes, directed at the stranger in their sanctuary. Therian noses twitched because we had to stink to high hell from our walk through the factory of death.

Astrid and Rufus met us inside Ops. Alejandro did an admirable job of not looking like he wanted to shit his pants when Astrid politely asked me to let them take it from here. I knew she only wanted to question him about Boot Camp and everything he knew about the goblin Queen he'd tracked, but he didn't. Poor kid.

Wyatt still hadn't called me back, so I took a few minutes to shower off the odor of death and change my clothes. Feeling a lot less grungy, I headed for the infirmary to check on Milo—not only for Marcus, but for my own peace of mind, too.

One person was in the infirmary waiting area when I walked in, curled up in a chair, looking as lost as I'd ever seen her. Gina Kismet didn't wear helpless well, and worse, she didn't try to hide it when I spotted her. She blinked at me through blurred eyes, cheeks streaked with tears.

My heart nearly stopped, and I stared at the door that led into the private rooms, panicked, until she said, "Milo's resting. Dr. Vansis is keeping him sedated for now."

That strangling fear loosened enough for me to get a solid breath. Damn her for scaring me like that. Milo wasn't dead, so—oh wait. I sat in the chair next to her, unsure what to say about Baylor's death. They'd been close for many years, and Kismet and I had just established a friendly truce a few months back. I wasn't any good at comforting grieving people, but the other people closest to her (Wyatt, Tybalt, Rufus) were busy elsewhere.

So I told her about Alejandro and the gremlin warehouse. She didn't have any particularly warm fuzzy feelings for the gremlins, but she'd helped relocate them to that location. A slaughter of this magnitude was affecting, no matter your species.

"When it rains, it pours," she said.

"I'd say we've left downpour and hit hurricane force weather."

She grunted. "It's funny, but I always kind of expected Adrian to outlive the rest of us. And by us, I mean me, Wyatt, and Rufus. We were the Mercy's Lot Handlers, the four of us."

"I remember."

"Carly and Paul are taking it pretty hard." They'd both been members of his Triad before the Triads ceased to exist, so I could imagine their grief.

"A Hunter never expects to outlive their Handler."

"Losing Hunters was never easy for us, either."

She didn't have to convince me of that. I knew how much she cared about the Hunters in her care—how much Felix's death last month had hurt. "We lose people we love," I said. "It's the life we chose."

"But when does all of that loss stop being worth it? When do we say enough?"

I slid my arm across Kismet's shoulders and pulled her in a sideways hug. "When there's no one left that we love to keep fighting for. Until then, we fight. It's who we are, Gina. Adrian knew that. He lived it every day."

"At least he can finally rest." The corners of her mouth quirked. "Did you know that when Adrian and Wyatt first met, they got into a fist fight?"

"No." The mental image made me laugh out loud. "Tell me."

She did. Reliving the past, and what must have been a pretty funny moment for the witnesses, loosened her up. Remembering her friend returned some of the brightness to her eyes and the light to her face.

After a while, Dr. Vansis shooed us out with orders to get our own rest while his patient got his. Since we weren't going to be able to visit Milo anytime soon, we both headed back to our sleeping quarters. I'd be going out with the hunting teams later, but could probably squeeze in a cat nap before we had to prep.

I woke in my bed with a warm hand gently shaking my shoulder. Before I opened my eyes, I knew it was Wyatt. He had sense enough to look ashamed of himself before I figured out what time it was. I punched him in the chest anyway.

"That's for not calling me for two fucking hours," I said.

"I'm sorry, Evy. I had to get the boys to trust me."

"Did you?"

"Yes."

"Where are they?"

"I set them up in a place with money and food. They're going to help us look for Vale and his family."

I perked up. "Well, that's something. Three more noses on the street is always helpful when we're looking for were-cats on the lam. What's Astrid think about it?"

"She isn't completely happy to be out of the loop, but she isn't fighting me for now. She's more concerned with finding Vale before he does any more damage to the Pride."

"Good."

"I hear you made a new friend tonight."

"Something like that."

I told him about my night while we both changed into hunting gear—black shirts and black cargo pants, boots, and plenty of hidden weapons. After four years of prepping while he watched from the sidelines, it still felt a little strange to head out hunting with Wyatt instead of leaving him behind. But we worked well together, and we'd always watch the other's back. Period.

All of the volunteered pairs met in the parking area, humans carrying all kinds of weapons and Therians dressed for easy stripping and shifting. Wyatt pulled out a map marked up with the site of each of the most recent attacks, plus Alejandro's sightings. The circle was kept mostly to Mercy's Lot and downtown, centered on the peninsula of land between the Black and Anjean Rivers. The goblins were rarely known to cross those rivers, so our hunting grid didn't surprise me.

"Report in every twenty minutes," I said. "If you can't verbalize, then text. The goblins attacked in broad daylight today, guys." I didn't have to tell them how significant today's events were; they knew.

"Is this kill or capture?" Paul asked. He was as cold and angry as I'd ever seen him, and it was a scary thing on someone who I'd accused only four months ago of being too young and twitchy to be allowed around live ammo.

"Goblin warriors are not big on talking or thinking. Even if we captured one it wouldn't tell us anything useful."

"So kill?"

"Kill or follow. If you can track a goblin that isn't about to murder or maim someone, do it. Find out where they're hiding."

"Queens are definitely in the capture category, but we aren't likely to see one," Wyatt added. "Questions?"

No one spoke. Mostly we were itching to get out there, do some goblin hunting, and avenge our friends.

"Then be careful," I said. "And happy hunting."

CHAPTER TWELVE

Tuesday, September 2
12:10 a.m.

Wyatt and I probably could have divided our collective knowledge and resources better by partnering with other people, but we worked best as a team. Plus Wyatt was still getting to know his Lupa side, and since Lupa society used to be matriarchal, as his mate I was the only person who could get him to stand down if his temper started to get the best of him. I think he also wanted to keep an eye on me, even if he'd never admit it out loud.

Goblins still make my stomach hurt.

Our search grid was the north side of Mercy's Lot, near the old Anjean River waterfront that was slowly being renovated and brought back to life. Goblins had been spotted there pretty frequently until the disaster that was Parker's Palace, and it was one of Alejandro's sighting spots. I hadn't been back to this particular area of the city since a bunch of half-Bloods tried to murder a theater full of humans during an Arts benefit. The evening was topped off by a four-story drop out a window in an attempt to save Phineas's life.

That had hurt like a son of a bitch.

It was the same night Tybalt had lost his hand.

We dropped two pairs (Marcus/Kismet and Paul/Autumn) off in their search grid on the way to ours. Wyatt parked in an alley at the edge the grid, and then we hit the pavement. Sometimes this sort of covert work was boring as hell—a lot of walking, watching and waiting for what could amount to absolutely no payoff. In my Hunter days, no payoff meant I was going home alive and sans injury. With the slaughter of the gremlins so fresh in my mind, tonight I was craving a little mayhem.

We moved through the streets without speaking, our actions communicating for us. A head tilt here, a jacked thumb there. I'd developed that sort of thing with Jesse and Ash back in our Triad days, and I loved having it with Wyatt. I loved everything about him, as a matter of fact, and it still startled me when thoughts like that bubbled up. I wasn't used to this kind of total love, and I wanted it as long as I could have it.

Older brick and stone buildings were mixed with steel and glass. Some were homes, other businesses and restaurants in what was as close as the city got to an historic district. We were still a good eight blocks from Parker's Palace, and a big system of sewer tunnels existed below us that had once housed goblins and allowed them to travel freely in daylight. As Hunters we'd avoided going into those tunnels. Entry points were difficult to find, the quarters were too close for fighting, and the chances of getting lost were high.

Still, it was tempting me tonight.

Over an hour passed with three check-ins from all the teams. No leads and no goblin sightings, although Carly and Shelby did kill a pair of Halfies.

Score one for us, I guess.

Around two a.m. my energy was starting to flag, and I briefly entertained the idea of sneaking into a nearby all-night coffee shop for a caffeine boost. Food wasn't a horrible idea, either. I bit back a yawn, and Wyatt noticed.

Before he could say anything, our phones vibrated with text messages.

Parker's Palace. Engaged. Backup now!

The text came from Paul's phone. We'd dropped him and Autumn off a few blocks north of our area. The car was in the opposite direction and too far away, so Wyatt and I ran. The streets were quiet enough that we avoided any collisions with traffic or pedestrians, and the noise of the fight reached us before we saw it.

The street in front of the Parker's Palace theater was swarming with about three dozen goblin warriors, all in various states of battle frenzy. Goblins are nasty looking creatures on their best days, but add in a little blood lust and they are the stuff of nightmares. About four-feet tall, they hunch at the shoulders, have sharp claws on their bony hands, ruby red eyes, scaly black skin, and mouths full of cone-shaped teeth that like to bite. They also tend to run around nearly naked, wearing little loincloths that don't hide anything during a real fight—especially when the beasts get aroused by battle lust.

They were lusting all right, with four of ours in the middle of it all. Marcus and Kismet had somehow gotten there before us, and they were as engaged as Paul and Autumn. Marcus had shifted, which gave our side a good advantage. Autumn's true form was a Bengal fox, only she hadn't changed. I figured out why pretty fast.

Autumn swung at the goblins with a short sword clutched in her left hand—probably given to her by Paul because I'd never seen her with a weapon like that before—and swinging poorly.

Her right arm was tucked close to her body, her face pinched and pale from pain, which meant something was broken or dislocated, and preventing her from shifting. Paul stuck close, protecting her as best he could. He'd forgone his usual weapon of an aluminum baseball bat in favor of butterfly knives that stabbed and cut with amazing precision.

Someone had been practicing.

The four of them should have been overwhelmed by the size of the goblin horde surrounding them, but the warriors weren't attacking en masse. They moved in waves, snapping at heels like rabid dogs, then backing out again. They were teasing, trapping, only occasionally trying to draw blood, but why?

Wyatt had bi-shifted as we ran, and his horrifying half-Lupa form barreled into the fight with a furious snarl. Some of the goblins actually shrank back from the sight of him, a brand-new monster to their very limited minds. Wyatt ripped two throats out with his clawed hands before they snapped into action. Instead of scattering, though, eight of them pounced on Wyatt at once.

Something slammed into me from behind before I could help him, and I rolled across the pavement. Got a knife out of my ankle sheath as I went. Came up on my knees in a half-crouch and shoved the blade into an advancing goblin's gut. Fuchsia blood spurted out, spattering my hand and arm, filling my nose with the stink of old seawater. The goblin hissed as it died.

Bitter fury filled me as I launched to my feet. Fury directed blindly at the goblins around us—soulless killing machines that existed for no other reason than to destroy and cause pain. Bits of old hurts bubbled up too, feeding that fury, and I launched myself into the fight. I rarely found any glee in killing these days,

but this battle brought all those old feelings back to the forefront.

Brought back old hates and prejudices I'd long thought buried.

The nasty little monsters deserved it. So I did my very best to protect my friends and kill every last one of the goblins.

A flash of golden fur caught my attention. Kyle, in his true dingo form, ran head-first into the back of a goblin and sent the creature flying into the side of a light pole. A glance to my left found Tybalt in the street, his face perfectly blank as he swung his prosthetic attachment at the goblins, eviscerating two with one solid stroke.

Paul shouted, then cursed, his voice practically in my ear. I turned. A goblin had latched onto Paul's back like a child getting piggy-backed, and its teeth were deep in Paul's shoulder. One of Paul's butterfly knives was already lodged in the goblin's side, and Paul couldn't seem to get a good shot with the other.

"Knees," I shouted.

He dropped immediately. I yanked the butterfly knife out of the goblin's side, then slammed it into the base of its neck. Severed the spine. It went limp. I pulled its teeth out of Paul's shoulder, and the body slumped to the street. Paul looked up at me, panting and pale-faced, his eyes glazed with pain.

"Thank me later," I said.

Kismet moved in to help protect Paul and Autumn, while I jumped back into the slaughter. My skin was smeared with goblin blood, and I was a sweaty, sticky mess, but I still managed to laugh when I stabbed another goblin in the eye. I think it was a slightly hysterical laugh. No one here would blame me for it.

The goblin bodies were piling up. Half a dozen took off for an alley. Dingo Kyle raced after them. We quickly cut down the last few standing targets, until all that was left was the carnage.

Wyatt stood apart from the group, his bi-shifted body heaving from exertion and battle lust. His eyes were perfectly silver, his canine teeth flashing in the streetlight. He looked very much like an ancient predatory beast—and like he could do this for hours yet. Personally, I was exhausted. He started growling. Jaguar Marcus hissed.

Oh hell no.

I moved to Wyatt's side and yanked his chin down so he was looking at me instead of over me. Our height difference in this state was a pain in the ass, but I'd be damned if I'd let him lose it. Ever. A small red pupil appeared in his silver eyes. Good, he was seeing me.

"Eyes on me, Truman," I said. "Fight's over. All that's left here are friends."

He blinked hard. It took a minute, but he worked himself down from the bi-shift and back to his regular self. "Are you hurt?" he asked as soon as his teeth were back to normal.

"For a change, no. You?"

"No."

We rejoined our people, who'd gathered around Autumn and Paul. Both looked a little shocky from their respective injuries. Tybalt had sacrificed his shirt as a bandage for Paul, whose own shirt was soaked with blood.

"—out of nowhere," Autumn was saying. "I didn't even smell them until after I'd been pushed."

"Pushed?" I repeated, since I'd missed the start of the story.

She nodded at the roof of a three-story building across the street. "Pushed. I damaged my arm in the fall. Think I dislocated my shoulder. Paul got down to me fast, and by then the goblins were swarming us."

"So no idea where they came up from?" Tybalt asked.

"No, just from the alley there."

The alley Kyle had gone down and not returned from. Kismet was missing, too. Before I could ask, Marcus (who'd shifted back) said, "Gina went for the car."

Kyle also appeared, limping out of the shadows of the alley. He shifted, as well, and winced as he put weight on his right ankle. "They disappeared into a storm drain behind the theater," he said. "It was too narrow to get down, and it reeked of goblin."

"Good thing you didn't try to squeeze in then," I said. "If it's a nest, you'd have been puppy chow."

He grunted. "I also found two human bodies in the alley."

Of course you did. I sighed in my head as Wyatt, Tybalt, and I followed him. The bodies were out in the open, unhidden, their skin and clothing flayed and torn. Eyes wide open. Both women, probably early twenties, but their faces were too damaged to be sure. They hadn't been dead long, maybe an hour.

One woman's leg had KEL scratched into it. Looked like our people interrupted another love note from Nessa.

"After we get the goblins cleaned up, we'll call the police," Wyatt said.

Despite the horrific way they died, those girls' families deserved to know they were dead. They deserved a chance to grieve.

Don't the Frosts deserve that chance too?

I shoved the voice of reason away. I had too many other things to worry about tonight, and the Frosts were nowhere near the top of my list.

Kismet returned with the SUV. Autumn and Paul needed to get back to the Watchtower for medical attention, while some of us stayed behind on cleanup duty. Wyatt was on the phone with someone at the Watchtower, reporting our activities of the last thirty minutes or so and requesting help with cleanup. The last thing we needed to do was leave a pile of goblin parts for the city police to find, and we only had about three hours before people started waking up around here.

Kyle was helping Kismet settle Autumn and Paul into the backseat. Autumn's phone kept buzzing, but she didn't seem in any hurry to pick up. I moved forward to answer the phone for her.

A warm body hit mine, and then I hit the bloody pavement. My right thigh shrieked with heat and pain. Something warm and wet spread over the small of my back. Wyatt was yelling my name from far away, so he wasn't the person flattening me. Bleeding on me.

Crap.

"The roof over there," Kyle yelled.

Sniper. Another fucking sniper.

The body on top of me rolled, and I turned my head to look into Marcus's pained copper eyes. I sat up way too fast, because agony seared down my right leg, blurred my vision, and I may have let out a little scream. Wyatt was suddenly behind me, holding me up, and I fell back against him.

Kismet knelt next to Marcus and pressed her hands against his right side, below his ribs.

"What the hell?" I asked.

"Saw a laser sight," Marcus said, voice strained. "Reacted."

"I didn't hear the shot," Wyatt said.

"Me, either."

Wyatt had somehow worked off his belt and was wrapping it around my upper thigh. I finally saw the hole. I'd been shot in the leg.

"How bad?" I said.

"Could have been worse." Marcus flinched when Kismet

increased pressure. "Damn, woman, that hurts."

"It'll hurt worse if you bleed out," Kismet retorted.

"It's not that serious."

"You have two holes in your body, Marcus, it's serious enough."

Wyatt finished cinching his tourniquet, and I hissed through clenched teeth. "Evy only has one. The bullet's still in there."

"Oh goodie, evidence," I said.

"I meant you can't start healing until it's removed."

"Right." I knew that. The pain was messing with my head. "Did we get the shooter?"

"Tybalt and Kyle went after them."

"Who were they trying to kill? Me or Marcus?" I kind of knew the answer but still had to ask the question. He'd jumped in front of a bullet for me. I still got shot, sure, but that didn't negate the gesture.

"The sight was on the back of your head, Evy," Marcus replied.

"Great."

"Could it have been the goblins?" Kismet floated the idea while she helped Marcus lay down in the back of the SUV.

Wyatt went a little overprotective and carried me to the front passenger seat. He even fastened my seatbelt, which I found both irritating and adorable. "I doubt it," he replied. "They don't have the coordination or body type to handle rifles like that."

"A Queen could have hired someone."

"Or it's another of Vale's cousins," I said, "and completely unrelated to the goblins."

No one had an answer to that.

Kismet drove us back to the Watchtower, and halfway there

we got an update on the sniper. No sign once they got to the roof. Kyle said he smelled Bengal.

Fucking fantastic.

My leg wasn't bleeding heavily, but the wound hurt worse than most stab wounds I'd received. Made me worry the bullet had hit bone, especially since there was no exit wound. The city blurred around me during the drive home. Kismet made use of the rule that cars could only drive down the wide mall corridors when delivering seriously injured people to the infirmary, so we didn't have far to walk once we got there.

Once again, though, I didn't walk. Dr. Vansis was a were-bear and strong enough to carry me right into the infirmary and deposit me on an exam table. Paul ended up on one next to me.

"How come whenever you and me battle goblins together, people standing close to me get shot?" I asked. The last time had been a big battle at a nature preserve. Before the battle against combined Halfie and goblin forces began, Paul had accidentally shot Wyatt in the arm.

The comment seemed funnier in my head. Paul gave me a weak smile before Dr. Vansis pulled the curtain between our beds and went about his doctoring. I stared up at the ceiling and tried to ignore the agony in my leg, which seemed to get worse as my body's instinct to heal itself was thwarted by the piece of metal still stuck inside.

At some point, somebody gave me a couple of pills for the pain. My head got very swimmy after that, and by the time my system worked those drugs back out and I became aware again, Dr. Vansis was standing over me with a scrap of metal clutched in a pair of super-long tweezers.

"You're lucky this didn't shatter your femur." He dropped both bullet and tweezers into a basin, then reached for some bandages. "I already anticipate you saying that you'll heal so don't bother, but I'm bandaging you anyway. Deal with it."

I snickered and let the grumpy doc do his job. He might have been abrasive and abrupt, but he was a damned good doctor of humans for being Therian himself. After another mild dose of painkillers, he left my cubicle. I checked my phone and discovered two new texts from Wyatt.

We think Vale is the shooter. Still tracking.

The second text made me smile: **Healing yet?**

I texted back that I was bullet-free and healing, even though the familiar itching sensation of my body's healing power hadn't kicked in yet. It didn't always start immediately, though, especially with serious wounds. My tumble out that fourth-floor window had taken a few days of unconsciousness to finally fix. So I dozed until the itching began, and then it was so intense that laying there started making me crazy. Like a million tiny ants were crawling in and out of my leg, all at once, on razor-sharp feet.

Autumn appeared at the foot of my bed, her eyebrows furrowed with worry. Her arm was in a sling, and she was giving me a funny look. "Evy?"

"I need to get off this bed. Like, now."

"But your leg—"

"Is healing, which is why I need to get up and move around. Can you find me a cane or something? Please?"

She didn't look convinced, but she left in search of a physical prop so I could limp around without falling over. She managed to produce an actual crutch. We adjusted it to work with my height, then she helped me stand. Blood rushed downward as soon as

I got vertical, and throbbing pain joined the itching. I let out a long, unhappy groan.

"Are you sure this is a good idea?" she asked.

"Yes." The infirmary seemed bizarrely quiet, considering how many of us were injured. "Where is everyone?"

"Joining the search for Vale."

"A lot of people are going to be looking for that cat today."

"True enough. Do you need anything else?"

"No, thanks. How's your arm?"

"I dislocated the shoulder. Dr. Vansis reset it."

"Ouch."

"Quite. I only need the sling for a few hours, though, until the discomfort passes."

After she left, I amused myself with a quick tour of the exam cubicles. Partly for the exercise and partly to see who else was still around. The beds there were empty, so I limped my way into the private area. Paul was asleep in the first room. An IV stand pumped blood and fluids into him, and while he didn't look like he was on death's doorstep, he still looked…fragile.

So often I forgot how young we were. Paul was only eighteen years old, and he lived with the cynicism and anger of someone twice that. He'd been badly wounded tonight, but he'd never backed down, never looked scared.

"You did good tonight," I whispered.

In the hall, I paused when a familiar voice rumbled out from the half-closed door two down from Paul's room. I shuffled over as quietly as possible just to make sure I was right.

"—blame yourself. I know you."

Milo. Awake.

Thank God.

Chapter Thirteen

5:15 a.m.

Milo's voice was thick and rough, someone in pain speaking through heavy doses of medication, but he was talking. He was awake. My heart leapt with joy at such a simple thing.

"I blame myself because it's my fault," Marcus replied.

Guess he was healing from his gunshot, too, if he was making bedside visits to other patients. I felt guilty for eavesdropping—not guilty enough to actually walk away from the door, though.

"Vale was going to hurt someone, Marcus. Just happened to be me this time."

Marcus growled. "I hate what he did to you."

"I'm alive."

"If I hadn't kissed you, Vale would not have targeted you."

"Maybe, maybe not. Rather it was me. I'm tired of seeing people I care about get hurt."

"You think I don't feel the same? I care for you, Milo, perhaps more than is advisable."

"Fuck that. You know my one regret about that kiss? That I was too startled to kiss you back."

Someone mumbled something. Fabric shifted. Okay, time to stop being a bad, eavesdropping friend and announce myself. I counted to ten in my head, then took two steps forward and knocked on the door.

"Yeah," Milo said.

I limped inside on my single crutch. Marcus had taken over a small chair next to the bed, and he was bare-chested except for the swaths of white bandages around his abdomen. He seemed alert and rested, unlike the owner of the hand he was holding.

Milo looked terrible and the sight of him made me want to cry for his obvious pain. A wide, blue-black bruise covered most of his throat, and his arms were littered with more bruises. A sheet covered the rest of his body, but I could imagine what his legs looked like. Both of his eyes were blackened, the pupils so spider-veined from burst capillaries that I saw the red from across the room.

Somehow, though, he managed a small smile.

I crutched my way over to the other side of the bed. I'd have hugged him if I didn't think it would cause him all kinds of additional pain. "You scared the shit out of me, buster."

"Sorry." His red gaze dropped to my crutch. "What'd you do?"

"Got shot in the leg. Same bullet that got Marcus."

"Huh?" He turned his head with effort and squinted at Marcus. Marcus scowled at me. Oops. "You're shot?"

Marcus cleared his throat. "Yes, but—"

"Where?"

"Just below my ribs."

For all the painkillers and muscle relaxers he was probably on, Milo looked impressively pissed. "You didn't tell me. You should be resting."

Marcus had the good sense to look contrite, and I had to hide a smile. Even horribly injured, Milo didn't want to be handled. "I'm sorry, Milo. I didn't want to add to your distress. You need your own rest."

"I'll rest if you rest."

He hesitated, then said, "All right. I'll check on you in a few hours."

"Okay."

Marcus couldn't hide a flinch as he stood. Therians healed pretty quickly, but not as fast as me, and not from a bullet wound. He leaned over and pressed a gentle kiss to Milo's forehead. They didn't say anything as he left. I stared at the empty doorway, impressed by the hitherto unseen tender side of Marcus Dane.

"How'd you get shot?" Milo asked.

I perched on the side of the bed to take some pressure off that crutch and my armpit. "Marcus tell you about our goblin hunt tonight?"

"No."

I filled him in on everything that had happened since our escape from Vale's hands, right up to checking on Paul. He worked hard to pay attention and seemed to be following along.

"Sorry I missed all the fun," he said.

"That's what happens when you get tortured, pal."

"Yeah."

"How's your pain?"

"Intense but not painful, if that makes sense. Dr. Vansis is worried about blood clots and…" He frowned. "Something about fluid building up in places. Don't remember."

"How about you let the doctor worry about all that, and you just rest? You're going to need it."

"Hate this, feeling so helpless."

"I know. We're Hunters, Milo. We don't wear helpless well. Any of us."

His eyes unfocused for a beat, then he blinked hard. "Evy? Tell me something."

"Sure."

"I don't remember much about us escaping Vale. Was Baylor shot?"

My stomach flipped. "Yes. There was a sniper outside the door when we tried to leave the building the first time." He waited for more, so I gave it to him. "He was down before we could do anything."

"He's dead." Milo didn't phrase it as a question.

I answered him anyway. "Yeah."

Grief worked its way through the fog in his eyes. "Gina must be a mess."

"She's taking it hard. They all are. You should have seen her out there tonight, killing those goblins. She was taking out a little rage."

"So who's stepping up?"

"To what?"

He somehow managed a perfect *Are you an idiot?* look. "In charge. Baylor was one of the Cerberus heads."

I hadn't given any thought to who would be taking over as one of the three head honchos now that Baylor was dead. Astrid and Rufus could certainly handle things for a while. I doubted they would remain a pair. Three worked better for decision making processes, in case two people got deadlocked. They'd need someone to step up.

"I have no idea," I said. "I think everyone's more focused on finding Vale, settling the discord he's sowing amongst the Clans, and trying to figure out what the goblins are up to."

"True."

His eyelids began to droop. He fought the fatigue and the drugs, but he needed to rest. Milo had a lot of healing to do, and I had a feeling it would be a long process to get him back to 100 percent.

"Get some sleep, pal." I gave his hand a gentle squeeze. "I'll make sure you stay informed, okay?"

He smiled gratefully. "Thanks, Evy."

I woke up later in bed, surrounded by blankets and a deeply-breathing body curled up next to mine. My leg ached and itched but not as badly as when I'd limped back to my room and passed out. I was still a bloody mess, which made the sheets a bloody mess, and it looked like Wyatt hadn't bothered to shower before going to sleep either.

The fact that sleeping in a gore-soaked bed with my filthy half-werewolf boyfriend didn't even seem strange made me laugh. Well, snort, anyway, right through my nose. The noise made Wyatt grumble and reach out. I let him curl around me from behind, grateful to have him there—and eager for him to wake up and deliver some news.

I grabbed my phone off the short bedside dresser that served as both clothing storage and a nightstand. After eight o'clock, still morning.

Behind me, Wyatt's breathing changed. The arm around my waist tightened and his nose pressed into my neck below my ear, not quite nuzzling but close. Some of his Lupa instincts were taking over, telling him his mate was near. He was getting hard and I didn't know if I should wake him up before he went farther, or encourage the attention. The walls between rooms in this part of the housing section weren't terribly thick, and we'd both been pretty vocal when we made love yesterday.

It was a lot easier to get loud with your mate when you have four-inch thick steel walls all around you. Maybe we could sneak back down to that bank vault….

He grunted, and I felt the tension in his body rack up the moment he came fully awake. I counted to seven before he relaxed enough that I could wiggle around to face him. If someone could look both exhausted and well-rested, Wyatt managed. He smiled, and I leaned in for a kiss.

"How's your leg?" he asked.

"Still healing but it feels better. Wound's probably closed. It hit bone. Dr. Vansis seemed impressed it didn't break my leg."

"I looked for you there first when I got back. Autumn and Marcus were discharged. He's keeping Paul for another day or two so he can watch for infection."

"Probably a good idea." Goblin mouths are not sanitary. "When did you get back?"

"About an hour ago." He exhaled hard through his nose. "We lost Vale's scent around Benton Street. Our best guess is he got into a car."

"Well, crap."

"Crap?"

"Fuck?"

"That sounds more like you. We did manage to put down a few Halfies while we were out."

"That's something."

"And Astrid spoke with the new Assembly Voice about Vale."

"Oh?"

The Assembly Voice is basically the public relations spokesperson for the Assembly of Clan Elders. The first one I met,

Michael Jenner, was killed last month during our pursuit of Walter Thackery and his Lupa pups. His daughter, Dawn, would start working here at the Watchtower in another month, when she finally reached the age of four—which is the age of maturity for Therians. The new Voice was a Cania named Oslo, and according to Kyle he shifted into a coyote.

"Oslo said that Vale, Starr, and two other members of the Tuck family have been named criminals and are officially wanted by the Assembly for their actions against the Pride. Assembly security representatives are also searching for them."

"Well, that's good news," I said. "I don't care who finds Vale first, as long as we get the scroll and the vampire cure back." I had a lot of friends who needed that cure.

"It's good and bad news. Word is that the declaration has riled up some of Vale's friends in the Pride, as well as a few other Clans. Astrid expects there will be some pushback, maybe even violence."

"Vale kidnapped five people, tortured us, and had one of us killed. Who knows what else he's done or will do next?"

"It's Clan politics, Evy, and I don't understand it all. We see Prentiss's attempt to steal the role of Alpha from the Danes as wrong, especially through underhanded means."

"Cheating."

"Right. Some of the Clans have operated that way for centuries, wresting control from one family to the next. The Elder on the Assembly usually remains the same, but internal leadership changes hands often."

"So some of the Clans don't care what Vale's up to, because it's what their Clan would do?"

"Yes."

"Even though he's challenging for Elder, not Alpha?"

"Yes. The only reason the Assembly voted in favor of labeling Vale a criminal was because he openly attacked the Watchtower and its members, which is supported by a majority of the Elders, including Elder Dane."

"So if he'd only gone after Marcus, the Assembly would care less?"

"Right."

"That's fucked up."

"A little. But it's our reality right now, and at least we have more eyes out there looking for Vale."

Something else was bothering Wyatt. I saw it in the way his eyes pinched at the corners and the way he pressed his lips together. "What else is going on?"

"Astrid told me she's heard rumors that more than one Felia may challenge Riley as Elder, and that Keenan may also see a challenge as Alpha."

Something cold trickled down my spine. "That's bad."

"Yes, it is. And it may be my fault."

"What?" I sat up, tangled, sticky hair falling in front of my face. I pushed it away and glared down at Wyatt. "How do you figure?"

"Lupa were made extinct for a reason, Evy, and when I was infected Elder Dane had every reason to have me executed. But he spared my life."

"Is Elder Dane taking shit for that?"

"According to Astrid, yes. Not all of the Elders agree that since I was human first I don't fall under their jurisdiction."

He looked so guilty that my heart ached. I swung a leg over his—the wounded leg, of course, which it reminded me of quite painfully—and settled my weight on his hips. He watched me, guarded. I put my hands on his bare chest and leaned down.

"Listen to me, Wyatt Truman," I said. "You were infected against your will. You survived the Lupa bite when everyone thought you were going to die. You are living with the changes and you are doing a remarkable job. Don't you dare ever feel guilty for living. Not ever."

I cupped his bearded cheeks in my palms, forcing him to maintain eye contact. "Your life was spared. Anyone who tries to come after you for any reason, Therian or otherwise, will have to kill me first. That's a promise."

He pulled me down into a hard kiss that lasted a little too long to end there. I slid back a few inches, reassuring myself that he was still hard. He made a noise that I answered with a well-placed rub of my hips. Fingers gripped my waist. His arm muscles tensed as he fought what was probably the very overwhelming urge to roll us over and claim me.

"I love you so much, Evy." His voice was a hoarse whisper that sent shivers through my belly and down my thighs.

"I love you too. All of you with all of me."

Another long, intense kiss like the first one, and I was scrambling in the bedside dresser for a condom. We didn't even shed all of our clothes. Just got his shorts down and my ruined jeans off, and then my body was sliding onto his, opening for him. The passion in his eyes swelled my heart to bursting. I leaned down to kiss him again as our bodies began to move together.

We existed in each other, in that moment, for as long as we could. In the last few months we'd learned to never take each other for granted or to take what we'd found together for granted. It could all be over in a flash—a lesson reinforced yesterday after our captivity. Every touch, every kiss, every ripple of pleasure we gave each other's body was treasured. Because as much as I wanted a forever with Wyatt, forever was not a guarantee, and I wanted no more regrets. Not with him.

Long after, we lay together in a tangled, messy, half-clothed heap, enjoying such a simple thing as holding each other. Sooner or later one of our phones would ring and remind us of the world outside those thin plaster walls. Until that happened, I held my lover close and dozed.

CHAPTER FOURTEEN

10:45 a.m.

Wyatt went ahead of me to Operations. I lingered a little longer while showering because my hair was a tangled, matted mess and required some extra attention—and not for the first time, I gave serious thought to just cutting it short. Maybe some other time. Once it was clean and I was dressed, I twisted it up into a messy bun so it was out of the way.

I didn't need the crutch anymore, but I still had a slight limp as I headed down the corridor to Ops. The leg ached, and I suspected it would for the rest of the day until the wound was fully healed. Considering the bullet had been half an inch from hitting my femoral artery, I'd take the limp over being dead.

Halfway there, Kismet stepped out of the shadow of an unused storefront. I jumped back, startled to see her lurking there. "The hell, Gina?"

"I need to show you something." Her tone left no room for argument, and it tweaked my nerves a little bit.

"Okay."

"In here." She pushed open the storefront door.

I followed her inside. The windows were papered over, which allowed some residual light from the corridor. Enough to see by, anyway. The store was small, the floors bare and walls empty. I didn't see anything unusual until Kismet presented me with her phone.

"This was sent to me from your old phone," Kismet said. "The one Vale took from you yesterday."

Oh great. "You've watched it, I take it?"

"Yes." Her face was unreadable, but I knew without asking that I wasn't going to like whatever Vale sent.

I pressed Play. The black screen flashed to life, displaying two frighteningly familiar figures huddled together in the near-dark. Each had a wrist handcuffed to a chain, which was wrapped around a wooden support beam of some sort, and they both looked terrified.

"Son of a bitch," I said. Vale had Stephen and Lori Frost. Judging by the shadowed shape of a water heater in the background, they were in a basement somewhere.

The light source shining on them cut off, plunging the room into darkness. Lori screamed. Wood creaked. The video jumped to a bright close up of Vale's face, looking righteously pissed and a little bit smug. Fury tickled at the back of my mind, aimed right at the were-cat onscreen for all the hurt he'd already caused, and for dragging two more innocent people into this clusterfuck.

"I'm uncertain if I should call you Evangeline or Chalice," Vale said. "Imagine my surprise when I saw your face on the news as a missing person, and imagine my further surprise when Mr. and Mrs. Frost willingly came here to meet me and speak with their daughter. They are far too trusting, and if you would like to see them alive again, call me back on this phone. You have until noon."

The video ended.

I didn't waste breath or energy expelling the dozen or so expletives roaring through my mind. I didn't even look at Kismet, who was hovering nearby. I hit redial, then put the call onto Speaker.

"You're prompt, Ms. Stone," Vale said. His voice sent cold fingers down my spine.

"You gave me a good incentive to call."

"Indeed. Are you alone?"

"Yes." I trusted Kismet to stay silent for this conversation. "Are you insane? There's a city full of Therians looking for you right now, and you're going to try and blackmail me with hostages?"

"Yes."

"What makes you think they mean anything to me? They aren't my parents."

"I've heard about your resurrection, and I'm not banking on a strong sense of daughterly duty. I'm banking on your training as a Triad Hunter. You protect innocents."

Dammit.

"If you don't want the Frosts hanging from chains like your Hunter friend, you'll pay close attention," Vale said, his voice darker. Angrier.

"I'm listening."

"Right now, Marcellus Dane is being challenged for the position of Pride Elder. Riley will, of course, answer the challenge in his place. I need you to ensure that the fight is lost."

I let loose a surprised snort before I could stop myself. "You can't be serious. I'm not Therian. The Pride won't let me anywhere near that fight."

Traditionally, challenges were fought in a similar manner as old-fashioned human duels. Both sides met in a neutral location, a thirty party—usually an Elder—was there to signal the start of the fight, and witnesses were there in the event that one fighter yielded before they were killed. Because the whole point was to kill the other person. I had no chance of successfully sabotaging Riley—no intention of trying, either.

Vale laughed. "Your perspective is too narrow, Ms. Stone, which proves how little you know about Pride politics."

If that was supposed to be an insult, it didn't deliver. Handling Pride politics was not my job. "So what is it you want from me exactly?"

"By Therian law, if the sitting Elder dies before the official challenge is answered, the position is open to Assembly control. The Assembly can hear nominations and vote on the replacement Elder."

"And let me guess? You have enough friends on the Assembly to get a good pal of yours nominated?"

"Nominated and voted into the position."

"So you want me to what? Assassinate Riley before the official challenge fight?"

"No."

I glanced at Kismet, a little confused. She shrugged. "What then?"

"Riley is simply a stand-in for Marcellus. Since Marcus refused to give up the security codes to the Dane compound, you're going in for me. You've been allowed onto the grounds as a guest because of your relationship with the Coni."

He was right on that count. Joseph, Aurora, and Ava lived with the Danes, and I'd visited them a few times since they had moved to the mansion. The security guards knew me, and they'd let me in without putting up a fuss. Vale was hot-headed and didn't plan well, but he did his research.

And then his plan for me today fell into place with alarming clarity moments before he said it: "Your job, once you're in the Dane compound, is to find Marcellus and kill him."

"No."

"No?"

"Hell no. Do I really need to list all the reasons why that will never happen?"

"You're clever, and you have a few handy powers in your pocket, or so I've heard."

"So you think I'll what? Teleport into Elder Dane's office, cut his throat, and then teleport back out? And no one will be suspicious?"

"I honestly don't care if you're suspected or not, as long as you aren't caught. If you are, you're rogue. One mention of me will result in more of this."

Wood creaked. I heard a sound that might have been fingers snapping, and then a woman screamed. Lori. I squeezed the phone as anger surged through me. Lori kept screaming.

"Stop!" My eyes stung with emotion I didn't understand. "Stop, please."

Her screams dissolved into deep sobs, and then the sound cut off.

"You were saying?" Vale asked.

The Frosts weren't my parents, but the knowledge didn't stop a surge of hate and grief from making my insides shake. I didn't look at Kismet. I had to make this decision on my own. "I do this and you let the Frosts go alive and without further harm?"

"Yes."

"I also want the items you stole from me yesterday."

"What items would that be?"

"The scroll and the leather bag."

"Sorry, Ms. Stone, you'll need to do another favor for those."

"Unless the Felia kill me first."

"That's your issue."

Fantastic.

"You have until noon tomorrow," Vale said. "If you tell anyone about this conversation, I'll be sure to take it out on your parents before handing them back."

"What about Kismet? The woman whose phone you send that photo to?"

"I've already reached an understanding with Ms. Kismet. Noon."

He hung up, and I very nearly threw the phone across the room. Instead, I forced my fingers to unclench and hand it back to Kismet. She watched me with a curious, cautious expression that I mirrored.

"What does he have over you?" I asked.

"That's my problem, Stone."

"Not if it affects the outcome of this whole clusterfuck."

"It won't. Vale thinks he has something to hold over my head and keep me quiet, so I don't connect him to whatever it is he wants you to do. But the bigger picture is more important, Evy. The Assembly, the Watchtower, the vampire cure, it's all more important right now. What happens next is your call."

My mind raced with a dozen different things I could do, different ways to go about solving this particular crisis. I wasn't the planner though. That was always Wyatt's job—to come up with a solution to problems, plan out our defense or offense. And I couldn't risk telling Wyatt what was going on. Not this time. He'd try to stop me or want to help, and I could not allow Vale to torture and murder the Frosts. They'd already lost their daughter; they deserved better than that. But how could I walk onto the

Dane compound and murder Marcellus without putting a giant target on my own ass?

"What now?" Kismet asked.

"For now, I need your word that you won't say anything about this. Not to anyone, even yourself. Life as normal. Please?"

"I promise." She frowned. "Evy, what are you going to do?"

"I need to figure out how to assassinate a were-cat without getting my throat ripped out."

Kismet impressed me by shutting up completely about the call and my new task. Two months ago, she would have questioned the hell out of my decisions, maybe even ratted me out to the others. Hell, two months ago I would have refused to let her stay in the room while I spoke to Vale. Showed how far our relationship had progressed from the days of her trying to murder me.

We walked into Operations to a lot of loud chatter. Wyatt looked up from his conversation circle with Astrid and Rufus. I met his eyes and managed to not react to the question in his—I'd taken more time getting to Ops than he expected. I winked, then smiled, and his curiosity settled.

"What's going on?" Kismet asked as we joined the trio.

"Elder Dane has been challenged," Astrid replied. "It's an official challenge through the Assembly, so Riley will fight in his place."

"Who challenged him?" I asked.

"A man named Silva. His true form is a lion."

"So not a Bengal?"

"At this point, none of the Bengals are stupid enough to step forward, but that doesn't mean Silva is unconnected to Vale."

She had no idea how connected he was to Vale.

"When's the fight?" Kismet asked.

"Noon tomorrow."

Of course it was noon tomorrow. Twenty-four hours before the fate of the Watchtower was decided. "So what are we doing?" I asked.

"The same thing we've been doing," Astrid said. "Searching for Vale."

"We don't just need him for the crimes he's committed," Rufus added. "He also has the items you received from the gnome. We need those things back."

Yet another reason I needed a good plan for this assassination job. I had to be alive in order to do this unknown second favor and get the scroll and medicine pouch from Vale. No pressure.

"I'd also like to send a team down into the sewers near Parker's Palace," Astrid said. "We know the goblins came and went from there last night, so it's possible there's a nest nearby. It may lead us to Nessa's location."

I avoided eye contact, which wasn't like me, but I didn't want her assigning that job to me today. I had other things to do.

"I'd like to take point," Kismet said.

Bless you, Gina.

"All right," Astrid said. "Take six people, good noses and good with blades. Let me know when you're ready to leave."

"Understood." She headed out without another word or look, and I made a mental note to thank her later—if I was alive to manage it.

Wyatt, on the other hand, cornered me as soon as I left Ops. "What's wrong?"

"Nothing except the obvious, why?" I said. I hated lying to him, but I didn't have time for an interrogation.

"I expected you to jump at the chance to do some goblin hunting."

"I think I got my fill last night." Which was partially true. The release of gutting a dozen goblins had felt wonderful, and it was very therapeutic. I'd probably benefit greatly from gutting a few dozen more. "Plus, I want to be available in case Vale is found."

Wyatt nodded. "All right, I can accept that."

"What does that mean?"

"It means I know you better than you know yourself, Evy. Something else is bothering you. Is it the Frosts?"

Oh, baby, you have no idea. "A little, yes. I still don't know how to deal with them."

"Maybe once this challenge business is over with tomorrow, you'll be able to sit down and talk with them."

"Maybe."

"Don't you think you should? Chalice was their daughter. They deserve some sort of closure." Grief flickered in Wyatt's eyes. He took family issues to heart, because his had been taken away so violently when he was still a teenager. His parents and sister were murdered by Halfies, and his twin brother died a few years later in a tragic accident.

On the other hand, I was an only child with no father in the picture. My mother died when I was ten. I probably loved her as much as a kid could love someone who ignored them most days and yelled at them whenever they were actually noticed. She had been more concerned with getting drunk, getting high, and having sex with anything with a penis. I had no frame of reference for loving parents who actually gave a shit about their kids, or a family unit that protected each other. All I ever had was Wyatt and my Triad.

"You're right," I said. "I'll make the effort to talk to the Frosts, I promise."

"Thank you."

"No problem. Listen, I'll catch up with you later tonight, okay?"

"Sure." His eyebrows furrowed. "Where are you headed?"

I swallowed and worked up a smile—if whatever plan I made up on the way went to hell, I might never see him again. *I love you, Wyatt, so much.* As much as I wanted to say it, the words would sound too much like good-bye. Instead, I simply said, "I'm going to go visit my goddaughter."

I made one stop in Mercy's Lot before heading south. The Dane compound was on the outskirts of the city, in an area south of uptown, full of fancy homes and gated communities. Not quite a mansion, but too huge to be just a house, three stories spread out over a good quarter acre of the five acre, fenced lot. The grounds were free of trees to preserve line of sight, decorated instead with fancily-shaped shrubs and bushes. A large barn in the back was where, according to Marcus, the family could shift and run around without chance of a neighbor spying them in their true form.

A man with black hair and sunglasses hiding what were probably copper eyes was guarding the gate. I identified myself, and he let me inside without question.

So far so good.

A stone driveway led up to the front doors, and I parked off to the side behind two other vehicles. As I climbed out of the car, my nerves hummed. So much was riding on me getting this right. I wasn't wired and wore no weapons, which left me feeling totally naked despite my clothes. Naked, exposed, and ready to jump out of my skin.

The front door opened before I could ring the bell. Aurora's delighted smile curbed some of my guilt over this errand. She threw thin arms around my shoulders in an unexpected hug. Her thick, corkscrew-curled hair was pulled back in a big messy bun, and her clothes looked thrown on without thought to matching. But she was happy, and more than anything, it made me smile.

"I didn't expect you today," Aurora said as she pulled back. "With so much going on in the city, I thought you'd be terribly busy."

"We're doing everything we can," I replied. I followed her into the house's giant foyer, careful to disguise my slight limp. "I was injured last night, so I'm taking it easy today. Don't faint."

She laughed. "You never take it easy."

"Exactly. I figured distracting myself with a visit would be therapeutic."

"And you can check up on the Danes?"

I shrugged. "Maybe. This all revolves around them."

"Too true." She linked her arm through mine and led me into the west side of the house. The hardwood floors gleamed with a fresh coat of polish, and the scent of roasting meat teased my nose. The Dane house always had a homey, lived-in feeling to it, and I'd never regretted my decision to move the Coni survivors here.

"Tell me Ava isn't napping," I said. Even though it wasn't my mission, I wanted to see my goddaughter. To hug her and experience the innocence of a child, if only for a few minutes.

"She's quite awake. Joseph is with her in the playroom."

We went upstairs on a grand, winding staircase. The playroom was the stuff of every small child's dreams: a jungle gym, dozens of toys, even a plastic ball pit, all crammed into a bedroom the size of two Cottage Place apartments. Joseph waved from his perch on one of the swings, his body swaying gently. He was one of the oldest living Therians I knew, and every moment of his life was etched into the wrinkles and lines on his face. His eyes remained sharp, though, and he'd die to protect the two ladies in his care.

A delighted squeal rose up from the ball pit, followed by an explosion of red, yellow, and blue orbs. Ava scrambled out of the pit and across the floor toward me, screeching my name. She hurtled herself at my legs, and I dropped to my knees so I could grab her in a proper hug. Ava had been born in May, putting her at three and a half months old. Due to her Therian physiology, she was the size of a sixteen-month old, steady on her feet and blurting out her first words. She was bigger every time I saw her, and I regretted not being a larger part of her life.

How often does a human get to be godmother to a Coni child?

"Evy, Evy," Ava said, over and over in her pipsqueak voice.

"Hey, cutie." I ruffled her thick curls, the same shiny auburn as her mother's. "I've missed you."

Ava smiled shyly, then raced back over to the ball pit. Had it only been a few months ago that I'd held her and she'd been a day old? It didn't seem possible.

"Hi, Joseph," I said.

"Greetings, Evangeline," he replied. His reedy voice was tighter, rougher than usual. "Have you word?"

It took me a moment to realize he meant word from Phineas. I wasn't the only one he'd left behind. "No, nothing, I'm sorry. This is purely a social call."

He nodded, then returned his attention to Ava and her antics in the pit.

"Phineas is missed," Aurora whispered when I stood.

"By all of us," I replied. "I wish he would send word."

"As do I. He's missing so much."

Ava was Phin's goddaughter, and he wasn't around to see her growing up—or to protect her, like he'd promised. He'd left me to do it for both of us, and a small part of me resented him for that. They were his people, his family, and he'd left them to chase the smallest hope of finding more Coni alive somewhere in the world.

Aurora took my hand and led me to one side of the playroom, out of earshot of the others. "What's troubling you, Evangeline?"

"That's a pretty long list." I wasn't about to unload the drama of the last few days on her narrow, overburdened shoulders, so I settled on a vague version of the truth. "Some friends are in pain, and I don't know how to help them."

"Do you blame yourself for their pain?"

"Don't I always?"

"Is it your blame to carry?"

"Some of it's mine. Some if it belongs to others."

"Then carry what's yours and leave the rest behind."

Easier said than done.

We watched Ava play for a few minutes in silence before Aurora said, "I hope he returns soon."

"Phin?"

"Yes. Joseph's dying."

Something in my chest squeezed. "He is?"

She blinked hard. "He's lived a long life. He'll pass soon, I think. My hope is that Phineas returns so that they may say good-bye."

"Weeks?"

"Days." She turned wide, tear-filled eyes to me. "I don't know if I can be here without Joseph. The Danes have been kind to us, but they're Felia. We're not natural allies."

"They scare you?"

"Very much. It's a silly instinct, but it's difficult to fight."

"If Phin is able, he'll come home."

"I know." She let out a long, shuddering breath. "It's the thought that he might be unable that terrifies me."

"Me, too." I hugged her, unsure what else to do. "Me, too."

I visited a while longer, until leaving was inevitable. I had a primary reason for coming to the Dane house today, and putting it off wouldn't make it go away. I hugged Ava extra fiercely before I excused myself from the playroom, careful to tell Aurora I could walk myself to the front door.

My heart hammered in my chest hard enough to hurt. Adrenaline made my fingertips shake. My skin crawled with awareness of what I was about to do. This plan could go to shit so easily if I wasn't fast enough. It was going to hurt a lot of people for a little while. Wyatt's face flashed in my mind's eye and I shoved him away. I couldn't think about him right now. I had to concentrate.

Marcellus's office was four doors down from the playroom, and I walked in that direction, each step sending a spike of fear through my gut. If this didn't work, I was royally fucked and the Frosts were dead.

I stopped outside the closed office door and listened—no voices inside. I checked for my tether to the Break out of habit, in case I needed to teleport out of a bad situation in a hurry—not that I had anywhere to run to, if this did go south. The Break was a comfort, and I let its power wash over me for a moment before I knocked. Two sharp bangs of my knuckles.

"Yes?" came a deep, growly voice.

I pushed the door open, glanced around to be sure no one else was in there, then shut it behind me. Marcellus Dane sat behind his desk, his aged face lined with worry and fatigue, the very image of an older, more mature Marcus. The left wall was decorated with four Japanese swords, placed at different heights. Easy to grab. Probably sharp.

"Ms. Stone," Marcellus said. "I don't recall us having an appointment."

"We don't, Elder," I said.

His copper eyes narrowed. "Then what can I do for you?"

I took a breath that did nothing to calm my racing heart and wished for a weapon of some sort in my hands. "A simple favor."

"From me?"

"Yes, Elder."

He leaned forward and propped his elbows on the wide expanse of his desk—the only thing between us. "And what favor do you require this day?"

I mirrored his stance, placing my palms flat on the desk's smooth surface. "I need you to die."

He moved first, but I was faster.

Chapter Fifteen

Evening

The sucky thing about dying is that you miss everything that happens while you're out of commission. I know this well.

To be fair, I didn't actually die this time around, but a few people helped me fake it so convincingly that everyone believed I had—and that's exactly what I needed. Vale had to believe Marcellus was dead. He also had to believe I was dead. But I'm getting a little ahead of myself.

Unconsciousness is never fun, and it's even less fun when you wake up with a stabbing headache, feeling like you're entire body has been crumpled up and left to dry like that. My abdomen was on fire. I struggled through a haze of fog and achiness, toward awareness, and blinked my eyes open in a totally unfamiliar room. It looked like an office of some kind, with a desk and chairs shoved against a wall to make room for the cot I was on. The place was impersonal, though, and it reeked of an indescribable odor—something scorched and old.

The vomit-inducing smell didn't clue me in until Tybalt walked in the door with a metal urn in his hands, and the pieces fell into place—the Therian-owned crematorium. My supposed final resting place. Because of their short life spans, Therians didn't do elaborate burials or funerals, and they didn't preserve bodies for viewing. Once someone was dead, they got cremated—which meant our deaths had been believable enough to get our "bodies" sent here.

Didn't explain Tybalt's presence, though. No one in the Watchtower except Kismet was supposed to be in on this.

Tybalt sat on the edge of the cot and handed me a glass of water. I sipped at it, glad to sooth my parched lips, but my stomach sloshed with nausea and pain. I didn't dare drink more.

"You?" I said, the first word I could manage.

"I know when Gina's lying," he replied. "We've known each other too long. Plus she was on the other side of town from the Dane mansion, and someone needed to help Demetrius get you two here."

Us two. "He's here?"

"In another room, resting comfortably."

"Thank God."

"You should be thanking God. I can't believe this worked."

"Me, too. My plans usually don't."

"You took a huge risk, Evy. Marcellus could have killed you outright."

"I know."

The look on Marcellus Dane's face when I stood in his office and said "I need you to die" would go down in history as one of the most shocked expressions ever. The shock had lasted only an instant, though, and I'd almost been too slow to knock his phone from his grasp before he could call for security. And then I'd talked faster than I had ever talked in my life, pleading from a child to a parent. He'd needed the entire story before he'd decided that I wasn't a lunatic and put me out of my misery.

Thankfully, he'd understood and agreed to help me.

"Is the Elder awake?" I asked.

"He is, indeed," Marcellus said from the office doorway. He'd changed clothes—which made sense, since the suit he'd been wearing a few hours ago was covered in blood—and seemed oddly relaxed, considering.

I sat up with Tybalt's help. The cot creaked dangerously, and I half-expected it to fold me in half as some sort of sick cosmic joke. My head still throbbed and my stomach felt woozy, but those things would fade quickly. The burning ache from my belly to my breastbone would take longer. The bandages beneath my baggy t-shirt itched where the tape pulled. "Thank you for trusting me, Elder Dane," I said.

He inclined his head in what looked like a nod. "My grand-children trust you, Ms. Stone, and while we don't always see eye to eye, I trust their judgment."

Wow. Probably the only time I'd ever heard him praise Astrid and Marcus. God, this must be killing them right now, mourning a grandfather who wasn't actually dead, killed by a supposed friend.

"I was also impressed by your courage," Marcellus continued. "It takes a strong heart to risk what you did, not knowing my answer to your proposal."

"They're my parents." The words slipped out without conscious thought, surprising me as much as they surprised Tybalt. "I couldn't let Vale murder them."

"I understand. Family is…complicated." He glanced at Tybalt, then returned his intense gaze to me. "How long will you hide here under the guise of being deceased?"

"Depends on what's happening in the outside world." To Tybalt I said, "You wanna fill me in on what I missed?"

"So far, everyone seems to be buying the setup," Tybalt said. "It's getting out that you entered the Elder's office and stabbed him in the heart with one of his swords. Before you could escape, his guard Demetrius walked in and killed you."

My hand went to the painful wound on my stomach. "And Demetrius is keeping his mouth shut?"

"He's loyal," Marcellus said. "It's why I chose him to assist us."

The Felia don't rely on modern forensics the way humans do, which gave us an advantage in creating this illusion. The only thing I'd brought with me to the Dane compound had been two vials of a serum that I'd procured from an apothecary shop run by an actual mage. It had cost every bit of cash I had to purchase the Juliet Potion, as well as the mage's promise to tell no one I'd been there. Once Marcellus and I swallowed the serum, it only took a few minutes to slow our heart rates and breathing to almost nothing—enough to fool anyone not looking extra close.

Actually stabbing Marcellus in the chest had been harder than I expected. Measuring my stroke so it caused blood loss without permanent damage had been nerve-wracking. I didn't like wounding allies on purpose, or causing pain to someone who wasn't an enemy. Demetrius hadn't been so tentative when he sliced me open from breasts to belly, deep enough to bleed heavily, but not deep enough to hit internal organs and kill me. My healing ability had once again proved itself immensely useful—and a serious pain.

A literal fucking pain.

Tybalt finished catching us up on the events immediately after our "deaths" with a surprising, "Do you remember Aurora being there, Evy?"

I blinked, horror turning my insides to ice. "No. Fuck, tell me she didn't see me like that."

"She was still holding your hand when I got there with Astrid."

No, no, no, no. After our conversation about Phineas, after finding out Joseph was dying, this would tear Aurora's delicate heart to pieces. I squeezed my eyes shut against bitter tears. I'd been too focused on saving the Frosts to see all of the collateral damage this plan would cause.

"Don't take this the wrong way, Evy," Tybalt said, "but her grief is what will convince everyone, now that there's no body."

I didn't reply. I didn't trust my voice.

"Gina told me to keep my ears open, so I was with Astrid when she got the call about the Elder's murder. I volunteered to drive her to the compound. You both really looked dead, you know." Something in his eyes told me that the sight had affected him on some level. I wasn't as close to Tybalt as I was to Milo, but he was still a good friend.

"I'm sorry," I said. I had a feeling I'd be saying that a lot, and to a crap-ton of people, in the near future.

Tybalt shrugged. "Part of the plan, right? Astrid was beyond pissed, thinking you'd gone nuts and murdered Elder Dane, so convincing her to have your body brought here was pretty easy. I told her I'd accompany Demetrius with the bodies, and then take your ashes back to the Watchtower."

"How long ago?"

"A few hours. I have to go soon, or someone's going to wonder."

"And you actually have ashes to present?"

"Yep. " He pointed at the urn he'd placed on the floor. "Demetrius called in a favor with the Therian who owns this place."

"That is really fucking creepy."

"How is your wound?" Marcellus asked, thankfully changing the subject.

"Hurts, but it'll heal," I said. The itch-ache all along my abdomen was starting to make me crazy. "How's yours?"

"The same. My worry now is for Riley."

"The Assembly knows the whole story," Tybalt said. "Kismet showed them the video Vale sent. They know that Evy killed Marcellus on Vale's orders, because of his two human hostages. Once that got out, the Clans got pissed."

"Because I tried to kill Marcellus?" I asked.

"No—well, yes, but more pissed because Vale involved humans in Pride politics and ordered a sitting Elder assassinated." He shrugged. "It's complicated."

"No shit."

Tybalt's phone rang. He held it up so I saw Kismet's name on the display, then answered. "Yeah?" After a brief pause, he smiled. "I'll tell her. Thanks."

"Tell me what?" I said before he could properly hang up.

"About thirty minutes ago the Watchtower received an anonymous call about the Frosts, supposedly their location. Nevada took a team to check it out."

My heart jumped. "And?"

"They're alive and well and on their way to the Watchtower."

Relief nearly knocked me over backward. Vale, that son of a bitch, had actually kept up his end of the bargain. He wasn't much of a criminal mastermind, but at least he kept his word—not that he had much of a choice, since the entire Assembly (and Watchtower, too, I imagined) knew he had them. "The Frosts aren't hurt? I heard Lori screaming on the phone."

"Bumps and bruises, as far as I know."

"So your gambit has paid off," Marcellus said.

"In more ways than one," I said. "The Frosts are safe, the Clans are turning against Vale for hiding behind humans and ordering your death, and neither of us is actually dead."

"For now."

I almost asked the Elder what he meant, but fortunately my brain caught up before my mouth went off. I'd forgotten he had the Shadow. He was dying, and he would likely die within the month. The Shadow was incredibly fast-acting once it took hold. We'd only delayed the inevitable for him.

"I can't tell you how grateful I am for your help, Elder," I said.

"You've given a dying old man some small measure of peace, Ms. Stone. From the moment I learned of my illness, I feared for Riley. I knew some weak coward would make an attempt on his life before the challenge was met, and I feared he would be assassinated. Now I can rest easy in my final days."

"How's that?"

"Because the position of Elder to the Felia Clan is in the hands of the Assembly. Riley's interest is known, and he's likely to be named, but we have removed the target from his back. With everything that has surfaced about Vale and the Bengals, if Riley receives so much as a wood splinter, the Clans will roar in protest. An attempt on his life would be suicide for anyone associated with the Tuck family."

Good news for Riley, but—"But you're not really dead, Elder. Won't the Assembly simply reinstate you so you can name your successor?"

"A house divided cannot stand."

"Huh?"

"I have never been silent in my disapproval of the choices made by Astrid and Marcus. They have both eschewed tradition and chosen their own desires above duty to their family." Before I could get riled up and defend Astrid and Marcus, Marcellus kept talking. "However, the steps they have taken with the Watchtower Initiative shows a strong desire to protect our Clan, as well as the interests of the Assembly. If they had listened to me and done as I asked, perhaps the Watchtower would not exist."

So fucking true. Up until a few months ago, Marcus and Astrid had both been Assembly enforcers (think CIA but for shapeshifters), their only connection to the human world a tenuous friendship with Tybalt. A lot of factors had to be considered, but it had been the Dane siblings who brought the Clans to the table when the Watchtower formed.

They had also saved Wyatt from himself once, while I was held captive and tortured for nearly three weeks. They gave him an enemy to fight while he mourned my second death. It was a debt I could never repay.

Wyatt.

Oh crap.

"If the Assembly votes for Riley, then so be it," Marcellus said. "If not, then there will be a change. The Danes have held sole power for too long, as both Alpha and Elder. It's time we relinquish some of that control."

His explanation made sense. I just wasn't used to hearing a man in power willing to give some of it up. "A house divided cannot stand" made more sense. The Felia was divided. The Bengals versus the Jaguars. Tuck versus Dane. Enemies and allies within the same community. If a change in Elder helped bring the Felia back together, Marcellus thought it was worth it.

"How long do you plan on staying dead?" I asked.

"Until after the vote."

"And how long does that usually take?"

"A maximum of three days."

Fantastic. Three days. I hated that number. Almost as much as I hated dying on my friends—again—and what it was doing to them. Hated that I would once again be proved alive and hurt them with my lie. But more than hurting Milo and Marcus and Rufus and Kyle, I was hurting Wyatt.

God, Wyatt, I'm so sorry.

"Where's Wyatt?" I asked Tybalt.

The only person I'd wanted involved in this cover-up was the one person whose help I couldn't have. More than anyone, Wyatt's reaction to my death would convince everyone else of the validity of it. His grief would be proof that I was dead. My second death had almost killed him.

I didn't know if he'd be able to forgive me a third death.

Tears stung my eyes, choking me, and Tybalt hadn't even answered yet.

"Gina said he was freaking out," Tybalt said. "Demanding to see your body for himself, that the photos weren't good enough. Aurora's words weren't enough. He's been threatening to kill Demetrius for touching you, snarling at every Watchtower Felia who gets near him."

"Fuck." I wanted to hit something really, really hard, and Tybalt wasn't saying something. "Spit it out, Leftie."

"He was losing control of his Lupa side, so Dr. Vansis sedated him."

Shitshitshitshitshit.

He needed me and I couldn't go to him. Some fucking mate I was, allowing him to believe I was dead and lose control, when he was still coming to understand his dual nature. I was a failure as a girlfriend and a failure as a mate—suddenly all of the positive things my fake death had reaped seemed small and insignificant next to Wyatt's pain.

"Can he be brought here?" I asked. "Wyatt needs to know the truth before it breaks him."

Tybalt squeezed my hand. "I'll call Gina and see what we can do. But Evy, don't forget. Vale still has the elf scroll and the vampire cure. If he suspects you backstabbed him, he might destroy them both before he tries to bargain with them."

Why did it always come down to a choice between my love life and my duty to the bigger picture? I was really starting to hate the fucking view. My head told me that Tybalt was right, but my heart decided to step up and tell logic to take a flying fuck. "I need him to see that I'm alive, Tybalt. It needs to happen today, before he does something he can't take back."

"Okay, I'll make the call."

I had him show me where the bathroom was before he made the call, because I had to pee and generally felt gross. The bathroom was functionally boring, just like the office had been—sink, toilet, paper towels, soap dispenser. I splashed some water on my face, then contemplated taking a look at the gash on my stomach. It itched like a son of a bitch, so I knew it was healing.

A grocery bag of items rested on the floor by the sink. I bent far enough to snag it with the tips of my fingers. Cheap toothbrushes, toothpaste, some generic soap and dry shampoo. Plastic comb. At the bottom of the bag was a second bag, and its contents surprised me—box of hair dye, black eyeliner, an eye shadow compact, burgundy lipstick, and a pair of scissors.

"Gina dropped off that stuff," Tybalt said from the doorway, which startled the shit out of me.

I held up the lipstick. "Tell her it isn't her color."

"For you, Stone."

"Me?"

"You're going to want to leave here and go after Vale. You figure now that you're dead, he won't be expecting you and you can use that to your advantage to find him and the vampire cure."

"How—?"

"We know you better than you think. Plus it's what me and Gina would have done in your place."

"So she wants me to hit the streets done up like a hooker?"

"I think she was going for emo goth."

"Fantastic. Wyatt?"

"He'll be unconscious for another hour yet, Gina said. Once he comes around, she'll try to get him here."

"Good, okay." I studied the box of dye. "You know, I've never actually done this before."

"Don't ask me."

"I wasn't. Just remarking on my lack of knowledge of a simple girl thing. Don't most girls dye their hair at least once by the time they're my age?"

"Which age?"

"Good point." Chalice had been about five years older than me when we died. I opened the box and began sorting the bizarre contents—instructions, gloves, bottle, plastic tip, another bottle—until Tybalt's continued presence dinged my discomfort meter. "Okay, out. This isn't a sideshow."

He snickered, but pulled the bathroom door shut when he left.

I removed the scissors from the other bag and ran my fingers down the cool metal blades. I had a love-hate relationship with my hair. The length and thickness had been so foreign at first, and now I saw *me* in the reflection, not just the face of another woman. I liked how soft and feminine this hair made me look, made me feel.

But if ever there was a reason for a change, sneaking up on Vale and pounding his ass into the pavement was as good a reason as any. I grabbed a hank of hair, angled the scissors to a length right above my shoulders, and cut.

Forty-five minutes later, the girl staring back at me was a strange amalgamation of the Evy who'd died in May and the Evy I'd been up until this morning. She had the same freckled nose and brown eyes and heart-shaped face. But this new Evy had shoulder-length hair, dyed a strange shade of blonde-brown that had been a pain in the ass to wash out.

Bending over a sink and ducking your head under a small, badly-angled faucet is not easy when you have a ten-inch healing cut on your belly.

The results were worth it though, especially combined with my attempts at applying heavy eye makeup that didn't cross the line from striking to trampy. Nothing I did could disguise my scent to a trained Therian nose, or hide the birthmark that all Gifted humans carried and I had thanks to my teleporting ability, but anyone looking for Chalice Frost would not see her in me.

I needed clothes, though. My previous day's outfit was cut up and blood-soaked, and no way was I running around the city in someone's oversized t-shirt. I opened the bathroom door, unsurprised to see Tybalt sitting in the hall opposite. His mouth fell open when he saw the new me.

"If you say anything, I will punch you," I said.

He snapped his jaw shut.

"I need clothes."

He pointed at the office.

I went inside and found another shopping bag, this one with jeans, a t-shirt, and a black hoodie. No underwear and no bra, which made me roll my eyes. Gina obviously hadn't bought these. The jeans were super-tight, a size too small, but the hoodie helped cover some of the second-skin way they fit over my ass. Under the cot, I found a pair of boots a size too large. Some paper towels stuffed into the toes kept them from clunking around too much. I didn't complain out loud, though, because the strange outfit played to the strengths of my disguise. I looked and felt like a completely different person.

"Evy, I have to go," Tybalt said from the doorway. His eyebrows winged up at the sight of me, but he didn't comment on the new look. "I need to drop Elder Dane off at a more comfortable location, and then the Watchtower is expecting me." He picked the urn up off the floor, then handed me a plastic package. "There's a pre-paid cell phone. I wrote mine and Gina's cell numbers on the box, so program them before you toss it. One of us will call you about Wyatt."

"So I'm supposed to hang out here until then?"

"If you want Wyatt to know you're alive, then yes. For an hour or two, okay? We'll keep you updated."

"Fine." I didn't like the idea of hanging around an empty crematorium, but if it meant seeing Wyatt in the very near future, I'd deal.

Tybalt's cell rang. He mouthed Gina's name at me before answering. His eyebrows winged up in shock almost immediately, which gave me a horrible feeling in the pit of my still-healing stomach. "How bad?" he asked. Nodded. "Yeah, you, too."

"Who's hurt?" I asked as soon as he was off the phone.

"Dr. Vansis."

Oh no.

"Wyatt woke up sooner than expected. When Vansis tried to dose him again, he attacked. Threw Vansis across the room and knocked him out before escaping."

"Escaping?"

"He left the Watchtower, Evy. No one knows where Wyatt is."

Chapter Sixteen

6:15 p.m.

Having a grieving, half-Lupa ex-Handler on the loose certainly added an extra layer of fun to my already fantastic day. The good news: Vansis was fine, but pissed, and the Dane household was locked up tighter than the federal Mint, so Wyatt had no chance of getting his claws on Demetrius. The bad news: no one knew where Wyatt was, and he'd disappeared into the city. Not even the super-sniffers of some of our Therian friends could pick up on his scent.

With no reason to hang around the crematorium, I had Tybalt drop me off on a quiet corner in Mercy's Lot before he headed off with Elder Dane. Despite my disguise, I still felt like everyone I passed knew who I was, knew I was supposed to be dead and wasn't fooling anyone.

Only I'd fooled the person I cared about the most, and he was in major pain because of that betrayal.

Tybalt had given me a switchblade to go along with my cell phone, and they were my only companions as I began my search. My first stop was the old apartment on Cottage Place. The pups had come here. Wyatt might, too. Small chance, since this was too obvious of a place, and Wyatt knew how to hide when he didn't want to be found. I still had to check it off my list.

The apartment was empty, no sign of anyone having been there today. The phone number he'd written in mustard had dried to a greenish-brown, and the air was musty-stale.

"Where did you go, Wyatt?"

I'd lived here with my Triad partners once, but Wyatt had kept his own apartment a few blocks away—close enough in case of emergency orders, but far enough to give him privacy and distance from his Hunters. In all my years of knowing him, I'd never actually been to his apartment, even though I knew the address. He probably didn't hold the lease on it anymore, since we'd both been living at the Watchtower full-time since July.

Worth a try, though.

I walked four blocks west, one block up, to Culpepper Street. His building wasn't much nicer than ours, but it had an entrance that wasn't stuck between the doors of two tiny businesses, or a led into stairwell that reeked of old urine. My nerves jumped when I reached the third floor, and I took a steadying breath in front of his number. Normally I'd have jimmied the lock, but I didn't know if other people lived here now so I did something slightly out of character. I knocked.

Nothing. I knocked again, harder, and figured what the hell. "Wyatt? If you're there, please open the door."

A lock turned. The door pulled back a few inches, stopped by the security chain, and a pale face peered out. A somewhat familiar face with red hair and freckles. One of the Lupa pups. Crap.

"Is he here?" I asked.

"No," the boy replied. "You're his mate?"

"Yes."

"You look different."

"No kidding. Have you talked to him today? I need to find him."

"I haven't seen him today. He hasn't called us." There was accusation in his voice. The poor kid had no idea what was going on in the outside world.

"May I come in, please?" My healing cut still hurt, and I was already exhausted. Going at this on foot so soon after being sliced open was not my best plan ever.

I also needed to regroup. I hadn't planned on revealing myself to anyone else except Wyatt, much less a twitchy teenager I simply did not trust.

He closed the door far enough to remove the chain, then let me in. The apartment was tastefully decorated in a very manly style—dark furniture, wood, perfectly matched fabric patterns, like Wyatt had pointed to a room in a catalogue and made it magically appear in his space. It was impersonal, too, lacking photos or books, or anything that told me about the man who'd lived here. The only sense of being lived-in came from the messy kitchen, with its collection of trash bags, food containers, and empty pizza boxes.

Three teenage boys could eat like nobody's business.

"Which one are you again?" I said to the twitchy pup.

He shut the door and turned a deadbolt, but didn't slip on the chain. "John. You're Evangeline."

"Evy."

"Can't you call Wyatt?"

"I tried." I sat down on the sofa, grateful for a chance to rest for a minute. "Either he doesn't have his phone, or he isn't answering for anybody." Or checking his voice mails, because I'd left one demanding he call his not-dead mate back immediately or else. "Where are your brothers?"

"Out getting dinner. We're allowed to leave for food, as long as we stay on this block and don't interact with strangers."

"Better than being locked up, I guess."

"It is. I like Wyatt. He's fair to us."

"Considering you infected him, I think he's being super fair to you."

John's mouth puckered up, and he stepped behind a nearby armchair. "I didn't infect him."

"Your brother did."

"Please don't assign his actions to me. It isn't fair."

True enough, but I was too tired and cranky to be fair, and I was scared out of my mind for Wyatt's mental state. I wanted him here so he could get pissed at me for hurting him, so I could see for myself that he was okay.

"Why is Wyatt avoiding contact?" John asked after a moment of awkward silence.

"Really long story, but he's upset and I need to talk to him. I thought maybe he'd come here."

Keys jangled in the door locks. John turned around, while I hauled my tired bones to my feet. Peter and Mark tumbled inside the apartment with two white plastic sacks of food I could smell before they were three steps in the door. And it smelled great. They noticed me right away and froze in place.

"Wyatt's mate is here," John said, earning him his own crown as King of the Obvious.

"Why?" Peter asked. I remembered him easily enough. He was the oldest, the one who'd spoken with Wyatt yesterday when he took them under his wing. The suspicious glare he was tossing my way did not endear him to me at all, but it did make me respect him.

"Because Wyatt's missing, he's upset, and I need to talk to him," I said.

Mark shut the door and carried the food into the kitchen, out of sight. Peter eyeballed me like I was part of his dinner, and I was very glad to have John between us. "Why is Wyatt upset? And why do you think he would come here?"

"He doesn't have anywhere else to go." As much as I hated to admit it, the pups were his family now.

John snapped to attention, followed an instant later by Peter. Both turned to face the door in the same moment that Mark appeared in the living room. The hair on my neck prickled with alarm. The front door slammed open, and all three pups dropped to their knees, heads down

Wyatt stalked inside, his face shifting in his rage, as though all of the control he'd maintained on the way here had finally snapped. I didn't move, barely had sense to breathe, while his face bi-shifted into the thing that terrified me the most. His silver eyes flashed as he looked over the boys, who were all trembling—with fear or from his shared rage, I didn't know. Words stuck in my throat as terror won out over love. I tested for the Break and found it waiting.

Wyatt snarled something, and Peter scrambled to close to the door. It shut with a bang that made me jump. Silver eyes turned on me, in a face so full of rage and hate that I lost all sense of the man I loved. He simply wasn't there. A monster had taken over, and it was all my fault.

The monster took a step in my direction. I fell into the Break and let it shatter me, carry me away. Too late I focused on a nearby location, someplace I could go without risking rematerializing inside of a solid object. The only place I summoned was the hallway outside, and that's where I landed a moment later. My wound screamed at me. Sweat popped out on my forehead and shoulders, and I dropped to my knees, dizzy from the exertion. Dizzy from having run from Wyatt like a coward.

I was down the hall from the apartment, near the stairwell door. I could leave, get away before his rage sent him into the hall looking for me.

An odd déjà vu struck me. Months ago, I'd done something very similar—teleported out of Wyatt's reach out of terror and shame. The circumstances had been wildly different that night in the motel where we shared so many secrets, but the result had been the same. I'd run from his touch, and the devastation in his eyes had torn me apart.

Running from Wyatt now wouldn't help settle his soul or convince him I was still alive. He told me once he'd never hurt me physically, even at his angriest, and I believed him. Time to put my money where my mouth was.

I stood on shaky legs and walked back to his apartment door. Froze at the sound of a mournful howl, so heartbreaking that tears tightened my throat and stung my eyes. The boys were talking, voices and words muffled behind the door. Were they calming him down, telling him I was alive? Did he believe them?

No sounds of furniture breaking or kids screaming in fright.

I steeled my spine and knocked.

Peter whipped the door open, the relief in his eyes stark and shaming. I stepped back into the apartment, surprised by its pristine state. Not even a throw pillow out of place. John and Mark hadn't moved from the floor, but their expressions were identical to Peter's.

Wyatt was sitting on the sofa in the exact spot I'd vacated, elbows on his knees, face in his hands. He seemed to have lost the bi-shift, if his normal fingernails and height were to be believed.

His shoulders were shaking, and then his broken sob sent me racing across the room.

"I'm so sorry, Wyatt, I'm here, I'm sorry." I wrapped my arms around him from the side. His entire body tensed, then pulled away.

He held me at a distance, wide eyes taking me in, tears I'd hope to see stop instead falling more thickly. He studied me, sniffed me, never losing that confused, stricken look.

"I'll explain everything, I swear," I said.

"You're alive."

"And you'd have known sooner if you hadn't assaulted your doctor and run off, you bonehead."

He blinked and something wonderful lit up in his eyes. "I didn't want to believe them. I felt you still, right here." He touched my chest, his hand warm over my pattering heart. "I knew you couldn't be dead if I still felt you, but Aurora said—I didn't know what to think."

I lifted the hem of my t-shirt and hoodie, showing off the bandages. "It had to look real. Vale had my parents, Wyatt. I didn't have a choice."

His fingers traced my cheeks and brow. "You had a choice, Evy, and you made this one without me." He sounded utterly confounded as to why I'd have done such a thing. Maybe when he was down off his emotional roller coaster, he'd understand why I made the choice I had.

"Marcellus is alive, too."

"He is?"

Ouch. That one kind of hurt. "Yes, he is. I never intended to kill him for real, dumbass, but Vale needed to think I did. The whole Assembly is out for Vale now." I straightened up and pulled away from his touch, finding some courage lurking behind my guilt. "I know I hurt people, and I hate how badly I hurt you today, but I can't argue with the results."

He turned that over, every emotional tic easy to spot because I knew him so well. Knew he felt pain at my betrayal, joy at my resurrection, hope that the plan worked, and confusion over everything as a whole. He had every right to be furious at me, to yell and throw things and call me names. I wouldn't care if he did. The only reaction I couldn't handle was dismissal.

I didn't want to do this—any of this—without him.

"Did you think about me?" he asked.

"Yes. I knew this would hurt you, but I couldn't risk telling you ahead of time. The more people who knew, the bigger chance Vale would find out it was all a fake."

"Who did know?"

"Gina knew, because Vale contacted her first. He had some kind of leverage, apparently, to keep her quiet, but she didn't care. She's the one who told the Assembly about my parents. And Tybalt found out because she can't keep secrets from him."

"A problem we obviously don't have." The ice in his voice scared me. "You already knew Vale had your parents when we spoke this morning."

Shit, now he was going to deconstruct the entire conversation. "Yes, I'd just gotten the information, but I hadn't decided what to do yet. I did go visit Ava after I left you and…then I kind of winged it. The only Felia who knew, besides Marcellus, was an enforcer of his named Demetrius. He helped smuggle us out of the compound and into a crematorium."

Wyatt's eyebrows went up.

"Tybalt is presenting my ashes to the Watchtower as we speak," I said.

The eyebrows went down into a deep furrow. "How long do you plan on staying dead?"

"Probably a few days while Elder Dane remains dead too. He wants the Assembly to vote in a new Elder intead of—I don't know, that's his thing. He says the vote should happen within three days, and that gives me plenty of time to go looking for Vale. The bastard still has the vampires' cure."

I was letting all kinds of important things drop in front of three pups I barely knew. But who were they going to tell? They were hiding out in Wyatt's apartment precisely because they had no one else.

"And that's the reason for the new look."

"Pretty much. You can thank Gina for thinking that far ahead. Because of the Frosts, my mug was all over the news for two days. I can move around more easily like this." I reached for his hand, but he pulled back. Stabbing me in the eye would have hurt less. I swallowed. "Tell me how to fix this, Wyatt. Us. I love you so much. You're the other half of me, and I need you. I've never needed anyone before, and I *need* you."

"I need you too."

"I hurt you today, and I can't apologize enough for that. I hate what I did to you, and I'm not asking for you to forgive me. That has to be yours to give, and I probably don't deserve it."

He flinched. "I can't pretend this doesn't hurt, Evy. A lot. We've been through too much to not be totally honest with each other, and I am pissed. I am so fucking pissed at you for putting me through that again."

"Okay." Pissed was an emotion I could deal with—and it was a very human pissed because his eyes retained only the thinnest ring of silver around the black.

"And as angry as I am, I do understand, and I'm so grateful that I didn't lose you for good. But I need a little time to get through the anger."

"I get it, believe me." I turned my hand palm up, and he pressed his hand into mine. The warmth of his touch traveled straight to my heart, and a hot tear slipped down my cheek. "I thought I'd totally fucked this up and you were done with me."

"Never." He yanked me into his lap, and I fell against his chest, grateful for the contact. To hear the solid thump of his heartbeat. To smell his skin and know he was still mine. "You're stuck with me, Evy Stone."

"Good, because you're stuck with me too."

We sat together for a while, existing without talking. I realized that the boys had made themselves scarce now that Wyatt's temper was down below critical levels. It had been interesting how his emotions had so intensely influenced theirs—probably a Lupa thing, since I'd never seen the same rage-share among the other Clans.

"So did you actually stab Elder Dane?" Wyatt asked.

The left field question made me snort laughter. "Yes. Not deeply though, and he took it like a trooper. Dane's a tough old bird."

"Cat."

"Whatever."

"And this Demetrius, he actually cut you open?" A dangerous growl inflected that question.

I tightened my hold on his waist. "Yes, exactly where and how I told him to. Hurt like fuck, but it's healing, and I'm fine. You don't get to hurt him back, hero."

He made a noise that might have been a raspberry. "Spoil sport."

My cell phone rang, which scared the crap out of me since I didn't know the ring tone right away. "It's Gina," I said to Wyatt before answering. "Dead girl walking."

Kismet groaned. "Really?"

"You can forgive a bad pun because I have good news. I'm with Wyatt."

"Thank Christ. How is he?"

"Moody but intact." That got me a poke in the ribs. "What's happening on your end?"

"Therians are pissed, humans are confused, and the only thing we can agree on is that Vale is an asshole who needs to be found immediately so the Assembly can deliver some much deserved justice."

"Sounds about right. How are the Frosts?"

"They're really confused and demanding to see you. I keep telling Astrid to put off telling them you're dead, but I don't know how much longer she can."

"Maybe it's better if they think I'm dead." My heart hurt to even suggest it, and I hadn't realized until that moment that I kind of wanted a chance to get to know them. To talk to Chalice's parents at length and see what they were like. Maybe it was selfish though. Their daughter was dead, and they needed to grieve for her.

Right?

"It's more complicated than that, Evy. They saw Vale shift."

Crap. "How was that explained?"

"It wasn't. Dr. Vansis is calling it a post-traumatic stress-induced hallucination, but I don't think Mr. Frost is buying it. We're going to have to tell them something, and soon."

"Yeah. I know." I needed another complication like I needed another death in my repertoire. "Listen, how's Milo?"

"Healing but still on a lot of drugs. We haven't told him about your latest death. Marcus doesn't think we should until he's stronger."

"If we're lucky, he doesn't have to know until I'm alive again."

"How's that?"

I explained Elder Dane's wishes for the Assembly vote and my need to stay under the radar.

"Well, if you want a shot at Vale, he's contacted us," Kismet said.

"What? When?"

"A few minutes ago. It's why I called. He wants to ransom back the scroll and the cure. I doubt he knows what the cure is, just that you wanted it. He asked for half a million dollars, cash."

"Are you serious?"

"Perfectly."

"Where does he think we're going to come up with that kind of money?"

"He doesn't care. He gave us twenty-four hours."

"The vampire Families might pay it."

"For a gnome cure that we can't guarantee will work?"

"Yes. Gina, go to Alucard Communications and ask to speak to a man named Eulan. He's engaged to Isleen and he wants to save her. He'll hear you out."

"All right, I'll do it. And I'll tell the others that I spoke to Wyatt."

"Make sure Demetrius knows he can stop looking over his shoulder."

Wyatt grunted.

Kismet snickered. "What are you going to do?"

"I'm going to do what I do best." I glanced at Wyatt, who nodded, supporting me without question. "I'm going hunting."

CHAPTER SEVENTEEN

7:45 p.m.

Hunting didn't happen as soon as I'd hoped. Mostly because I didn't have clue one where to start looking for Vale.

Scratch that. I had a pretty long list, including the decrepit police station where we were held and the old motel where the Marcus/Prentiss showdown happened, but Astrid knew about those places, too. She'd have Watchtower people scouring the locations, plus the homes and businesses of the rest of Vale's family and social circle. I needed to go somewhere my friends wouldn't notice me, and I couldn't think of anyplace.

The pups invited me to join them for dinner, and even though I was still a little queasy from the Juliet Potion, I sat down with three red-headed teenage boys and watched them devour box after box of Chinese food. Wyatt ate a healthy portion of food, too, while I picked at plain white rice with a pair of chopsticks. My lack of attention to the food gave me a chance to watch the men in the room.

Peter was definitely the alpha of the brothers. When we assembled in the small dining room off to the side of the kitchen, Mark had laid out the dozen or so white boxes, as well as a few wax-paper bags, packets of sauces, and pairs of chopsticks. The three of them waited until Wyatt and I had seated ourselves before taking chairs on the other side of the table.

Wyatt helped himself to pork lo mein and fried rice, and once he finished, Peter picked up a container, put a small amount of vegetables on his plate, then handed it to Mark. Mark sniffed and curled his lip. He gave it over to John without comment. They went like that with every container of food. Sometimes Peter took a lot, sometimes he didn't take anything, but he always served himself first. The whole thing was kind of strange, but it also fit with them letting me and Wyatt get our food before serving themselves.

No one really talked at first, beyond grunts and simple commands to pass the soy sauce.

"Mark?" Wyatt said. "In what year was the Treaty of Versailles signed?"

I nearly dropped my chopsticks. I definitely flung some rice across the table. Wyatt was watching Mark over a half-eaten spring roll, intently waiting on an answer to the most left-field question of the month.

Mark picked up a piece of pork with his chopsticks, as though the answer was written on it in brown sauce. "Um, 1918?"

"John?"

"June 1919," John replied promptly.

"Peter, when did the U.S. officially end our involvement in the first World War?"

Peter squirmed.

Wyatt sighed. "Anyone?"

"1921, after the Knox-Porter Resolution was signed," John said.

"I'm so confused right now," I said. "What's with the history quiz?"

"Being cut off from Thackery meant their education stopped," Wyatt said. "They might be orphaned Lupa, but they're teenagers and they still need to learn. We're picking up with an easy subject."

"History is easy?"

"Those who don't study history are doomed to repeat the past."

"Thank you, Aristotle."

"Actually, it was George Santayana," John said, "and what he said was—"

"Will you turn it off before I fong you?" Peter asked. "Geez, we know you're smart, okay?"

John flushed red and looked down at his plate.

"Fong?" I said. "Do I even want to know?"

"It's from a movie," Peter replied. "It's slang for kicking or beating up. Wyatt doesn't have a TV, but we had one when we lived…um, with Dad." He looked away.

Dad meant Walter Thackery, may he rot in hell.

"So is John the only one who did the reading assignment?" Wyatt asked.

"I tried," Peter said. "I really did but I'm not good at that stuff. I never was, even when Dad—Thackery, taught us."

"You didn't like anything he taught you?"

"I liked learning how to fight."

"And I said we'd work on that together."

I almost flung more rice across the room with that little nugget of information. Wyatt was going to teach the kids to fight? He was taking this "under his wing" thing seriously. More seriously than I thought, and that might not be good for him, considering they were wanted by the Assembly. A month ago,

I'd have loved to see all three of them dead, and now Wyatt had practically adopted them.

Thumping my head against the table wouldn't change anything, so I refrained.

"We'll find something you enjoy studying more than world history," Wyatt said. "As long as you promise to try."

"I do promise," Peter said. "We all did."

Wyatt pop-quizzed them a little bit more while they cleaned their plates and divvied up what was left in the containers. John got everything right. Peter didn't know a thing. Mark was about fifty-fifty. The entire production was sort of adorable in an alternate universe kind of way. Wyatt sounded like any parent making sure his kids were ready for a big test.

"I don't want to die." Words spoken in earnest by a sobbing, terrified boy I'd watched being tortured for information at an abandoned construction site. A boy identical to the three eating dinner with me. A boy who'd died sobbing in a pool of his own blood, sweat, and piss because I'd thought Wyatt was dying, and now we were protecting that boy's surviving brothers.

"I don't want to die."

I pushed away from the table and found the bathroom tucked down the hall from the living room. Closed the door, turned on the faucet, and then sat down on the toilet as the emotion bent me in half. So much that it wasn't able to manifest as tears, because I wasn't sad. I'd done my job, like I always did my job, but the end result was that I'd participated in the capture and murder of a teenage boy. No, three teenage boys. Brothers to the boys I was trying to help now. Boys Wyatt saw as family—he didn't have to say it, because I saw it.

I wrapped my arms around my aching middle and rocked a while, letting the regret worm its way up and out. The shame of looking Peter, Mark, and John in the eye, knowing I'd done the same thing to their brother—I'd looked Daniel in the eye while his fingers were being cut off.

"Shit." I pressed the heels of my hands into my eyes, needing to rub those images away.

Someone else had done the cutting. Someone else had landed the killing blow. But I'd been complicit. I'd done the asking, and I hadn't stopped anything. I didn't have the stomach for that kind of torture anymore. I could kill goblins all day long to keep them from hurting innocent people and never bat an eyelash at the slaughter. Halfies, too. This was completely different.

Thackery had been given these children to raise as he saw fit. He made them into the villains I'd once hunted. Had they been given to a loving parent, someone who wanted them to grow up sane and happy, they might all still be alive. Their family wouldn't have been ripped in half. They wouldn't be hiding out in the apartment of the man they'd tried to kill and only succeeded in changing.

For the first time, I hated myself for the thing I'd become—the killer that Boot Camp had created and unleashed on the world.

"Evy?" Wyatt knocked. "May I come in?"

"Yeah."

He pushed the door open far enough to slip inside, then shut it. He didn't ask, simply knelt in front of me and gathered me into his arms, a solid presence I'd come to depend on more than I ever thought possible. The tears still wouldn't come, so I clung while he stroked my back.

"What happened?"

"Bad memories," I said.

"Of?"

"Killing their brothers."

"Oh, baby." Wyatt pulled back and cupped my cheeks in his palms. "That was a lifetime ago. You can't—"

"Blame myself? That ship has sailed around the world, so try again."

"You reacted to a situation. You had no choice."

"Didn't I? There's always a choice, Wyatt."

"Thackery had Ava and Aurora. You were protecting your family."

"They thought they were doing the same thing."

"Maybe, but you know more than anyone that you can't change the choices you've made. You have to live with them." The soft growl at the end of told me he was also addressing my most recent choice to "die" without telling him first.

Wyatt knew about living with choices better than almost anyone—except maybe Rufus, who was still withholding a whopper of a secret from Wyatt. "I know," I said. "Really. I guess it hit me all at once, sitting across from the disciples like that."

"The disciples?"

"Peter, Mark and John. Don't tell me it never occurred to you?"

He chuckled. "I guess it did. Evy, there's a lot of blame to go around, but the important thing is that those three are safe, and they want to stay that way."

"They definitely seem to like you."

"I'm an easy guy to like."

I rolled my eyes, which made him laugh again. "You're good with them, Wyatt. I mean that."

"Some of it is Lupa pack instinct. They're young and they want to be led by someone stronger and older."

"Or they need a father figure, and they like you for it." Something warm flashed in his eyes, an affection that wasn't directed at me. "Did you ever want kids?" The question bubbled up and out before I could think it through.

His eyebrows winged up. "I don't give it a lot of thought, since Gifted can't have children."

One of those weird side effects of being able to tap into the Break and its magical energy source was sterility—boys and girls. Biologically, it made the question moot, especially as a "couples topic." But it didn't do a damn thing to stop adoption. Literal or figurative.

"The Lupa are your family now, Wyatt, whether we like it or not. And even if you don't see yourself as a dad, at the very least you're the handsome, fun uncle who feeds them sodium-laden fast food on a regular basis."

"A high-speed metabolism helps with the sodium and MSG."

"And seriously depletes your bank account."

"No kidding."

"How long are you going to hide them?"

He released a long, uneasy breath. "I don't know. If I can prove they aren't a danger to humans or other Therians, then maybe the Assembly will rescind their kill order."

"What if they don't?"

A flash of silver in his eyes hinted at danger if that happened. "One crisis at a time. They're safe here for now. Our first priority is Vale."

I could live with that. "Okay, so if you were a were-cat wanted by your own people, where would you hide?"

"If I was Vale, I'd leave the city altogether."

"But not before you get your ransom money. So where do you hide while that's happening?"

"Fleabag motel?"

"Plenty of those around here. Vale isn't the smartest big bad ever, but I don't think he's stupid enough to use his real name. It'll take forever to flash his picture at every front desk, and who knows if we'll be lied to."

"You're forgetting one advantage we've got."

"What?"

He tapped the side of his nose. "I know what the bastard smells like."

Sometimes having a half-Lupa boyfriend was kind of awesome.

With no computer on the premises and my pre-paid phone only a few years past the Stone Age, we figured out our motel search grid the old-fashioned way: a piece of paper and a phone book. It took a while, but between the five of us we knew every single street and location, and their relationship to the others. The pups seemed eager to help and disappointed when we told them they couldn't go with us.

"Too many people affiliated with the Watchtower will be out tonight," Wyatt said. "You're still wanted by the Assembly, so I want you to stay here. Promise me."

"We promise," Peter said, and that seemed good enough for Wyatt.

Not me. "You so much as go outside for a pizza and I'll bust your ass, kid," I said.

Peter blinked and nodded vigorously. "We'll stay here."

"Good."

Our next problem was the issue of transportation. Wyatt had fled the Watchtower on foot, and I'd left my car at the Dane compound. Stealing a car was on the list of possibilities, but we both preferred saving that one as a last resort. Stolen cars meant police attention when the owner noticed it was missing.

As I was considering calling Kimset to see if she could help us on that front, Tybalt called me. "Hey," I said.

"I knew you weren't dead. I told you she wasn't dead."

Oh crap. "Milo?"

"Yeah."

"Why aren't you resting?"

"Been resting all day, and then everyone started acting weird. Avoiding questions. Marcus finally told me what was going on, but I didn't believe him. I made him steal Tybalt's phone, since I can't walk."

The mental image of Marcus pickpocketing Tybalt made me snort hard through my nose. "How did you know Tybalt knew anything?"

"Because he came to see me a while ago, and he's not that great of an actor. If he thought you were dead and did what you're accused of, he wouldn't have been so calm."

True. Milo's deductive reasoning skills scared me sometimes. "Is Marcus with you still?"

"Um, yeah. He actually looks kind of steamed, and—"

"Put him on the phone."

My end of the conversation had earned Wyatt's undivided attention, and his expression asked if I thought this was a good idea. I thought it was a fantastically bad idea, but I couldn't let Marcus keep thinking I'd murdered his grandfather and gotten away with my own life. Hell, I hated lying to everyone about my latest death, but especially Marcus. I respected the hell out of him, even though I'd never say so out loud.

The only reason I knew Marcus was on the line was because he breathed really loudly, almost a growl.

"Marcellus is alive, too," I said.

I swear I heard his eyebrows hit his hairline. "What?"

"We cooked up the plan together in about five minutes, but he's fine, and I totally owe him for going along with this."

"Can I speak with him?"

"He isn't with me."

"Your parents are safe now. Why haven't you both come forward? Do you know how many people this is hurting?"

I flinched because, yes, I knew, and for once I actually gave a damn. "Marcellus wants to stay dead for a while longer, and his reasons are his own. I'm playing along for him, and it gives me a chance to sneak up on Vale."

"You have to find him first."

"No kidding."

"I have to tell Astrid."

"That's your call, Marcus, I can't force you not to tell her. But no one else, please. Promise me that, at least."

He grunted. "I promise to keep your confidence, and I'll ensure the same from my sister."

"Thank you. Give me Milo again."

The phone switched hands. "I promise to keep quiet, too, Evy," Milo said. "But goddamn, don't do that to me again."

"Sorry, pal."

"I'm glad your parents are safe."

"Thanks. Now listen up and stop playing junior detective. Your only job right now is to heal, you hear me?"

"I hear you."

"Excellent." Wyatt was making turning gestures with his hands, and I remembered why I'd wanted to make my own phone call. "Actually, while I have you, I need a favor."

With our transportation's ETA still thirty minutes out, we had some time to kill. Wyatt decided to kill it by staring at me like he wanted me to guess exactly what was on his mind, but I was too tired and stressed to play guessing games.

"What?" I snapped.

"Are you really certain that keeping up this charade of being dead is worth it?" His voice was measured and calm, asking without being confrontational. "Your parents are safe now, Evy."

"Elder Dane wants it this way."

"I understand that, and I understand his reasoning. But his decision affects Assembly politics much more than it affects the Watchtower. If Therians and humans begin fighting amongst themselves within the Watchtower because they believe you killed Elder Dane, it could have far reaching consequences."

Marcus's tense breathing on the phone before my announcement that his grandfather was alive came back like a slap of cold water. He'd been furious, and I could only imagine those few moments of thought between hearing I was alive and hearing I hadn't murdered Elder Dane.

Wyatt also had the uncanny ability to reframe a question in a way that got me to think harder, to really question my decisions. Had faking our deaths been correct at the time? Yes. Was keeping up the charade a good idea now?

"It's only for a day or two," I said.

"Lives change in a day or two, Evy, you know that. I know that the list of people you really trust is about as long as my index finger, but being part of an organization again is about trusting the people you work with to watch your back."

He was pulling an old Handler trick on me. "Being a Hunter was different."

"How?"

"We were—" I almost said "all human," bringing back a beaten-down prejudice that had sustained me for four years as a Triad Hunter. Hunters were always human, and we were trained to believe specific things about non-humans. We were to never trust them, and even the few non-humans I'd considered tentative allies were never really trusted friends.

"You were what?" Wyatt asked.

The Watchtower was very similar to the Triads in many ways: strength in numbers, in secrecy, and in maintaining anonymity. It also worked on trust—trusting the guy working with you to not get you killed. Everyone who was part of the Watchtower was there because we had a common goal, and we had promised to work together as a unit.

Shit.

"You have to be able to trust everyone at the Watchtower or this thing can't last," Wyatt said. "Telling them, your allies, that you and Elder Dane are alive won't affect the ransom demand from Vale. Keeping you off the radar and out of sight is still the plan. We'll just have a few more people in on the plan."

He was right. Very right. "I should still ask for Elder Dane's permission," I said.

"Agreed."

So I called Tybalt's phone, and the correct person answered. Once I explained why I was calling, he promised to pass my message along to Elder Dane right away and to call back as soon as he got an answer. It was better than nothing.

"Faking my own death was probably the most rash, un-thought-out plan ever," I said to Wyatt after I hung up with Tybalt.

"Your intentions were honorable." His words couldn't hide the twitch in his jaw that said he agreed with me and that he hadn't quite worked through his anger. Not that I blamed him. Wyatt deserved all kinds of emotional slack over this mess.

"At least this way I'll get to talk to the Frosts." Not that the idea thrilled me in any way, shape, or form. I had no idea what I was going to say to them about any of this. The whole "your daughter killed herself and I reincarnated into her body" truth wasn't happening. They'd have me committed to a nut house faster than a gargoyle turned to stone in sunlight.

"You look like you'd rather go six rounds with a shifted were-bear than talk to the Frosts."

"Am I that obvious?"

"Only to me."

My phone rang. The number was local, but not in my phone's memory. I hesitated, then answered, "Joe's Pizza, will this be pickup or delivery?"

"Is this Evangeline Stone? It's Demetrius."

Someone who had absolutely no reason to be calling me. "Yes, it's me. What's wrong?"

"The Coni are gone."

I jolted to my feet, heart pounding, stomach twisted hard. "What? Were they taken?"

"No, there is no sign of forced entry or removal. They simply left."

"Why the fuck would they leave? Joseph's dying."

Wyatt's raised eyebrows reminded me that I hadn't passed along that information yet.

"I don't know," Demetrius said. "I truly don't. Another guard told me he saw them shift together, and then fly away to the northwest."

This was bad in so many ways. Aurora felt abandoned by Phineas. She was waiting for Joseph to pass away from old age.

She'd held my hand while I "died" in front of her—shit. "Shit! This is my fault."

"You don't—"

"Yes, I do. I should have told her I wasn't really dead. Fuck!"

Wyatt grabbed the phone before I sent it sailing across the living room. He spoke quietly to Demetrius while I raged at my own stupidity. I could rationally explain this to the people I worked with at the Watchtower. I hadn't given proper thought to what this must have been doing to Aurora. The poor woman had been through so much these last few months—the death of her husband, as well as her entire Clan. Being kidnapped twice. Enduring her child's kidnapping and watching Ava tortured into shifting too soon for her age. Losing Phineas to some idea of finding long-lost Coni relatives. Joseph's mortality.

I seriously considered giving the living room wall a fist-sized hole, but Wyatt got in my way. I didn't realize I was shaking until he pulled me into a hug, and the soft fabric of his t-shirt absorbed the tears that began falling. God, I was getting soft. But Ava was my goddaughter, and I couldn't protect her if I didn't know where she was.

"We'll find them, Evy," Wyatt whispered.

"How? What if Aurora takes them out of the city?"

He didn't reply.

"I did this, by not telling her I was alive," I said. "If anything happens to them, it's on me."

"Leaving the safety of the Dane compound was Aurora's choice."

"She wouldn't have left if she hadn't seen me die."

I knew he wanted to make me feel better, to make it all right, but he didn't patronize me by arguing my very valid points. "I don't know how we'll fix this, Evy, but we'll do our best. We'll try."

"Ava's still so young."

"I know, but she's strong like her mom. Like her *Aluli*."

"I wish Phineas was here. She'd have stayed if he was here."

Wyatt tensed only a fraction, but I felt it. "Probably. Again, leaving was Phin's decision. We can't change what's happened."

"We just have to deal with it, yeah, I know."

"Demetrius had one bit of good news. The Assembly is calling an emergency meeting in the morning to discuss the new Felia Elder. Apparently with everything happening with Vale, electing a new Elder is a priority."

"That's something, I guess. I'm sick of sitting here in your apartment, hearing about everything second-hand. I hate not being part of things."

"I know." He kissed my forehead, and I inhaled the earthy, wet leaves and cinnamon scent of him. "But you have to admit, this is some personal growth for you."

"How's that?"

"A few months ago, you'd have barreled off on your own, caution be damned, and done what you thought was best. Now you're letting other people handle things and take the lead."

"I don't have a lot of choice." I saw his mouth open, saw the bon mot about to drop, and beat him to it. "Yeah, yeah, there's always a choice. Fine."

"Good."

"My personal growth is your new ulcer, you know."

"I'll take my chances."

Chapter Eighteen

8:55 p.m.

Wyatt and I were on our way downstairs when Tybalt called me back. Marcellus had agreed with my decision to tell our Watchtower allies that we were both alive. He knew the Assembly vote would happen tomorrow, and he understood my need to mend fences with my coworkers. I told Tybalt to pass along my thanks, and then gave him the heads-up about Aurora.

"We know," he said. The noise from his end of the line suggested he was in the field somewhere—sounded like music. "Someone from the Dane compound called and told Astrid. I'm sorry."

"Don't be sorry, pal, I just want them found."

"I know. We'll do what we can."

"Thanks."

"So when are you making your grand resurrection?"

"Officially in a few hours, I think. Wyatt and I are checking out some leads first. Tell Astrid she can let the cat out of the bag."

"So to speak."

"Exactly."

"Be safe."

"You too."

We hit the sidewalk and made tracks straight for the black SUV idling by the curb. Marcus flashed us a droll look from the driver's seat. He'd surprised me by offering to pick us up and help with the motel search. "Two noses are better than one," he'd said.

I'd accused him of working too soon after being shot—I still hadn't thanked him for knocking me down that night—and he had said it was the perfect cover for getting out of the Watchtower for a few hours. He was off-duty, officially, so he could come and go as he pleased.

I took shotgun so I could navigate, and Wyatt sat behind me. Our first stop was only four blocks away, on the edge of Mercy's Lot, a pay by-the-hour place I wouldn't have slept in if I was wearing a full-body Hazmat suit. Wyatt went inside to talk to the clerk while Marcus sniffed around outside. It didn't take long for my pair of Therian noses to suss out that Vale hadn't been there.

Motel number two was ten blocks north.

Marcus cast frequent glances in my direction, none of them hostile, but they were intent enough to make me squirm. He was entitled to be unsettled, considering what I'd put him through today, so I endured the discomfort for four more motel checks. The boys alternated who went inside and who stayed outside, and this was Marcus's turn to stay put.

While Wyatt went into the office, I pinned Marcus into the driver's seat with a frustrated stare. "Okay, what?"

"I understand your reasons for faking yours and the Elder's deaths today," Marcus said, his tone tinged with danger. "Family is important, and I know that fact well."

"But?"

"Today I found myself in the unique position of having to lie to Milo, and I'm furious at you for putting me there. He's seriously hurt, and he didn't need the added stress of hearing that you'd died. He values your friendship, Evangeline."

"Milo's my best friend, you know that. I didn't want to hurt anyone, Marcus, especially him and Wyatt." I hadn't properly thought this plan through today—that was becoming abundantly clear as I cleaned up the damage I'd done. Not that I'd had time to consider the consequences of my actions beyond saving my parents.

"I'm grateful that he didn't believe you'd died. I didn't want him to carry that emotional pain, along with the physical pain he's battling."

"Why did you kiss him?" I hadn't meant to ask the question, and especially not in the middle of an investigation. It slipped out without conscious thought.

My pulse raced when his face twisted into an epic frown. Marcus was genuinely scary when he was angry. "He told you?"

"I knew something was up between you two, so I kind of pushed."

Marcus studied the steering wheel with intense concentration, then looked at me with perfect calm. "I care for him a great deal."

"As what?"

"That's for us to define." With that, he climbed out of the SUV and checked the perimeter of the motel.

He was pissed and entitled to it, given everything he wasn't saying out loud. No matter where their fledgling relationship did or didn't go, I was glad that Milo had him. I was far from an expert on relationships, but they seemed good together. I didn't have to warn Marcus about handling Milo with care. We'd both seen Milo fall apart when Felix died; he wouldn't give his heart away so easily again.

The motel check has seemed like a good idea at the time, but when we were three motels from the end of the list and nothing had panned out, I'd added this little adventure to the long list of Shit I Did Wrong This Week. We hadn't even rustled a nest of Halfies to take the sting out of several wasted hours.

"At least we know where he isn't," Marcus said.

"Yay," I replied with an eye roll. "A city this size and we've deduced he's not in one-thousandth of a percent of the square yardage."

"We still have three locations left to check."

I gave him the next address, and he pulled out into the street. I glanced behind me at Wyatt, who'd been quiet since returning to the car. He was frowning at the back of Marcus's seat, eyebrows furrowed in a deep vee. Silver flashed in his eyes, and something about that drew Marcus's attention.

"Wyatt?" I said.

He pinched the bridge of his nose, then blinked hard. "I had the oddest feeling just now."

"Like what?" We were still discovering the nuances of his half-Lupa state, and I needed to know if he was about to go all wolfy on us so we could find a deserted building or something.

"I don't know. A sense of dread, but not mine."

"Have you been in contact with the Lupa children?" Marcus asked.

We both stared at him, surprised Astrid hadn't clued him into that particular subterfuge. "I have," Wyatt replied.

"Lupa Clans have a powerful sense of each other, even when not in proximity. Few other Clans have such a sense. It could be their dread—"

Wyatt yanked out his phone and dialed.

"—you're experiencing," Marcus finished.

I leaned between the seats, barely able to hear the electronic sound of the phone ringing. And ringing. Wyatt's face turned to stone. It rang until the service transferred him to a generic voice mail. He hung up.

"Take us back to my apartment on Culpepper," Wyatt said.

Marcus immediately made a right onto a connecting street. "They're in your place?"

"Yes. Something's wrong. They know to pick up when I call."

I squeezed Wyatt's shoulder. He reached up to twine our fingers, and I held on. I couldn't take away his anxiety for the three boys he'd adopted into his life, but I could be there for him. I'd fight for him, and I'd fight for them, because they were important to him.

Marcus pulled into the first free space he found on Culpepper, and we three tumbled out. We were a block away from the apartment building. Wyatt strode with purpose, desperate to get there, but unwilling to break into a full-out run with so many unaware pedestrians around us. This close to midnight, Mercy's Lot was just waking up.

At the door to the building, Wyatt froze. If he'd had hackles, they'd have raised on-end. "Vale," he said, the word almost a growl. "I smell the bastard."

Marcus made a noise in his throat was almost a hiss. "As do I."

"Evy?"

"I'll cover you both," I said.

As we went inside, I drew the pistol I'd kept tucked in my waistband. I preferred fighting with knives and that would never change, but I'd rather not have to get up close and personal with a were-cat's claws tonight. I'd much prefer to just shoot one between his damned copper eyes.

Wyatt went up first, and at the third floor landing, he paused to listen. Gave the all-clear signal before opening the door. We filed out into a quiet hallway. Wyatt growled again, and I could see the effort it took to not let the Lupa take over. To keep the bi-shift under control. He listened at the door. Held up two fingers.

Two people inside.

I swallowed down a flutter of fear.

Wyatt tested the door—unlocked. He pushed it open and charged inside. The kitchen and main rooms were empty, but the place was a disaster. Chairs overturned, books off shelves, pottery shattered on the floor. Two pizza boxes were broken open, their contents spilled on the carpet. Something about the chaos was too ordered, as if the ransacking was for show. A distraction.

We found them in the bedroom.

Mark and Peter were unconscious on the bed, stripped and beaten, their pale skin livid with blossoming bruises. Their hands were cuffed behind their backs, and those awful silver collars were blistering the delicate skin on their throats. A blast of fury ripped through me so unexpectedly that I almost hit my knees— and it wasn't only my fury affecting me. Wyatt's rage filled the small room.

"Where's John?" I asked. If Wyatt only heard two heart-beats—no. Not going there.

Wyatt let the bi-shift take over, and I avoided seeing it by grabbing some blankets from his hall closet. Marcus left us alone to search the apartment, and when I returned to the bedroom, Wyatt had snapped the cuffs apart. We turned the boys onto their backs, then covered them up. Their heartbeats seemed strong, their pulses steady.

"Vale's scent is all over them," Wyatt said, his voice horrifying and rough through his bi-shift teeth. "And another scent I don't know."

"So two Felia took down three Lupa?" It seemed a little impossible. Even if the pups couldn't fight, they should have left more of Vale's blood on the floor. Unless...

I pulled Mark's blanket down and checked his arms and torso. On his left shoulder, I found the puncture sight. "Wyatt, sniff that for me."

He did without question. "Medicinal."

"Fucker used the same tranq darts on them that he used on us. I bet you a year's salary."

"No bet. It's the same odor." Wyatt's eyes went flat silver. "Which means the coward beat them after they were unconscious."

Oh shit. I grabbed his hands before he could move away and punch a hole in the wall. Yanked him down so we were at eye level, and stared into the twisted face of my partner. "I need you to stay calm and focused, Truman. Calm and focused, do you hear me?"

His answer was a rumble from deep in his chest.

"We will take care of Mark and Peter, and then we fill find John. Okay?"

He nodded.

"Good. We have to get those collars off. Can you summon them?"

He blinked hard several times and some of the silver went away. I let go of him. He backed away and worked to return to human form.

Marcus appeared in the bedroom doorway, his face impassive. "There's no sign of the third boy," he reported. "But both Vale and a second scent permeate the place. I smelled it before, at the Tuck house. And I found something else."

I followed him back into the living room. He pointed at the apartment door, which was closed, and my stomach dropped to my knees. Painted on the door in dripping, splotchy red letters was a note: *I don't like being lied to, Stone.*

Shit, shit, and double-shit.

"It's Lupa blood," Marcus said.

John. The bookworm of the bunch. Oh God. Wyatt was going to rip Vale's guts out with pliers and feed them to him a bite at a time.

"How in the blue fuck did Vale find out I'm alive?"

Marcus's stare had *are you an idiot* all over it. "He'd have smelled you in this apartment."

I gave him an identical glare. "Maybe, but Vale is being hunted by the Assembly and the Watchtower. He'd be laying low, waiting for his ransom demands to be met, not randomly beating and kidnapping teenagers. Coming here makes no sense unless he was looking for leverage over me and Wyatt."

"Perhaps he is attempting to punish those of us he held captive."

"Still seems too risky." The power of the Break rippled the air of the apartment, standing the hair on my arms on end. Wyatt was using his Gift to get those collars off. "No one except the people at the Watchtower knew Wyatt left the compound, and no one outside the Watchtower except Elder Dane and Demetrius knew I was alive—shit."

"What?"

Ice scraped up my spine. "Marcus, what if Vale has a mole inside the Watchtower? What if someone is telling him everything we're up to?"

He looked like he wanted to deny the possibility, then bit off the thought. "Who?"

"I have no idea, but up until a few hours ago, everyone except a few very trusted people thought I was dead. Now Vale shows up here, kidnaps John, and leaves me a love note? Vale has proven that he acts recklessly when he's cornered or seriously pissed off, and I'm guessing right now it's the latter. I played him, and then I sicced the Assembly on his sorry ass."

So much for Wyatt's song and dance about trusting everyone I work with equally.

"Evy, what are you—?" Wyatt's words stopped, as did his footsteps. He was two paces inside the living room, eyes fixed on the door and those horrible words. He looked exhausted, but that disappeared under a brand new wave of hate.

"I'm sorry," I said.

Surprise flashed in his eyes. "For what? Vale did this, not you. He attacked defenseless children."

Marcus snorted at something, probably "defenseless children." The Lupa pups were hardly defenseless, but I understood Wyatt's meaning.

"Vale knocked them out with drugs and then beat the shit out of them," I said.

That got a flash of anger out of Marcus. "Vale continues to prove himself the worst sort of coward."

"Are the collars off?" I asked Wyatt.

"They are," Wyatt said. "Marcus, did you find a cell phone anywhere?"

"No, I haven't," he said.

"You think Vale took it?" I asked.

"Likely," Wyatt said. "He can't use John against us if he can't contact us." His head snapped in the direction of the bedroom, and then he took off.

I followed him. Mark was waking up, groggy and disoriented. The collar line on his throat was red and weeping, and he had a bruise on his jaw the size of an apple—or a grown man's fist. A surge of hate for Vale filled me to bursting, quelled somewhat by the sight of Wyatt climbing onto the bed and pulling Mark into his arms. Mark clung to him, to the familiar body and scent, even as his mind fought to catch up.

"Peter," he mumbled. "John. Where's John?"

"Hush, Mark, you're in shock," Wyatt said. "Peter's right here. I'm here."

"John?"

"He'll be fine. I'll make sure he's fine."

I backed out, giving them their privacy, my heart aching for their pain. People I cared about were still suffering because of me, and I hated that. Hated it so much. And I had no way of taking their pain away.

"They need medical attention," I said to Marcus, who was photographing the apartment with his phone.

"I assumed as much," he said. "I'll call Astrid and inform her of the situation. If she agrees, we'll take them back to the Watchtower. Under careful guard, of course."

"Of course." I didn't expect them to attack unless something happened to Wyatt, but I understood the need for caution. A few weeks ago, they'd topped our Most Wanted list, and for most people, nothing had changed.

Marcus moved away to make the call. I walked into the dining room and sat in a chair. Stared at the table where, six hours ago, I'd eaten Chinese food with Wyatt and the pups. Three teenage boys who craved love and attention—two of whom were hurt, and one of whom was missing. A long chain of events had led to this moment, and the chain always linked back to me. My resurrection. My refusal to lay down and die once and for all. I had more things in my life to live for now than I had four months ago, and a lot more to lose. A lot more to save, too, if my death meant they could live and be safe.

The pups deserved a chance to be safe. And loved.

The table blurred and I blinked back tears. They'd get that chance, dammit. No matter what.

Imagine two teenage boys who are terrified and in serious pain, and who are trying very hard to not show it to the adults around them. Add in the fact that two of those adults are Therians, and the boys are teenage werewolves, and it's not a pretty picture. When Peter came around, he freaked out so badly that I thought we'd have to knock him back out. Wyatt banned me from the bedroom, afraid of me getting accidentally bitten, while he dealt with them.

A while later, all three came out of the bedroom. Mark and Peter were dressed in sweats too big for them, and they were clutching each other, limping and sweating from the pain of moving. Therians healed faster than humans, but they were also dealing with the affects of the silver collars they'd worn. They glared suspiciously at Marcus, but tried to smile at me.

"They know we're leaving," Wyatt said.

So we left. It took a while, because the pups moved like old men who were trying hard to not let you know how much their arthritis pained them. Marcus went ahead to bring the car closer. Wyatt climbed into the backseat with the boys, so I took shotgun.

"I told John to not answer the door," Peter said, his thin voice reedy and furious. "Guy said the people across from us ordered pizza and then weren't answering. Asked if we wanted to buy it. John loves pizza."

Classic move to get someone to open the door to a stranger, and the evidence was staining the floor of Wyatt's apartment.

"We didn't think you'd mind if we bought the pizza," Mark said to Wyatt. "Honest. We couldn't go out, you know?"

"You couldn't smell he was Therian?" Wyatt asked. A question, not an accusation.

Mark flinched. "I didn't think to try. All I smelled was the pizza. John opened the door. They shot him."

"With a tranquilizer?"

"I think so. He wasn't bleeding, just unconscious. Peter yelled. I tried to get the phone to call you. Everything happened so fast, and then he must have shot us too."

"The men at the door. What did they look like?"

"I think they were both Felia. They had copper eyes." Mark glared at the back of Marcus's head. "One had reddish-brown hair. He was big, muscular. Taller than Wyatt."

Sounded like Vale.

"The other man?" Wyatt asked.

"Woman," Peter said. "The other one was a woman."

I met Wyatt's eyes, both of us surprised. I don't know why, though. Chicks could be turncoats too. "What did she look like?" I asked.

"Pretty. Tall. Blonde hair, all tied back."

Not a super helpful description, but it was something.

"Possibly Starr Tuck," Marcus said.

Roof sniper's sister. Did that entire family inherit a crazy gene? "What time was it?" I asked the boys. "Do you remember?"

"A little after nine," Peter said.

Not long after we'd left. Damn.

"I'm sorry," Mark said.

"For what?" Wyatt asked.

"We screwed up."

"You were attacked without provocation, Mark. This wasn't your fault. It was my fault. I left you in an obvious place, and I wasn't there to protect you boys. I should have been more careful."

We both should have done a lot of things differently today.

Mark and Peter tried to remember everything they could about the attack, but they'd both been knocked out pretty quickly. They were embarrassed and in pain, and they were worried about their brother. I was worried about John too, more than I expected to be. The pups had been six strong once, then their numbers were cut in half. I didn't know what they'd do if they lost John.

I didn't know what Wyatt would do.

A small group of curiosity seekers (and enforcers) were waiting in the parking area when we returned to the Watchtower. Astrid and Rufus were there, along with Kismet, Tybalt, and Autumn, her arm free of that sling. They were the official welcoming committee, and I wasn't surprised to see a pair of human recruits nearby with side arms. Tranqs, probably, in case someone flipped out.

A lot of them were glaring at me, too, and I ignored the looks. They had a right to be pissed. My pressing concern was for the pups, and to find Vale. Wyatt and I walked on either side of them, offering support and a physical shield from so many other Therians, all the way to the infirmary. I didn't try to listen to the conversation Marcus and Astrid were having as they followed.

Mark and Peter took in their surroundings as they limped between us, curiosity overwhelming their pain, keeping them sharp. Once inside the infirmary, we settled them onto exam beds, careful to keep the curtain between them open. I didn't think they'd take well to being separated right now, even by a thin piece of cotton.

Dr. Vansis approached from the back and introduced himself. He gave the boys the same bland, disinterested look he offered to all of his patients, seeming unimpressed that these were the Lupa whose bite had caused such radical changes in Wyatt's physiology.

"How long ago was the silver removed?" Vansis asked.

"Less than an hour," Wyatt replied. "They wore them for about three hours prior to that."

Vansis snapped on a pair of gloves, then approached Mark first. Mark's nostrils flared, but he allowed Vansis to probe at his neck. "It appears to be healing. I can apply a topical ointment to help with the pain. Where else are you injured, son?"

Mark glanced at Wyatt, who helped him take the sweatshirt off. His thin chest was a palette of blue, black, and purple, and seeing the depth of those bruises sent my temper boiling. He was just a kid, dammit.

Peter watched with sharp, angry eyes while Vansis examined Mark's bruises, starting every time Mark flinched from a rough touch. He even growled once, a sound cut short when Wyatt put a hand on his shoulder. Vansis listened to Mark's breathing, then had him lay down. He pressed around his belly, which made Mark squirm. He asked questions about pain levels and did this or that hurt.

The hushed voices of our shadows had continued beyond the curtains, but they stopped now. I peeked out to find the waiting area empty, except for the two guys and their guns. I might have tried to remember their names (Dallas? Austin?) if I cared enough to expend the energy, but I didn't.

"There is no obvious swelling in the abdomen, nor are any bones broken," Vansis said. "I'll observe the injuries for a few more hours, but I suspect young Mark will heal without complications."

A flare of something hopeful lit Wyatt's face. No permanent physical harm done. Didn't mean there wouldn't be emotional scars, though—not only for Wyatt, but for Mark and Peter, too.

Vansis moved on to patient number two, which took all of Wyatt's concentration. Peter flinched and growled every time Vansis touched him. He was definitely the more high-strung of the trio. While doctor and patient went through the motions, I slipped out to check on some of the other wounded haunting the infirmary.

Paul was asleep in his room, his color better than the last time I saw him. The bandages on his shoulder were clean, not seeped through with fresh blood. He'd probably have a hell of a scar, but he was alive. The little bastard was too stubborn to die.

Maybe we weren't really all that different.

In the next room, Milo was sleeping, too, but a lot less peacefully. A sheen of sweat covered his face, and his eyes twitched. Caught up in a dream or nightmare, I didn't know. I slunk over to the bed, as silently as possible. Touched his cheek with the back of my hand, felt the damp, clammy skin. I smoothed the hair back from his forehead, a light stroke that seemed to settle him.

My best friend was hurting, and if all I could do was chase away a bad dream, I'd take it. I'd do anything for him, and I hadn't felt that sort of loyalty to one person in a long time. In some ways, Milo and Tybalt had become my Jesse and Ash. My friends and partners. I needed them in my life.

When Milo slept peacefully again, I returned to the exam rooms. Mark and Peter's necks were both shiny with ointment, and they'd settled onto their beds to rest.

The compound intercom buzzed, and then Astrid's voice came over. "Stone and Truman to Ops, now."

"I'm not going," Wyatt said.

I blinked. "You're not?"

He planted himself between the boys' beds and crossed his arms over his chest. "No. I won't leave them alone." *Again* hung off the end of his sentence. I got it, and I agreed. If he left and one of the boys—namely, Peter—panicked, they could get hurt.

Or hurt someone else.

He probably also needed a break from me for a while. He couldn't work through his anger at me if we were attached at the hip. "I'll let you know what's going on," I said.

"Evangeline?" Peter said.

I stepped a little closer to his bed. "Yes?"

His silver eyes flashed. "Find our brother. Please?"

"I'll do everything I can to bring John home. I promise."

I hoped that I could keep my promise and bring John not just home, but home alive.

Chapter Nineteen

Wednesday, September 3
1:30 a.m.

Just when I didn't think anything else could surprise me tonight, I walked into Ops and found Eulan conversing with Astrid, Marcus, Rufus, Kismet, and Tybalt. All eyes turned on me, but I only had eyes for the vampire in our midst.

"Greetings, Ms. Stone," Eulan said. "I am pleased to see that rumors of your death were exaggerated."

"That happens to me a lot," I replied. "I didn't think you made house calls."

"In a situation such as this, I would entrust the task to no one else."

"So you're paying the ransom?"

"We would pay ten times the asking price to save our people."

"You don't know it'll work. All you have is the word of a gnome."

Eulan tilted his head, as though indulging a stubborn child—I hated it when vampires did that. "It is a risk worth taking."

"Where's Wyatt?" Astrid asked.

"Babysitting." Before she could argue, I added, "They trust him, Astrid. They're scared and hurt, and he can keep them calm better than a couple of armed guards and an Ursia doctor can."

"All right. Marcus gave me his report. Gina and Tybalt have too. You want to fill us in on what you've been doing since you pretended to kill my grandfather?"

Ouch. I deserved that. I recapped my day, which sounded really long and a little bit insane the more I talked. I touched on everything up to and including the Lupa pups' exams. "No permanent physical damage," I said. "But they're scared for their brother."

"Do you believe Vale will insist on trading the Lupa for you?" Astrid asked.

"It's likely. We played him and he's pissed. Now he has leverage."

"Does he really?"

I blinked, unnerved by her hard stare. "He's a kid, Astrid, and he's important to Wyatt. And before you start, no, I have not forgotten what they did last month. Neither has Wyatt. But he's protecting them because he's part of their bloodline now. They're family to him, which makes them important to me."

Good lord, I'd really said that out loud.

Kismet and Astrid looked at me like I was crazy. Tybalt and Rufus both seemed more curious than appalled. I couldn't read Marcus or Eulan at all.

"What I want to know," Rufus said, "is how Vale came upon knowledge of Wyatt's apartment and the fact that he was harboring the Lupa?"

"Add that to list," I said. Since no one else was addressing the elephant in the conversation, I did. "Right after the question of how Vale found out I was still alive in the first place. A scant handful knew, until Elder Dane and I agreed to share it with the Watchtower. An hour later, the pups are attacked and John is kidnapped."

I don't like being lied to, Stone.

Marcus caught my eye, a gentle warning there. So he hadn't floated this to his sister yet.

Astrid's face went first white, then her cheeks flushed. "You think someone inside the Watchtower is loyal to Vale?"

"Or being paid to feed him information, yes," I said. "He knew we were at the Lincoln Street Bridge. He knew about the pups. He knew I wasn't dead. Maybe the pups weren't as a big a secret, but the other things? It was privileged information."

"Is there anyone from the Felia Clan whose loyalty could be called into question?" Kismet asked.

This time, Marcus and Astrid shared a look. "Perhaps," Astrid said.

"Who?" I asked.

"Lynn Neil."

I couldn't make that one fit. Lynn was a were-lioness with the aggressive personality of a newborn kitten. She was also Kyle Jane's girlfriend, and they were the only inter-Clan couple in the Watchtower. She had to have one hell of an interesting past for them to suspect her right off the bat.

"Back in May, when Aurora and Joseph were kidnapped by a group of Felia intent on keeping her and her unborn child safe," Marcus said. "Do you remember?"

As if I'd forget. "Hell, yes, I remember. I was the one they tried to kill in the process. I shot Belle and another one of her pals."

"The pal you killed was a jaguar named Kiefer Foss."

"You stabbed me with a nail file." I remembered that night clearly, and I remembered being told later that Belle had been executed for treason against the Assembly. "The name doesn't ring a bell."

"That's because it wasn't released beyond Assembly records," Astrid said, shooting her brother a glare that said he probably shouldn't have released it now. "At the time, Foss was living with Lynn. They weren't mated, and when she was questioned, Lynn denied all knowledge of Foss's activities with Belle."

"You believed her?"

"Yes. Kyle believed her too, and his faith in Lynn convinced the rest of us."

"But how does that connect Lynn to Vale?"

"It doesn't, not directly. Even Belle isn't directly connected. She was a Siberian Tiger, and Vale is Bengal. Vale was never, to our knowledge, connected to Belle's movement."

"So Lynn could be a dead end?" My head was spinning a little with all of the dot connecting going on, and we had no clearer picture than when we started.

"Perhaps," Marcus said. "We should still question her."

"Kyle's going to shit kittens." So to speak.

"He'll understand."

"And alibi her, as well," Rufus said. "They've been in the field for hours, aiding our efforts to locate Vale. I doubt she's found time to leak information to him."

"Call her back in," Astrid said. "We should still talk to her."

"Tell me you have other suspects," I said.

"Not on the tip of my tongue, no. Every Therian at the Watchtower is here because I trust them to be discreet and to keep what happens here within these walls. I despise the idea of anyone I hired being a leak." Her copper eyes flashed with hurt and anger, and I believed her.

"The leak could be human," Tybalt said. "I couldn't guess as to a motive, but there are two species working here."

My brain jumped to Alejandro, the new kid who'd been brought into our compound today, but that didn't fit for two reasons. First, he wasn't even a blip on my radar when Vale attacked us on Lincoln Street. Second, the kid had been searched for all electronic or tracking devices, and he didn't have access to anyone's phone. He was new and twitchy, but that didn't make him a plant.

Tybalt went still, as if something had occurred to him. "What?" I asked.

"I thought of someone who might be able to give us a little information," he said. To Astrid, he said, "Castle."

The look she shared with him and Marcus told me that the name meant something to them. Not to the rest of us though. Even Kismet seemed confused. "Do you know where he is?" Astrid asked.

"No, but I can find him."

"Take Shelby with you."

"Will do."

Tybalt headed out. I kind of wished I was going with him, but for now, my place was here. Vale wanted me dead, which would make Tybalt a bigger target than he already was with me running around the city in his pocket. And Wyatt still needed me close. His mood was as volatile as the pups'.

"So what next?" I asked.

"I'll question Lynn when she returns," Astrid said. "Other than that, we wait for Vale to call about the ransom."

And if we really had a mole in the Watchtower, he'd know that Eulan was here with his cash pretty soon—if he didn't already.

I excused myself to the cafeteria. I desperately needed a caffeine boost, and the pups could probably use a snack. Their metabolisms were already high, and the stress of the beatings would only add to that. More people were milling around in the cafeteria than I expected, considering it was after two in the morning, but we all kept bizarre hours. I'd go crazy if I was ever shackled into a 9 to 5 kind of job.

I poured a mug of coffee for myself, added a few ice cubes, then gulped. Repeat. The hot liquid burned into my stomach, a pleasant heat that reminded me of how empty it was. I put half a dozen sandwiches on a plate, then turned to take the food back to the infirmary.

A skinny, dark-haired figure hunched alone at a table made me pause. Alejandro. As much as he wasn't a suspect, he also wasn't a member of the team. He was alone here, and he looked like he'd just seen his favorite pet creamed by a car. I carried my plate over and plopped down in a chair next to him.

He jerked, startled. "Oh, hi."

"Oh, hi," I parroted. "Making friends is easier if you talk to people."

"I'm not very good at that."

"Talking?"

"Making friends."

"Me either."

"Hard to believe."

I laughed at the sass. The kid had guts for sure. "Really, though, why the funk? I thought getting involved was what you wanted?"

"Is was. It is, I mean."

He stared at the table while I stared at him. I was too tired to guess, and I had better things to do than try to puzzle this out. Alejandro seemed like a nice kid, but he had serious trust issues and they weren't my issues to fix.

"Are you eating all those?" he asked, nodding at the sandwiches.

"Delivery for friends, and don't change the subject. You've got thirty seconds."

"It's just…I'm new."

"Duh."

"And I don't want to rock the boat, or get anyone into trouble because I don't really know what's going on."

Okay, he had my full attention now. I kept my pose casual while checking our surroundings. No one was close enough to listen in. "Alejandro, I need you trust me. I need you to trust that anyone you might have overheard, anything that seems off? You need to tell me right now."

He considered me a moment. "I do trust you."

"Then tell me what's going on? Did you hear something?"

"Yes."

"Okay, what was it?"

He took a moment to look around before lowering his voice to a bare whisper. "I heard someone on the phone. They didn't know I was there."

"Saying what?"

"Telling somebody that you were back here, along with Truman and two of the puppies?" He seemed unsure about the last bit. "Why would Truman bring puppies here?"

"Long story." I tried to keep myself from exploding with impatience, because it was quite possible Alejandro—bad-at-stalking, Boot Camp recruit, and generally jumpy teenager—had overheard our mole talking to Vale. "Who was it? Who did you hear on the phone?"

After securing Alejandro's promise to deliver the plate of sandwiches to the infirmary, I ran back to Ops. His admission was burning a hole in my brain, and I needed to discuss it with Astrid before the potential mole tried to flee the premises.

The earlier crowd had dispersed itself, but Astrid hadn't moved from her desk. She glanced up when I walked into Ops, and something in my demeanor alarmed her because she stood up. She'd taken one step in my direction when her cell phone rang.

"Vale," she said, waving me over. Marcus and Rufus appeared out of nowhere, and we four gathered around her phone as she accepted the call. Set it to speaker.

"Not even a hello?" Vale said after a pause.

"We have the money," Astrid said. "In cash like you asked."

"Excellent. You sound pensive, Astrid."

"Long day."

"I think perhaps you're waiting for me to change my demands, and you're correct. They've changed."

I stifled a groan. Of course they'd fucking changed.

"The cost of returning the potion and scroll hasn't changed," Vale went on. "The delivery system, however, requires a personal touch."

"Explain that."

"If you want the mongrel dog returned safe and sound, then Evangeline Stone will bring me the money. Alone. She's there, I take it? Not a pile of ash blowing in the breeze, as she should be?"

"I'm here," I said. No sense in denying it.

"Then your presence in exchange for the boy."

"No fucking way."

Three pairs of eyebrows went up, and I imagined Vale's did too. My heart thudded heavily, alarmed at my choice, but also confident in the decision.

"No?" Vale repeated.

"No. There's nothing to stop you from killing me and John, and then taking off with the money, the scroll, and the potion."

"I kept my word about releasing the Frosts."

"Yeah, well, you also had the Assembly screaming for your sorry striped hide. You had nothing to gain by killing them. You have nothing to lose by killing me. In fact, I think you'd take great joy in it."

"You're right on that count, Ms. Stone. You broke our bargain by not killing Elder Dane as requested."

"As demanded. We didn't have a bargain, we had blackmail. And considering you beat two kids while they were unconscious, I'm not inclined to believe a fucking thing oozing out of your mouth."

"Then we are, as they say, at an impasse."

"Not necessarily. You keep hiding behind other people, Vale. So come at me face to face. In front of witnesses. You get the money for the stuff you stole, and then we fight for John, one on one. You and me, pussycat."

Astrid and Marcus stared at me like I was insane, and I probably was. If Vale shifted, I'd never beat him in a fair fight—not even with my healing and my teleporting ability. Bengal tigers, especially Therian Bengals, were huge and had big teeth. But I'd do this for John. I'd do this for Wyatt.

"No," Vale said.

"Can't take me?"

He laughed. "I'm very certain I can, actually, and as much as I'd enjoy it, I'd rather expend the energy fighting someone I hate more than you."

"Who?"

"Marcus."

The were-cat in question blinked once.

"Why Marcus?" I asked.

"He led the charge in May. He's responsible for my brother's death."

"Prentiss was executed by the Assembly for being a dirty traitor."

"He wouldn't have been caught if not for Marcus." The logic of cowards—blaming the cop who arrested them instead of taking responsibility for committing the crime in the first place.

I couldn't ask Marcus to do this, not for the life of a Lupa, an enemy to his own people. We'd find another way to save John.

"What are your terms?" Marcus asked.

My mouth fell open. His quelling glare kept words from tumbling out.

"You are listening," Vale said. "Good. We'll keep this brief. We meet at dawn. I'll tell you the location twenty minutes beforehand. Three witnesses for each of us, in the old style. To the death, Marcus."

"Unacceptable."

"Not interested in fighting to the death?"

"I'll kill you any day of the week, Vale, I promise you that. The location is unacceptable. We speak again at six o'clock, and we agree upon a neutral location at which to meet by six-thirty. No one gains the advantage in this."

Vale grunted. "Acceptable. You bring my money, and I'll bring your valuables."

"All three?"

"All three."

"I want to speak to John," I said.

"Impossible. I'm keeping him sedated so he doesn't lose it on me."

Smart bastard.

"I want your word, Marcus," Vale said, in a forceful tone I didn't expect. "Your word that this will be our duel, and ours alone. No Assembly enforcers waiting in the wings, no Watchtower stooges ready to pounce on me."

"You have my word, Vale," Marcus said.

"I'll call at six." He hung up.

"A duel?" I said. "Seriously?"

Marcus shrugged, unable to pull off casual when he was that tense. "It's a tradition of our kind, to settle disputes. Although we usually fight over mates and not to the death."

"I can't believe you agreed to this," Astrid said.

"You don't think I can beat his ass?"

"I know you can, but then I won't get to kill him."

"Get in line," I said. "But at this point, I just want the asshole caught or dead."

"Agreed," Marcus said. "And if this gains us the vampire cure, as well as the safe return of the Lupa boy, then it's worth a few scratches."

"You won't feel that way if he bites your ear off," Astrid said.

"You can glue it back on if he does. I want you there."

"So I can kill him after he kills you?"

"Exactly."

Affection passed between the Dane siblings. Something was coming full circle for both of them, and they were united to stop a threat to their Clan. It was kind of awesome to see.

"You don't have to agree," I said, "but I'd like to go as a witness. I want to be there to ensure John's safety, and if he's awake and scared, he'll react better to a familiar face."

Marcus considered me a moment. "All right. The boy will need someone to ground him, and there's no way Wyatt is going."

"No kidding." He was too damned volatile right now. Peter and Mark needed him here. "Who's your third?"

"I'd like it to be Tybalt, if he's back from his errand in time. He was with us when Prentiss was captured. He's part of this."

"Speaking of Tybalt, who is Castle?"

"Someone who helped us locate Prentiss when he was holding Keenan. If Castle's still around, he may have information on Vale. It's worth a try."

Informant. Gotcha. And speaking of valuable information… "Astrid, can I speak with you? In private?"

In private was somewhat relative when it came to Therian hearing. Since we had no one currently residing in our re-built jail, we walked down the corridor to speak there. Astrid kept pace, probably full of thoughts of her brother's impending fight, no idea of the bomb I was about to drop in her lap.

The interior of the jail had seen some damage a few weeks ago, when a Halfie blew himself up inside of it. The three reinforced cells were good as new, the desk had been replaced, and not a sign of gore remained. The only thing still haunting this place was the memory of that Halfie. He'd been a friend of mine once, suffering through a brief, uneasy existence as a monster he'd once sworn to eradicate.

"What's going on, Stone?" Astrid asked.

"Remember the newbie, Alejandro? I think he identified our mole."

"What? How?"

"Apparently he was sneaking around, getting to know the place, and he was snooping around the old vampire quarters when someone came inside to make a phone call. This person told someone about me and Wyatt coming back with the Lupa. Called them puppies."

"It could have been a personal call."

"Done in secret? Who the hell would care, at one in the morning, that I'm back at the Watchtower?"

Astrid's expression darkened. "Who was it?"

"Our very own flying fox. Autumn."

Chapter Twenty

2:45 a.m.

Our search for Autumn lasted exactly the two minutes it took to turn a corner and run smack into Shelby, sweaty and dressed in gym clothes.

Astrid and I stared at him, dumbfounded. "Why aren't you with Tybalt?" I asked.

Shelby wasn't one of my favorite people socially, but he could turn into a huge polar bear and was an asset in a fight. It was why I tolerated the impatient look he tossed my way. "Because I was working out when he asked for my assistance."

"Did he go alone?" Astrid asked.

"Of course not. Autumn was there, and she said she'd go with him."

"Shit."

My heart jumped into my throat. Astrid pulled her phone first and dialed. Shelby gawked at both of us. "What is going on?" he asked.

I waved him off and followed Astrid down the corridor. "Voice mail," she said. "Damn it."

I tried with my phone. Same thing. "I can't believe this. Would she take Tybalt to Vale?"

"I don't know, Stone, I really don't." She dialed again. Listened. "Autumn isn't answering, either."

"Does that really fucking surprise you?"

"Stone—"

"I'm sorry, I'm worried, okay? In case you missed it, I get mouthy when one of my friends is in trouble."

"We don't know for certain that Tybalt is in danger."

"We don't know that he isn't. God, Gina is going to flip out."

"Come on."

"Where?"

"Ops. I want to reread Autumn's file. Perhaps there's a clue in there as to what she's up to. In the meantime, we'll get all our eyes in the field looking for Tybalt and Autumn."

I hovered while Astrid did her leadership thing. She made calls to the teams in the field, telling them to report back if they saw Tybalt or Autumn, and she never had to explain why. The team leaders did as asked without question. She then gathered the small group of me, Eulan, Marcus, Kismet, Rufus, and Alejandro into the large conference room.

Then she explained what we thought was going on.

"Son of a bitch," Kismet said. Her expression fluctuated between horror and anger. "Why would Autumn feed information to Vale? She's not even Felia, she's Kitsune."

"I don't know," Astrid said. "We're still speculating, but the evidence is stacking up against her. Until we hear from one or both of them, we're going with this scenario."

"Do you think Vale will use Tybalt to pull something at the duel?"

"It's possible. Vale is a coward. He's shown that many times these last few days. He won't leave victory to chance, and he knows Tybalt is important to the both of us." She glanced at Marcus, who was equally furious and... well, no, just furious. I didn't know the complexities of the relationship those three shared, only that it extended back to childhood. More theirs than Tybalt's, considering the Therian aging thing, but they had a history.

We all loved Tybalt. We'd fight for him.

Rufus, our computer guru, was typing away at a laptop on one end of the table. "I may have found the connection we're missing," he said. He connected the laptop to the monitors on the far wall, and one of them flickered to life.

Three children, each with pale green eyes, mugged for whoever had taken the picture. Two girls had auburn hair, and the boy blond. They seemed the same age, but the identical eye color made me wonder. "Kitsune?" I asked.

"Correct," Rufus said. "The girl on the left is Autumn at her first year."

Explained why she looked like she was in pre-school. The resemblance was there, but I wouldn't have pegged her right away. Her face was thinner, hair darker. The other girl didn't seem familiar, but the boy... the boy did.

"If you make us guess the other two, I'll punch you," Kismet said. "Wheelchair or not."

Rufus gave her a wry look. "I won't drag out the suspense, Gina. The other two children are Snow and Rain."

"Fuck me sideways," I said. No wonder the boy had seemed familiar. "Snow is the asshole who tried to kill me."

"You may be required to narrow that down more," Eulan said.

Holy shit, the vampire made a joke.

"Five years ago, under orders from the brass, Wyatt killed a Kitsune woman named Rain," I said for those not in the know. "He was supposed to kill her human lover, too, Wyatt's own Hunter. His name was Cole." Rufus and Kismet knew this story, but by the expressions of horror on Astrid and Marcus's faces, they hadn't heard it. Maybe it wasn't my secret to tell, but the connection had to be made. "Wyatt faked Cole's death, tried to wipe his memory of the whole thing, but Cole remembered and he came back this spring for revenge. He called himself Leonard Call then."

A light went off for Astrid. "The man responsible for the attack at Parker's Palace?"

"That's him. He was working with Snow, because Snow was Rain's brother. They both wanted to bring down the Triads, and they were willing to do a hell of a lot to make that happen." I looked at the photo again. "Autumn has a past with Snow and Rain. Is she related?"

"Impossible," Astrid said. "We are well aware of Snow's crimes. We would not have allowed a relative into the Watchtower without proper scrutiny."

"They aren't related," Rufus said. "At least, not as far as I can find. But this proves a connection of some sort, and it lends itself to motive on Autumn's part."

"To go after Wyatt, maybe, if she's pissed about Snow and Rain," I said, "but not Tybalt. And why work with Vale?"

"Vale represents the same ideals that Snow and Call did, Evy. Radical change. The Watchtower Initiative was probably the largest shift in paranormal power that this city has seen since the inception of the Triads. It's more balanced, but it is still a system of government, and no government will ever be without its opponents."

"We don't have to understand their motives to stop them," Astrid said.

"No, but it gives us a clearer picture of our enemy," Rufus said. "Vale is our current target, but what if his actions are a small part of a larger organization? What if it's more than simply the Bengals working with a vengeful Kitsune?"

"I say it's worth considering when we have evidence that this organization still exists."

"We've seen it in bits and pieces, haven't we? Call and Snow. Belle and Foss. They're all symptoms of a larger problem."

"Like what, Rufus? Humans and Therians just can't get along? That's bullshit."

"No." Rufus gripped the edge of the table, his face set. He did something then that I rarely saw. He used his powerful forearms to lever to his feet, keeping a strong hold on the table for support. "The larger problem was one designed by the Fey, something they continue to manipulate from wherever they've fled to. They want us to destroy ourselves. I'm sure they'd have preferred the fast method of allowing the Tainted to cross the Break and kill us all in one fell swoop, but we threw a huge wrench into those works.

"The Fey live for hundreds, if not thousands, of years. They'll let us break ourselves down, piece by piece, by whispering dissension in our ears, as they have for the last decade. We cannot allow that to happen."

I hadn't seen Rufus get worked into a lather over anything in a long time, and the sight was welcoming. I only wished Wyatt was here to see his old friend getting his groove back. Rufus slunk back into his wheelchair, having said his piece. And he was absolutely right in his words. We were fighting a nearly incorporeal battle with an enemy that would outlive all of us.

"None of this helps us find Tybalt," Kismet said after a moment's silence.

"Something tells me Vale won't stick his nose out again until the duel," Astrid said. "Autumn strikes me as too smart to take Tybalt any place she knows we'd be likely to look for him. We'll be extremely lucky to find them before six-thirty."

"So we sit on our asses for the next three hours, waiting for Vale to call?"

"I won't risk sending anyone else out searching tonight. The city is too big, and we don't know how many other eyes and ears Vale has."

Kismet didn't reply. The tightness in her shoulders, the press of her mouth, was answer enough. She'd lost Felix. She'd lost Baylor. She nearly lost Milo. Tybalt was more a brother to her than a coworker. I could see her pain radiating across the table.

"If Vale calls again in the meantime, I'll let you know," Astrid said. "If he contacts any of you, I expect the same." The final comment was directed at Kismet, who nodded blandly.

I followed Kismet out of Ops and halfway to the infirmary before saying, "We'll get him back, Gina. He's gotten through worse scrapes."

"I know he has." She stopped walking and sagged against a storefront. "We all have, but everyone's luck runs out at some point. We all pay for our choices."

The penny dropped. "You think this is Vale's payback for you not going along with him this morning?"

"Yes, I do. Vale is fucking insane, Evy, and I didn't play ball, so Tybalt gets to suffer for it."

"Vale already had a grudge against Tybalt."

She shook her head, and I saw something in Kismet that I often did myself—taking the blame when a loved one is in danger, even if it's not directly her fault.

I leaned against the wall next to her, so I wasn't hovering over her shorter frame quite so much. I ran a hand through my hair, startled to remember it was cut so short. The ends ran through my fingertips above my shoulders. I was all about trying new things lately, so why not pull out the Supportive Friend Card and play? She was my friend, after all.

"Gina, what was the leverage Vale had over you?" I asked. "Because if it's something I can help you fix, we'll fix it."

She laughed through another harsher sound that was almost a sob. "It's nothing you can fix, Evy, but thanks. It was information."

"That he was holding over you?"

"That he offered to give me." The corridor was quiet, our voices low enough to not echo. Even so, Kismet opened the nearest door and I followed her inside. The interior was empty, freshly painted, its purpose unclear. But it was also private, and this chat seemed to call for serious privacy.

"Vale said he had information on the whereabouts of someone I've been looking for," Kismet said. "Vale knew the information was important to me, but saving the lives of the vampires is bigger than my grudge, so I refused."

"How do you know the info was legit?"

"I don't. I don't know how he found out my connection to the man, since I've kept that a secret from everyone except one person, and he's dead."

I took a stab at that. Kismet once told me about the Hunter she'd fallen in love with and lost about two years ago—that she'd told him details about her past that very few people knew. "Lucas Moore?"

"Yeah. Lucas is the only person who knew certain things about my past, things I've never told Wyatt or Tybalt, or anyone else in my life right now."

"Your past before you changed your name?"

She gave me a shrewd look. "Yes."

"The man you're looking for hurt you?"

"Hurt is a very small word for what he did to me." Hate rippled through her, followed by a shiver. She closed her eyes briefly, opening them again to blink away a sheen of tears. "I was a fifteen year-old runaway, Evy. And he was a grown man."

She didn't need to say more. My heart hurt for Gina Kismet, and for the unnamed horrors she'd endured. I didn't press. I never would. We had both survived terrible things. Gina had reinvented herself, become one of the fiercest warriors I'd ever known. She was my friend, and I didn't have a lot of those.

"I got away with help from a friend," Kismet said after a moment. "I got away, but so did he."

A roar of fury hit me. "He never paid?"

"He disappeared. I pushed it aside, joined the Army, began a new life as someone else. It was almost ten years after the fact before I finally told Lucas everything. But it put the man back in my mind, and I started putting out feelers. Nothing ever came back with results."

"Until Vale."

"Yep."

"Fuck, Gina. I'm sorry you gave up the chance to find that fucker and feed his balls to him."

Her lips twitched. "So am I."

"I won't say anything to anyone."

"I know you won't. Thank you."

"You're welcome."

"About Tybalt—"

"Don't say anything because it will upset Milo, right?"

"Exactly."

Milo hated being handled as much as I did, but if he found out Tybalt was in trouble, Vansis would have to sedate him to keep him in bed. He didn't need that stress. I just hoped he slept the night and I didn't have to lie to his face.

The sandwiches had, indeed, been delivered to Wyatt and Company. The pups were sleeping in their shared cubicle. Wyatt roused himself from a doze and came out into the hall so Kismet and I could fill him in on our night. He took everything with a surprising amount of calm, because Wyatt didn't generally do calm well, especially when left out of important discoveries and discussions. His primary concern, even while listening to us, was on the two boys sleeping in the next room and their missing brother.

It made me love him more than ever.

"We have two-ish hours until Vale calls again," I said. "I hate waiting."

"I know you do," Wyatt said. "Has Marcus chosen a third yet?"

"I don't know. Not that he's told us."

"It should be you," he said to Kismet.

"I don't have a stake in Clan politics," she replied.

"No, but you do have a stake in Tybalt's life."

"It's Marcus's choice."

"So put a bug in his ear. He's inside, probably sitting with Milo."

She shook her head. "I don't want Milo to know about Tybalt. And I doubt Marcus does, either."

"Sparing someone bad news often backfires, Gina."

"If Milo could do anything other than lay there suffering, in pain because of what Vale did, then I'd tell him. Milo has a long recovery ahead of him, Wyatt. If something happens to Tybalt tonight, he'll be grieving enough by morning."

Kismet pivoted and walked back toward Ops and the sleeping quarters. I watched her go, wishing I could do something for my friend.

Wyatt sighed heavily, then folded me into a warm, welcoming hug. I rested my cheek on his shoulder, grateful for his heat, his love—every single thing he gave me every day.

"You be careful at that duel," he whispered. "Don't give Vale the benefit of the doubt. Expect him to double-cross you."

"I do, trust me. How are the boys?"

"Comfortable now, but they're worried about John. They can't sense his fear and it's making them a little crazy."

"Vale says he's keeping John unconscious. Maybe that's why they can't feel him."

"Could be. Evy, when are you going to talk to the Frosts?"

I groaned and tugged away, putting him at arm's reach. "What the hell, Wyatt? Now isn't exactly the best time to have a heart-to-heart with my non-parents."

"We both know more than most that tomorrow isn't a promise. They deserve to hear from you, in case tomorrow never comes."

"I don't know what to say to them. The truth is insane."

"Alex believed you."

"Yeah, and then the truth bit him on the ass and killed him."

"What about Leo?"

"The truth tried to bite him, too, in Alex's apartment, if you recall." In the shape of a big damn were-cat. "And then he got the hell out of town."

"Do you blame him?"

"Not a bit." His significant look made something click. "So you think if I come clean with the Frosts, they'll freak, then accept, and then get out of town before one of them gets eaten by something ugly?"

"It's worth a shot. They've been kidnapped once for being in this city."

"Yeah, well, everyone close to me gets kidnapped at one point or another. It was just their turn."

"Don't condemn them for caring about you."

"They don't care about me, Wyatt. They care about their daughter, a damaged and frightened woman who killed herself in the bathtub. I'm not her."

"So tell them that. Tell them the truth and let them decide who they care about. Maybe they'll make tracks for the nearest bus station or maybe they'll surprise you."

"I don't want them to surprise me. I want them out of this fucking city before it devours them too." I wanted Stephen and Lori Frost out of harm's way, period. Even if it meant bullying them out.

We didn't have guest quarters in the Watchtower. Astrid had apparently seized an empty store, installed cots and a pile of books, and left it guarded. The store was on the same end of the compound as the regular sleeping quarters and the main bathroom facilities. Sandburg, a likeable guy whose true form was a ferret, was sitting in a chair outside the store, seemingly bored out of his skull.

"I was wondering when you'd show up," he said.

"Yeah, well, my schedule's been pretty full."

"Mine, too, of escorting people to the toilet. That woman has a bladder the size of a peanut."

I snickered. "Take a break, Sandburg. I'll watch them for a little while."

"You don't have to ask me twice."

He handed me the door key, then scurried off. As I slipped the key into the lock I took a deep, cleansing breath that did shit to settle my jumping nerves.

Here goes nothing.

I tapped my knuckles on the door. A polite warning before I opened it.

The room was lit by a pair of bare bulb floor lamps. The cots stood close together near a wall, and the Frosts were sitting side by side, resting but not asleep. They came to life the moment they realized I'd intruded. They blinked at me from a distance of about twenty feet, unsteady. The haircut and newfound emo goth look was probably throwing them for a loop.

"Chalice?" Lori asked. "Honey, is that you?"

"Kind of," I said, shutting the door and pocketing the key.

She looked like she wanted to rush me, to yank me into a bone-crushing hug, but refrained. She did seem a bit green around the edges. Shock, likely. Next to her, Stephen stared at me like I might attack, pissed off while Lori was simply baffled.

"What is going on here?" Stephen asked. "First we don't hear from you for months. Your records disappear from the face of the planet. You leave the apartment. You don't tell us Alex is dead. You barely spoke to us the other morning, and you were with that strange boy. And then we… we…."

"Got kidnapped by a were-tiger?" I said. "Is that the phrase you were grasping for?"

"No, because shapeshifters don't exist."

"You are so wrong about that. The guy who's been guarding you? He shifts into a ferret. The doctor you saw when you first got here? Grizzly bear."

Stephen frowned. "And I suppose you'll tell me the boy who came to the diner with you shifts into a bald eagle."

"No, Milo's totally human. I've never met an eagle-shifter, but one of my best friends is an osprey."

"Chalice—"

"My name isn't Chalice." I closed half the distance between them in slow, measured steps, stopping when Lori inched away. She was definitely freaked. "Look, I know this is going to sound incredibly insane, but I need you both to keep an open mind and hear me out."

Stephen wrapped his arms around his trembling wife, and I wished I had Wyatt here to back me up. I held my ground, and I held Stephen's distrustful gaze.

"On May 20th of this year, around four o'clock in the morning, your daughter, Chalice Frost, drew a hot bath in her apartment, got in, and sliced both her wrists open. She died before her roommate, Alex Forrester, came home and found her."

Lori choked, a hand covering her mouth. Stephen looked disgusted, like I was making up the whole thing.

"A few days earlier, a young woman was being tortured by goblins and left to die. She was a kind of paranormal bounty hunter, and her death was part of a bigger plan, something I'm not getting into right now. But a man loved her, this woman, and he refused to believe she was gone forever. So he went to an elf, who gave him a spell to bring her back to life. But since her body was gone, she came back in the body of someone else who had just died. She was resurrected in Chalice's body."

"You're on drugs, aren't you?" Stephen said. His voice betrayed grief, though, and less anger than before.

"I wish. I'm the woman who was tortured to death and brought back. My name is Evangeline Stone, and I have been this person ever since. Chalice's wasn't supposed to be my body, but that's how it turned out."

"No. No, Chalice, if you're angry with us, we can fix it. We can get you help."

I snorted. He thought I was certifiable. Maybe so, but not for this. This was the God's honest truth. "Alex didn't believe me at first either, until he got up close and personal with my life. Shapeshifters aren't the only creatures that exist. Vampires, goblins, trolls, gargoyles, fairies, gnomes, sprites…they're all real. And some of them are very dangerous. The man who was holding you prisoner and threatening to kill you unless I did him a favor? He's a shapeshifter."

Lori made a soft, choking sound behind her hand.

"Alex didn't die in a fire. He was bitten by a half-Blood vampire and he turned. He died from a bullet to the back of his head to release him. To set him free from the monster that had taken over his mind and body. To keep him from killing." My heart pounded hard. I couldn't make myself tell them that I'd put the bullet in Alex's head, and it had been one of the worst moments of my afterlife. Alex had deserved so much more than he got.

And I would forever live with the uncertainty of those few hours he was a Halfie, loose on the streets, free to attack and feed. I wanted to believe that he wasn't, but I'd never know if Alex died a killer.

Stephen was shaking his head. "No. Chal, honey, we can get you help. Professional help."

"Okay, how about a few tricks of my own? Did you know magic is real? Real as you and me, but not all humans can manipulate it. Your daughter, Chalice, was one of those people. She could teleport, but only when she was close to a magic source, like in this city. When she was a kid and you moved away, she lost that ability, and being separated from her source is what caused her depression later. I don't think she ever realized what she was."

"Will you stop? Please stop, for your mother."

Lori was sobbing loudly, clutching at her husband. I felt horrible for her, but I wouldn't recant anything I knew to be the truth.

"Fine, give me a second." I closed my eyes and felt for the Break. Latched onto its static-like caress and let the power rush through me. I drew on my emotional tap, on loneliness, and let myself shatter apart. Everything tingled, sparked, and I focused on a spot six feet to the right. Pulled myself to that spot and let go of the Break.

The world focused in a blink and a snap.

Stephen and Lori stared at me, slack-jawed and open-mouthed. Lori's tears fell silently. Stephen looked like he wanted to vomit.

"That was easy," I said. "I can go further and through solid objects." A tiny headache beat between my eyes. "Look, I'm sorry you lost your daughter. I wish I could say I always intended to contact you, but I didn't. I didn't give much thought to Chalice's old life, to the people who might be missing her. I was selfish in that, but I have spent almost every day since she died battling for my own life. I've lost a lot of friends, people close to me, to a battle that I don't know if we can ever win. But I fight every day, because that's what I do."

Chalice may have lain down and died, but I would never do that. Not while I had breath in my lungs or a beat in my heart.

"I'm sorry," I said because I had no more words for them.

"Will you leave us alone please?" Lori asked, her voice broken and rough.

"Yeah, of course."

I nearly teleported out to drive my point home, but with my luck I'd land right in the middle of Sandburg, and we'd both be fucked. So I walked. Walked out the door, handed Sandburg his key, and kept on walking. Right to my and Wyatt's room, where I face-planted in our bed, too emotionally drained to handle anyone else right now. Marcus could find me when it was time to leave for his epic duel.

The last forty-eight hours had sucked major ass. Something had to start going in our favor soon.

Didn't it?

CHAPTER
TWENTY-ONE

6:02 a.m.

I don't think I slept. My mind wandered in indistinct ways for a while and my body never moved. I heard footsteps and twisted around to sit up before Kismet found me. "They're discussing location," she said. "Come on."

We quick-stepped it to Ops. Marcus, Astrid, and Kyle were chatting intently and I cleared my throat to get their attention.

"So where's the duel happening?" I asked.

"Black River Ferry port, so we need to leave as soon as possible," Marcus said.

"How'd you determine that location?"

"Privacy and space."

The Black River Ferry hadn't been in use for nearly fifty years. Two passenger boats and one freight boat had been tied up and left to rot, part of the landscape of a dying industrial section of town west of Mercy's Lot. Last month, we'd tracked Walter Thackery to the port and he'd sunk one of the ferries in an effort to kill the Therians he'd kidnapped. It gave us two boats or the Terminal Station as actual fighting arenas.

It also gave Vale several places nearby to stash Tybalt.

"Do we have any teams close by who can scout ahead for us?" Kismet asked.

"Already on it," Astrid said.

"Who's your third?" I asked Marcus.

"Kyle," he replied.

Okay, that answer surprised me. Kismet didn't seem upset about being left behind, and since I wasn't known for my tact—"Why Kyle?"

"Insurance."

"Are you going to expand on that for me?"

"In the car, yes. We have limited time right now."

Too true. "Did Vale happen to put any limits on us bringing weapons?"

"As a matter of fact, no." Marcus smiled. "Why do you ask?"

"Because I need to swing by the armory before we hit the road."

"Did he mention Tybalt at all?"

"No," Marcus said as we headed for the corridor, "and I did not tip him off. If he believes his mole is yet undiscovered, he may attempt to send her back to us."

Good point. I'd have been on the phone demanding to know where Tybalt was and how Vale was planning to use him. I hate surprises, especially in fights.

I strapped myself down with knives—the best use for knee-high boots, in my opinion, is for hiding long blades, and hide them I did. I also selected two guns and backup ammo, just in case. Shooting in an enclosed area was a last resort option, but I didn't want us to be caught without one if the situation required covering fire. Astrid, Kyle, and I were not there to fight, but that meant nothing.

These things never went as planned.

Marcus, Astrid, and Kyle were waiting in the car when I arrived in the parking area—along with almost every Therian in the Watchtower. They stood in a line, at attention, in a silent salute to their brethren. I didn't understand a lot about Therian duels and codes of honor, but this seemed like an even bigger deal than I'd thought. Wyatt stood to the side with Kismet, Rufus, and Alejandro.

I didn't have time to do more than wink at Wyatt. He mouthed the words "Be careful." I gave a thumbs-up before climbing into the backseat with Kyle. I was anxious, but not scared. For once, this wasn't my fight. I was going along purely as backup, not as the primary contestant.

The change was pretty novel.

The drive to the Black River Ferry port took all the time we had. Marcus's explanation of Kyle's presence took about five minutes, and I was totally on board with the plan. Good plan that, again, went beyond my knowledge of Therian politics and cemented the reasons why I was a soldier, not a general.

The hulking glass building of the Terminal Station came into view at exactly six-thirty. A weed-strewn, cracked parking lot spread out around the Station and dock, which was surrounded by a chain-link fence. Ostensibly, the fence was meant to prevent vandalism and trespassing, which was kind of hilarious, considering. Even after Thackery sunk one of the ferries last month, police rarely patrolled the area. The security entrance remained broken.

We rolled through the gate at the same moment that a blue SUV with tinted windows turned into the parking lot. It followed us inside. Marcus drove around behind the Terminal Station to hide our vehicles from street view. The SUV stopped a dozen yards from us, at almost the other end of the Terminal Station.

The downside to this particular location smacked me in the nose the moment I opened my door. The stink of tepid water, oil, and burned things combined in a nostril-tingling odor that turned my stomach. The smell would also make it impossible for Therian noses to tell if Tybalt, or anyone else, was lurking nearby.

We assembled at the rear of our car, while Vale and his entourage moved to the front of his SUV. I hadn't looked Vale in the eye since the moment he tried to turn Wyatt on me in that jail cell, and I curbed the impulse to stride across the asphalt and plant my fist in his eye. Vale stood tall, straight backed, a nervous man pretending he was bold. I couldn't guess as to his backup until our two groups began walking toward one another, and their eye colors flashed in the brightening morning light.

The blonde woman to Vale's left had copper eyes—female Felia, probably the same one who'd tortured the pups. Starr Tuck, if we were lucky. An older, silver-haired man also had the copper eyes of a Felia. The third man, barely a teenager, had the bright green eyes and multiple-shades-of-brown hair of the Ursia Clan.

What the hell?

Not that I had room to judge, since Marcus's backup was a Felia, a Cania, and a human.

We all stopped with a safe distance of five feet between us, give or take. Marcus stood in front of us, Vale on point with his own group. A low, feline growl came out of them both, and something rippled in the air between them, as though their hatred had become a tangible thing.

"Where are the items you stole?" Marcus asked. His voice was deeper than its usual baritone, dripping with violence.

Vale snapped his fingers. The Ursia boy scampered back to the SUV and retrieved something from the rear compartment. He left that door up, open, then rushed back to us with the leather pouch and cylinder in his hands. The boy took a moment to show us that both the scroll and the powder were intact.

Kyle returned to our car and grabbed the briefcase of money that Eulan had provided. After showing Vale the cash, we made the exchange. A tiny part of my heart lightened, knowing we had the vampire cure back in our hands.

"And the Lupa?" Marcus asked.

Vale's eyebrows twitched, as if to say Marcus was pressing his luck. "Ben, show the human."

A bear named Ben. Sure, why not?

I followed Ben to the SUV, aware of each of my weapons and their distance from my hands. Aware of Ben's proximity. He led me to the rear compartment, where a thick green blanket covered a large lump. He stepped aside, seeming as eager to keep me at a distance as I was to return the favor. I yanked back the blanket.

John was wearing what looked like an entire roll of duct tape—around his arms, legs, ankles, wrists, even his mouth. He'd been trussed up like a hog in the most uncomfortable backwards position possible. Both his eyes were blackened, and a few other bruises peeked out from beneath his layers of tape. Layers over naked skin. Fuck, that was going to hurt coming off.

He was unconscious, and the only thing that kept me from flying into a rage was the lack of a silver collar. Eight hours in one of those things when already beaten up might have killed him.

"Stone?" Marcus hollered.

I stepped around the SUV and headed back for the group. "He's alive."

Ben slammed the rear door shut, then shadowed me to Vale. So far, Vale was being way too cooperative. He had a Tybalt-shaped ace up his sleeve somewhere so why hadn't he played it yet?

I was still a good ten feet away when Vale stepped forward, his hand extended. I thought he was offering to shake Marcus's hand because Marcus likewise reached out. Only Marcus withdrew quickly, holding something bright and metallic. He glared at the item, then passed it to Astrid without ever breaking Vale's gaze. Vale was speaking, but he shut up before I reached Kyle's side.

All three of my friends were livid, anger blazing in their eyes. Astrid handed the metal item to me, and I nearly dropped it—the prosthetic knife attachment Tybalt had been wearing when he left last night.

"Son of bitch," I said.

Marcus angled toward me, careful to never give Vale his back. "My life or Tybalt's. If I kill Vale, then Tybalt dies."

Vale had played his ace, the fucker. But we still had one move he wasn't expecting and—

The gentle rumble of an approaching car engine put Vale's group on high alert. We were expecting the black sedan that circled around Vale's SUV and parked between our two vehicles.

Elder Macario Rojay of Cania stepped out of the front passenger seat. He was a young Elder, with wild brown hair, coffee-colored eyes, and a ruddy complexion. He wore a snappy suit and carried a tablet in his hands. He was one of the few Elders actively involved in Watchtower activities and he had pledged the support of the Cania Clan to our cause. Kyle's Clan.

"Elder Rojay," Vale said. He looked stuck between wanting to cower and wanting to stomp his feet in a tantrum. "What are you doing here?"

Stupid question, really, since Vale was a fugitive wanted by the Assembly of Clan Elders. But he was pretty baffled by the Elder's planned appearance.

"This is a duel of honor," Kyle said, speaking up for the first time. "Duels are often fought in the presence of the Clan Elder in order to ensure all promises are kept. As the Felia Elder is unable to perform his duties, my Elder graciously agreed to oversee the fight."

Vale sputtered, clearly knocked on his ass by our little trick. He'd couldn't object because Marcus was completely within his rights to retain an Elder as a kind of referee. Vale's blonde touched his shoulder and whispered something that seemed to calm his indignation a little bit.

"Shall we observe the fighting grounds?" Elder Rojay asked.

He led the way. The doors to the Terminal Station weren't locked—someone had broken that long ago. We walked into a cavernous room three stories tall, mostly glass walls with a high tin roof. A line of boarded up ticket windows was on the left, and a dusty, linoleum floor spread out in front of us. Broken benches had been shoved to the side, piled up against walls in a feeble attempt to store them for some purpose or another. The air was stale, despite a few broken panes of glass. The rising sun shone through on the east-facing side, creating partial glare and partial darkness.

"Is the arena acceptable to both participants?" Elder Rojay asked.

Vale and Marcus both agreed.

"And what are the terms of the fight?"

"If I win," Marcus said, "Vale releases the Lupa boy named John back into my custody without further harm."

And Tybalt dies.

"And when I win," Vale said, "he remains in my custody, and we leave this location without interference from the Assembly or Marcus's witnesses." *And Tybalt lives.*

Maybe.

This was one of those times I was glad to be human, rather than Felia, because I wasn't bound to these little rules. If Marcus was killed, nothing would stop me from putting a bullet between Vale's eyes—after I had Tybalt safe and sound.

"Are these terms acceptable to both combatants?" Elder Rojay asked.

The combatants agreed.

"And this a fight to the death."

More agreement.

"Who are the witnesses for Vale Tuck?"

The trio stepped forward without introducing themselves. The Elder looked them over, then nodded. He turned to our little quartet.

"Who are the witnesses for Marcus Dane?"

Astrid, Kyle and I stepped forward.

"A human woman is not an acceptable witness to a Therian duel," Elder Rojay said. "Not even a Gifted human. She must wait outside until the matter at hand is decided."

I pretended to be affronted by the exclusion. Even Astrid mustered up a good dose of outrage on my behalf. But this was going exactly as planned. I wanted to be there and give Marcus my moral support while he fought for his life against the biggest coward to wear a fur coat, but my time was better spent on the hunt.

Hunting was what I did best.

"Rip his fucking heart out," I said to Marcus in a harsh whisper purposely loud enough for Vale to hear.

Vale hissed at me. I flipped him the bird.

"Out," Elder Rojay said.

I stormed outside, falling easily into my role as the excluded human. This side of the Terminal Station faced west, putting me in shadow. It also faced the river. A cement dock jutted out into the water, covered by a tin awning. The aging, rusty ferry tied up on the south side of the dock was smaller than the other two ferries on the north. The first ferry was half in the water, its lower decks fully submerged. I imagined a few Halfie corpses were down there somewhere, slowly being eaten by fish and other bottom feeders. A little farther down, the second passenger ferry was listing sideways, as though it had sprung a leak.

If the order was to kill Tybalt the moment Vale lost, then the person holding him must be within watching distance, as well as have a line of sight into the Terminal Station. Given its construction and the solid wall that faced north, the listing passenger ferry was unlikely. The half-sunk ferry was a decent option, but the dock awning blocked a good portion of the view.

The biggest problem with them being on the ferries at all was timing. Unless Vale was already in Mercy's Lot, he couldn't have gotten Tybalt and his captor here before he arrived—maybe. He could have been counting on the stink of the river hiding any fresh scents of arrival from Marcus and Astrid.

My best bet was the other side of the Terminal Station.

The scream of two furious felines shook the glass panes behind me. I squinted through the grimy window. A hulking black jaguar body-slammed a gorgeous Bengal tiger, and the pair went flying. As much as I wanted to watch the battle, I had a friend to find.

I sneaked around the north side of the Terminal Station and crept to the corner so I could peer across the parking lot to the street that ran parallel to the river. It was sparsely traveled. The block east of the ferry port housed a line of abandoned stone buildings, probably factories at one time. Anyone watching would be looking with the rising sun on their back and have a pretty clear view of the interior of the Terminal Station. And Vale had used a sniper more than once.

Marcus would do his best to make the battle last, to wound Vale without killing him, so I had time to search. None of us wanted Tybalt to die; all of us wanted Vale to pay for his crimes. Marcus would gladly kill Vale for what he did to Milo, but Vale's crimes didn't end there—Baylor, the Lupa pups, the hit on Elder Dane. Tybalt would hate for Vale to go free in exchange for his life. He'd cite the needs of the many.

As much as I wanted my friend back, I agreed with him. I'd sacrificed myself for the "greater good" once because I had no other choice. Today I still had time.

I closed my eyes and felt for the Break. It snapped and flickered all around me. Loneliness was easy to find. I thought of Tybalt, alone and hurt, a pawn in a larger game, probably anticipating his own death. The Break grabbed me and I fell into it, shattering and flying. I focused on the roof of one of the buildings, imagined a gravel surface warmed by the morning sun, and I hurtled that way.

Pulled out of the Break. Came back together.

I hit my knees in the gravel, arms pinwheeling for balance before I went face-first into sharp stone. A persistent throb between my eyes thanked me for the distance traveled. I blinked around the roof, grateful to not find myself staring down the barrel of someone's gun. The sounds of the city and stink of the river seemed far away up here, six stories off the ground.

Keeping low, I crept to the south side of the building. The factory next door was quiet, empty, half the east wall collapsing inward in a heap of stone and brick. Not an ideal spot for hiding. I went to the other side to check out the stone building on the north. It was one story shorter, its angle more directly facing the Terminal Station.

A body dressed in brown to blend into the roof colors was crouched near the ledge, a sniper's rifle propped and aimed, at least forty feet from my position. All they had to do was look a few degrees to their left, and they'd see me. The rest of that roof was empty, except for the small shed that had to be stairwell access. No one else, no Tybalt.

I could take out the sniper easily from here with a bullet to the brain. The problem with that solution was if someone else was guarding Tybalt, the noise would alert them and anyone else Vale had lurking about. Teleporting over would leave me disoriented for a few seconds after I rematerialized, and if the sniper noticed before I righted myself, I was dead.

I glanced at the Terminal Station, wishing I knew how the battle was progressing. All I saw were vague shadows moving behind glass.

I had to chance getting down there. The roof was smooth cement, instead of gravel, which would cut down on the noise. I chose a spot on the side of the stairwell access opposite the sniper's position. Even if they heard me, they wouldn't be able to see me right away.

Teleport number two left me with an actual headache, as well as a little bit of dizziness. I hadn't eaten in twelve hours or slept decently in twenty-four. This was going to bite me in the ass in a big way later, but I had to chance it. I leaned against the metal shed wall, grateful I'd landed on the side with the door, and listened. No detectable movement from the sniper.

I pressed my ear to the metal door. Silence, as far as I could tell. I gripped the cool knob in my left hand, then pulled a gun with my right. Turned the knob a degree, then another. It didn't squeal or squeak. I twisted it a bit at a time until it would move no further.

Please.

I pulled the door by degrees, scared the hinges would squeak and alert the sniper. Far enough so I could release the knob. A little more gave me a space of six inches to peer into the gloomy stairwell.

And into a pair of familiar brown eyes that narrowed in suspicion before widening in surprise. I didn't have to shush him because duct tape covered his mouth. I opened the door enough to slip inside. His ankles were bound. His arms were likewise taped behind his back, right above the place where his left arm ended. I checked the stairwell quickly, but saw no one lurking. Knelt next to him and put the gun down long enough to peel the duct tape away from his mouth.

He made a disgusted noise, then whispered, "Autumn."

"We know. How many here?"

"Just her."

Well that evened the odds nicely. Time to take Autumn out, then get us back down to the Terminal Station so Marcus could kill Vale.

I slipped a serrated knife from my boot and reached behind Tybalt to cut his arms free. Pressed the blade to the tape. The stairwell got instantly brighter, and my stomach tightened with dread.

"Evy!"

Tybalt's warning came as my hair was brutally yanked from behind. My scalp was on fire. The knife slipped. I fell backward, stumbling in the direction my head was being pulled. Out into

sunlight. I swung inward with the knife. It sank into flesh, and a woman screamed.

She shoved me into the ledge. My head cracked off solid stone, and I hit the cement roof like a sack of wet sand. My mind reeled, but I was very aware of the woman glaring down at me with a bloody knife in her hand.

Autumn.

"You shouldn't have done that, Evy," she snarled, then lunged.

CHAPTER
TWENTY-TWO

6:55 a.m.

Autumn was fucking *strong*. Intellectually, I knew that, because all Therians, in their human forms, are strong—stronger than the average human. I'm not the average human, and I've trained in hand-to-hand combat with were-cats, but the she-fox hadn't just had her brain scrambled by a brick wall.

I avoided her lunge with a quick tumble to my right. I came up on my knees, another knife in my hand. She tackled before I could get my weapon up. Her body slammed me back-first against the cement roof. Fire raced up my spine from the hard hit. She pounded my hand into the hard surface until the battered muscles released the knife on their own.

Certain I'd regret it later, I found my very active tap to the Break. She scooped my fallen knife, poised it over my throat. I felt into the Break, disappearing at the same moment cold heat sliced at my neck. She yelled.

I yanked hard to stay close, to pull out of the Break on the other side of the stair access. A mallet beat behind my eyes, threatening to liquefy my brain. Blood oozed from a painful spot on my throat. It wasn't gushing, so I ignored the wound and struggled to stand. The roof tilted. I palmed my second gun, aware I'd left the other in the stairwell, and stepped around the side of the shed.

No Autumn.

Tybalt shouted.

Oh shit, I'd left him defenseless.

I bolted, then skidded to a stop.

Tybalt must have shimmied his way to the first dropped knife while she-fox and I duked it out, because his arms were free. Autumn was straddling his waist, pressing down against his one-handed grip, the second knife she'd gotten from me pointed straight down at his chest.

I aimed for her head.

She ducked at the exact moment I squeezed the trigger. The bullet ricocheted off the stone. It gave Tybalt the upper hand though. He shoved her away, toward me. Autumn used the momentum to roll into a crouch. I followed through the gun's sight, waiting for her to clear Tybalt before I squeezed the trigger again. She flung the knife as I fired.

We both screamed.

Agony speared my gut, low and to the side. Nerveless fingers dropped the gun, and it skittered away. Instant shock sent me to my knees. My left hand coiled around the hilt the knife. At least three inches had gone in.

Movement in front of me stole my blurring vision from the wound. My bullet had caught Autumn in the left shoulder, and she screamed with a furious, unholy chittering noise that must have come from the fox inside of her. Tybalt sawed through the tape around his ankles. He twisted around to his knees.

Desperation brightened Autumn's eyes.

I saw it—the gun, at equal distance from all of us.

Autumn lunged first. I tried, but the pain in my hip turned the effort into a face-plant on the hard ground, and I shrieked as the knife shifted position.

Tybalt must have changed his mind on the gun, because I watched them engage in a sideways scuffle from my spot on the ground. The pair of them punching and rolling around. He got a few solid whacks in with the business end of his artificial arm attachment. Blood spurted from her nose.

I gave the knife in my gut a yank. First I felt the cold. Then the searing pain. I pressed my palm over the wound to stop the blood flow—it wasn't a fatal wound, but damn if it didn't hurt like hell. I scooted toward the gun. Just a few feet away.

Thud. Thump. Scrape.

Something squealed, a sound like a phone alarm. Not from my phone, though, and Tybalt had probably been relieved of his.

"Damn it!" That was Autumn.

My fingertips brushed the gun's stock. I scooted again. Wrapped my fingers around it.

Tybalt made a noise that sent ice down my spine.

I lurched up into a sitting position, immediately dizzy, one hand beneath the other to brace my unsteady grip. I'd missed their fight, but the outcome was horribly clear when I blinked them into focus.

Autumn had taken possession of the serrated knife, and it was planted to the hilt in Tybalt's chest. He was on the ground, her crouching above, dripping blood onto him from her nose and mouth. She snarled once, then scrambled away. I fired twice, missing both times, as she disappeared around the other side of the stairwell shed.

Let her run, the fucking coward.

I crawled to Tybalt's side, careful to keep my grip on the gun. Couldn't lose it again. He was trying to get a look at the wound, but couldn't manage to raise his head to the required angle. His eyes were wide, shocked, and he breathed in shallow gasps through his mouth.

"Don't you fucking move," I said.

"How bad?"

"Bad enough, so don't make it worse."

The knife was nearly centered, just below his sternum, which meant potential lung puncture. He wasn't foaming up blood though, and that gave me hope. I had to get him off this roof and to—

"No hospital," he wheezed. "Watchtower."

"Tybalt—"

"No."

As weak as his body was becoming, his eyes and voice meant business. The question of hospitals came up often when someone was wounded. Hospitals meant police, and police meant questions we couldn't answer.

"Autumn?" he said.

"On it. Don't go anywhere."

He crossed his eyes at me. I squeezed his hand, then lurched to my feet. Felt instantly sick to my stomach. Every joint ached and my skin felt scraped raw. I do not recommend fist fights with Therians, now or ever.

Autumn was back in her sniper spot—albeit trying to position the rifle with one bad shoulder. As I raised my own gun to take aim, she squeezed off a round. Fear seized my insides. God, who did she shoot?

I steadied the gun with my left hand, took a slow breath, and aimed at the back of Autumn's head. Squeezed the trigger.

I was no marksman and I was wounded. The bullet struck her in the neck. She slumped to the ground, completely boneless. I limped across the roof and kicked the rifle away from her hands.

She blinked up at me, expression totally blank.

"Why?" I asked. "Was it fucking worth it? Turning against us?"

"Change is necessary." She struggled to get the words out. Blood trickled from the corner of her mouth.

As much as I wanted her to suffer, I didn't have time to enjoy a slow, painful death. I put another bullet in her, right between the eyes.

With the immediate threat neutralized, I pulled my phone out with shaking, unsteady fingers. By some miracle, it had a cracked screen but the damn thing still worked. I sent a concise text to Kismet, because I didn't know who else: *East of ferry, Ty bad shape. Medical stat.*

I left Autumn and her rifle and returned to Tybalt's side. He was struggling to stay awake, to stay here. "Listen to me, pal, you have to fight a while longer, okay?" I said. "No checking out, not over this mosquito bite."

He pulled a face.

"I'm going to teleport us down to the ground, so it's easier to get you help. Remember what that's like?"

He made another face. I'd teleported him once, months ago, and he hadn't been a big fan of the experience. Today he didn't have a choice.

I carefully pressed my palms on his shoulders, then scooted so my thighs touched his leg. As much contact as I could manage for this. The Break was harder to find because I was so damned tired. My concentration was fried. And it always hurt extra when I was wounded.

"You're lucky I love you," I said.

Tybalt found my left wrist and squeezed.

The teleport was a special kind of excruciating—partly from the previous two teleports, partly from my injuries, and definitely because I had extra weight along. Bringing someone with me taxed my body more than teleporting alone, and using the Break always comes at a price. By the time I realized we'd safely rematerialized on the broken sidewalk east of the ferry port, someone was already shouting my name.

I tried to speak, to shout back, and ended up lolling sideways onto the ground. My body hurt all over, a constant throb that was harshest in my head. My hip was on fire. The cut on my throat felt like it was bleeding more heavily, and it hadn't seemed that deep before.

Rough fingers curled around mine. Tybalt's hand.

I held on tight.

Things got fuzzy for a while. Lots of voices talked around me. I struggled to identify them. Astrid. Kyle. Marcus, thank God. Elder Rojay.

Kismet.

What's Gina doing here?

Sudden movement made my stomach clench. I wanted to be violently ill, but my gorge never rose. I held on until the movement stopped, only to be replaced by a steadier motion.

Car.

Oh good. Home. Bed.

I wanted to sleep for a month, but I couldn't. Not until I knew Tybalt was okay. He had to be okay. "Tybalt." Getting that word out hurt my throat.

"He's in another car." Kyle. He sounded close. "Relax, okay? You did good."

"Vale?"

"Which piece?"

I think I smiled. I'd have cheered if I had the energy.

"John's fine, too," Kyle said. "He'll be back with his family very soon."

More good news. Wyatt would be thrilled. Then he'd get pissed at me for coming home wounded again. The man should have been used to it by now, but no.

I allowed the motion of the car to rock me to sleep, and I didn't wake up again until Wyatt's voice and heat surrounded me. He touched my face, whispered in my ear, was everywhere, and I basked in how wonderful it was. The antiseptic odors of the infirmary placed my location before I peeled my eyelids apart. Wyatt hovered above me, his relief plain, but still unable to mask the bitter frustration at having to worry over my near-death yet again.

"Hey, beautiful," he said. "There's my kick-ass warrior."

"Got her ass kicked," I rasped. My throat itched like crazy as my healing ability took over. The wound in my gut ached, the itch of healing on the cusp of becoming real, not quite there yet because of the depth of the wound. The headache was hiding behind a haze of drugs that made my tongue feel thick, my brain fuzzy.

"You did good this morning. Autumn was given orders to shoot Marcus from her position if Vale lost."

"Then Tybalt."

"Yeah."

"How is he?"

Wyatt's eyes shuttered. "In surgery. Dr. Vansis is doing what he can."

"It's bad."

"Yeah, it's pretty bad."

He brushed his lips over my cheek. "Thank you for bringing John home."

"Didn't Marcus technically do that?"

"Yes, he did," said the man in question. Marcus hobbled over to my bed, leaning hard onto a crutch. White bandages swathed his chest and abdomen, and long claw marks scored his left cheek. He looked worn out and wrung dry, but very much alive.

"Should you be up?" I asked.

"Probably not, but I'm an impatient patient. Thank you, Evangeline, for finding Tybalt. Vale was a formidable opponent, and twice I forwent a killing blow in order to buy you time. The tactic paid off."

"Maybe."

Marcus frowned. "We brought Tybalt home, as we intended. The Prince of Cats is quite strong. He'll pull through this."

"Anyone else hurt?"

"Astrid took a bullet protecting Elder Rojay from a sniper round. She's resting, awaiting her turn with Dr. Vansis."

Astrid was shot because I was too damned slow in taking Autumn down. Perfect. "Where was she hit?"

"Lower back."

"God, we're a mess. Tell me Kyle, at least, wasn't injured."

"Kyle wasn't injured."

I looked at Wyatt. "Is he telling the truth?"

"Yes, Kyle's fine," Wyatt replied. "Marcus, on the other hand, has a chest that looks like raw hamburger, and if he passes out from blood loss I'm not hauling his heavy ass onto a bed."

Marcus grunted, then slumped down into the plastic chair that Wyatt had probably been using while waiting for me to wake up. The verbal exchange was one of the most normal they'd had since Wyatt was infected. It actually bordered on friendly, which they'd always been until their warring genes made them snap and hiss at each other on a regular basis.

"What time is it?" I asked.

Wyatt checked his phone. "A little after nine."

Tybalt had been holding on for two hours, and that gave me hope. "Hey, what happened to Vale's posse?"

"Elder Rojay is taking them to the Assembly for trial and punishment," Marcus said. "Their roles in the events of the last few days will be evaluated during this morning's meeting."

"Are they going to pick a new Felia Elder?"

"Perhaps. Much has happened in the last twenty-four hours."

"No kidding."

I was getting tired of laying there like a salami, so I made Wyatt into my personal pillow. He scooted onto the bed behind me and helped me into a sitting position. Pain shot through my abdomen, followed by a deep throb with the vaguest hint of itching. Healing always took longer to start when I'd overextended my Gift, and boy had I overextended today.

He brushed my hair behind my ear, then rested in his chin on my shoulder. A perfect heat all around me. "Still not used to this short hair of yours," he whispered.

"Me, either."

A shuffle-creak, shuffle-creak beyond the curtain got my attention. Low voices murmured. I couldn't figure it out, but Marcus perked up, head snapping in the direction of the noise. He tried to rise, grimaced, and stayed put.

Below the fall of the curtain, two pairs of feet appeared, one sneakered and one slippered. The slippered feet stood between the front wheels of a walker, and I started grinning before the curtain was drawn back.

Milo held the sides of the walker in a white-knuckled grip, his arms trembling with the stress. He wore loose pajamas that hid the bruises giving him pain even as he stood there, in front of us, on his own two feet. Kismet hovered next to him, grinning like a proud mama whose cub had taken his first steps.

"Should you be up?" Marcus asked.

"Doc's orders," Milo replied. His voice carried the strain of standing. A line of sweat trickled down the side of his face. "Circulation or something."

"He isn't supposed to be up for long," Kismet said.

"Walked to the bathroom a few hours ago. Surely an announcement was made." Milo's mock outrage and returned sense of humor was a beautiful thing.

I laughed. "I'd go over there and kiss you, but getting up seems like too much trouble."

"Save your strength. You look like hell."

"Thank you."

"You, on the other hand," he said to Marcus, "look like shit on toast."

Marcus snorted. "You're too kind."

"You almost got yourself killed." Milo's frustration was palatable, and it seemed to reach six feet across the cubicle and slap Marcus in the face. Because Marcus did the impossible—he actually looked chagrined.

Marcus didn't hide the pain it caused him to stand up. He wobbled a bit, and Kismet's hand jerked toward him, as though she wanted to help. She drew back instead. Marcus was too proud to lean on her, and this was something he seemed determined to do. Each step was an effort for his battered, abused body, but I'll be damned if he didn't seem to stand taller the moment he was in front of Milo.

"Vale deserved his fate and more for what he did to you," Marcus said. "I would suffer this and worse to see your pain avenged."

Milo was dumbstruck. He blinked at Marcus, a little saucer-eyed, until something clicked home. The blank stare became a tender smile, and suddenly I felt like an intruder on a private moment. Even Kismet shuffled away from the pair, coming closer to the side of my bed. Wyatt's arms tightened around my waist, and I squeezed his hands.

The moment stayed suspended in time, a beautiful thing shared by two lonely souls who'd found something that made them happy. And then Marcus brushed his knuckles across Milo's cheek on his right hand's trip around to clasp the back of his neck. He kissed Milo. An action both consoling and possessing, gentle and harsh. Marcus was making a statement to everyone that Milo was his.

And Milo, bless his battered heart, kissed right Marcus back.

Wyatt stayed with me long after Kismet and Marcus took Milo back to his room to rest. We sat together while my body slowly healed itself. The cut on my throat was long gone, the various scrapes and bruises distant memories. My gut, on the other hand, felt like someone was pinching and twisting the skin and muscle, with tingling for good measure.

"I can't decide if this is a record for me," I said.

"What's that?" Wyatt asked.

"In the last forty-eight hours, I've been shot, stabbed, and julienned, not to mention the whole Juliet potion and the beat-down Autumn gave me."

He sighed, then kissed the side of my neck. "You're giving me gray hair, you know that, right?"

"I know. I'm sorry."

"It's the life we chose, Evy. Every single day, I'm grateful for the healing gift that Horzt gave you. It's kept you in my life this long."

"Hopefully it'll keep me around a while longer. If that's what you want?"

"It is. I may be angry at what you did, but I'll get over it at some point."

"I hate that you have to get over anything."

"I know. I also need your help with something."

"Oh?"

"I have three teenagers to take care of now."

I twisted a little in his arms to look him in the eye. "What the hell do I know about raising teenagers? I was a hellion when I was sixteen."

"So was I. I figure between the two of us, we know everything we don't want them to do."

"Good point. So do you think Astrid will let them stay here?"

Wyatt shrugged. "I don't know. I hope so. I hope the Assembly grants them mercy. If not… I'll deal with it."

Meaning: I go where they go.

And I went with Wyatt.

CHAPTER
TWENTY-THREE

11:40 a.m.

Bad news always seems to ride the coattails of good news.

The good news came when Wyatt returned to the infirmary with a tray of sandwiches and bottled water for the small group of us holding vigil in Milo's room.

"Eulan called," he said as he deposited the tray on the rolling side table. "They removed Eleri from stasis and dosed her with the gnome cure. He says she's showing signs of improvement."

Relief burned in my chest, and it bubbled up in a burst of laughter. "Really? It's going to work?"

"So far so good. If Eleri continues to improve, they'll slowly reawaken the other vampires and give them the cure, too."

I was too tired to jump up and down so I did a few mental gymnastics to wear out my excitement over the news. More than saving the lives of vampires I considered friends, this meant that Walter Thackery didn't get the last laugh. He didn't win.

"We owe Horzt a huge debt," Kismet said. She'd brought a bunch of chairs into Milo's room for all of us: me, Wyatt, Marcus, herself. Even Astrid had joined the group, her midsection bandaged tight from the bullet she'd taken. Milo had been given a big dose of painkillers after his adventure into the exam area, and he dozed in and out of the conversations.

Astrid and Marcus had been treated a little while ago by a Therian doctor named Hunt who'd been brought in to assist while Dr. Vansis was otherwise occupied saving Tybalt's life. The only news we'd had on Tybalt in the last few hours was a terse "He's hanging on" from Hunt when he joined Dr. Vansis in the operating room.

Tybalt wasn't going out without a fight.

We ate while we digested the news that the vampires had a chance to come through this. I had no idea if the infection would cause lasting damage or side effects. No one would know right away. All we could do was hope for a positive outcome.

Others wandered in and out, seeking news we didn't have, and offering their respects to Marcus for kicking Vale's ass so solidly. Kyle and Lynn, Leah and Jackson, Shelby, Sandburg, Rufus, Nevada, Morgan, Carly, even Paul with his bandaged shoulder—all familiar faces.

Astrid watched everyone with a new glint in her eyes that worried me: distrust. Autumn had broken our trust, wormed her way into our organization, and then tried to kill our own. Human or Therian, we were part of the Watchtower. We were a family. Autumn had placed a fracture at the base of that family, forever altering the solidity of its foundation. And I didn't know how to start repairing it.

Finding that sense of trust again was only one item on a long list of things that needed my attention. The Frosts were still in the compound, under guard, hopefully coming to grips with everything I'd told them earlier. Aurora, Ava, and Joseph were still missing. Nessa and her goblins had slowed their attacks on humans, but once word got out that my latest death had been faked, I knew she'd be at it again.

The one thing we were waiting for word on, the thing I had no hand in affecting one way or another, was the naming of Elder Dane's successor. The Assembly was in session. We'd know as soon as a decision was made.

For now, the only thing getting my full and undivided attention was Tybalt. And the people around me. The people who cared about him the most.

Dr. Vansis appeared in the doorway like a ghost, standing where no one had been an instant before. He wore stained scrubs, and I tried to ignore the splotches of red in favor of studying his face. His expression was completely neutral, even his eyes empty of any actual emotion.

My insides churned, and I reached for Wyatt's hand.

"There was a complication," Dr. Vansis said. The tension level in the room skyrocketed with those four words. "Tybalt's injuries from the knife were serious, but not catastrophic. However, as I repaired the damage his heart rate and breathing became dangerously erratic. Keeping him stable was difficult. His internal systems were shutting down."

"Why?" Kismet asked, her voice sharp, cold, begging him to not say what he was taking care to explain.

"Dr. Hunt found an injection site behind Tybalt's ear. I won't know for certain without further testing, but I believe he was poisoned."

"Vale." Marcus's voice cut like a blade, fury blazing in his eyes. "The coward."

Vale had played his final wild card, a trick none of us had expected.

"Do you have an antidote?" Milo asked, startling me. I hadn't realized he was awake and listening. "Something that will help him?"

Dr. Vansis shook his head. My throat tightened, certain without having heard the words yet. Wyatt held my hand tighter. I couldn't breathe.

"I'm sorry," Dr. Vansis said. "But Tybalt passed away a few minutes ago."

"That's not funny," Milo said.

"I assure you, it was not a jest. Perhaps if I had known about the poison earlier, the outcome would be different."

"It can't be true." Milo's helpless gaze swung from Marcus to Kismet, to everyone in the room. I wanted to comfort him, to tell him it was a joke, that Tybalt was fine, but I couldn't. I was too stunned to move, much less offer support to Milo. Or Kismet, who looked like she'd been punched in the stomach.

"I'm very sorry," Dr. Vansis said, and I suspected he meant it. He left an extremely stunned group behind.

A heartbeat later, Kismet bolted after him.

My vision blurred. I blinked hard and didn't bother to wipe away the tears that trickled down my cheeks to my neck. Tybalt had fought so hard, overcome so much to take his place in the Watchtower's elite. He would have survived the knife wound. He deserved better than his body shutting down from the effects of an unknown poison.

He deserved a warrior's death, goddammit.

Rage and grief bubbled up, and I started to cry in earnest. I didn't care who saw. The distant sounds of choked sobs told me I wasn't the only one breaking down. Wyatt surrounded me, pulled me to the floor, into his arms. I clung to him and cried, hating the unfairness of it all. Hating the idea of facing this constant war without a capable colleague by my side.

Most of all, I huddled there and mourned my friend.

CHAPTER
TWENTY-FOUR

Thursday, September 4
10:00 a.m.

Tybalt's memorial service at the Watchtower was held the day before, giving friends and coworkers a chance to celebrate his life and mourn his passing. We held a private funeral for him on Thursday, at Kismet's request. She arranged for him to be interred in St. Matthew's cemetery, right next to Lucas Moore, and she paid for it all herself. Memorials for two men she'd loved deeply, and in very different ways. One of them a lover, the other as a brother.

"I owe Tybalt nothing less," she'd told me yesterday.

A handful of us gathered around the freshly turned earth to pay our respects to our fallen comrade. Astrid and Kismet stood together, finding solace in each other's company. Kismet had aged these last few days, the stress of it all adding a weight to her shoulders and lines around her eyes. Green eyes that had gone cold.

Milo had been allowed to come, under strict instructions from Dr. Vansis that he keep his butt in a wheelchair and not over-exert himself. Marcus stood beside him, a hand on his shoulder, ever the protective warrior. They both looked beaten, exhausted. They'd each lost a brother.

I'd lost one too, and I didn't know what to do with my emotions. Tybalt had joined the Triads only a few weeks before I did. He'd been one of the Mercy's Lot Hunters. We hadn't always been friends. I'd punched him in the face once, years ago, when tensions were high between his Triad and mine. Hell, he'd even tried to kill me under orders from the Triad brass.

None of that mattered, because we'd fought side-by-side for months, and I'd seen his heart. And now he was gone. One more friend I'd outlived.

Wyatt's arm slipped around my waist, and I leaned into the heat of him, grateful for the support. The Lupa pups, healing and nervous as ever, were waiting in the car just down the hill, near the cemetery entrance. He didn't like leaving them alone for an extended period of time, and the Assembly hadn't made a ruling on them yet. Until he knew something for certain, he was keeping them close.

I didn't mind it as much as I thought I would. They were good kids. John was especially sweet and eager to please, and they knew the stakes were high. Good behavior was their best chance of not living as fugitives from all Therians everywhere, forever. Wyatt would never let them be executed. He'd take them and leave.

And I'd go with him.

No one read Bible verses or sang hymns or recited poetry. There was no need. We'd planned a very simple service.

Kismet picked up a small box from the ground. From the box, she handed each of us a shot glass. She kept one for herself, then placed the seventh on the small stone marker that simply said "Tybalt Monahan, Brother and Protector." She produced a bottle of whiskey from a paper bag and carefully poured a shot into each glass, including the seventh.

With the whiskey poured, we six raised our glasses.

"To Tybalt," Kismet said.

"To Tybalt," we said in unison.

The whiskey burned its way down my throat to warm my stomach.

We left the seventh glass behind, untouched.

Wyatt didn't lead me straight back to the car, which surprised me. We detoured into another part of the cemetery, and he stopped in front of a simple headstone with the word Petros on it. I studied it, not comprehending, until I looked down at the other words engraved in the marble. Delius. Corissa. Dates of death exactly the same, almost twelve years ago.

"My parents," he said. He pointed to two smaller headstones on the left. Salena. His sister, who died with their parents. Nicandro. His brother, who died almost a year later.

"I don't come here often," he said when I didn't speak. I had no idea what to say. "The past is the past, and I need to let it go. Andreas Petros died a long time ago. Even Wyatt Truman, the person I became after, died with the Lupa infection."

Hearing him say that hurt something deep inside of me, even though I knew more than anyone how true it was. How death wasn't always physical or permanent. Sometimes it left you changed and all you could do was adapt.

"I want to let go of everything, but I can't. Not yet."

"Why can't you?" I asked.

"Because I still don't have one answer that I've wanted since my family was murdered."

Oh God. "The second bounty hunter."

"Yes."

Twelve years ago, a group of Halfies had stormed a Greek restaurant and begun killing and torturing the occupants, including Wyatt's parents and sister. A pair of bounty hunters who'd been tracking the Halfies found them, killed the Halfies, and then made the awful decision to burn the place down—survivors included. The knowledge of vampires couldn't get out, and no one would be able to forget what they'd seen. That was how the bounty hunter in charge justified murder.

Ten months later, Andreas and Nicandro Petros had found the lead bounty hunter, and he paid with his life. The second bounty hunter had never been identified.

At least, not until a few months ago, when Rufus St. James told me in confidence that he had been the second bounty hunter. Young, inexperienced, deferring to the guy who'd taken him in and was teaching him the ropes, he'd gone along with the slaughter of innocents. Rufus had kept that secret from Wyatt for a decade. Now both of us were keeping it from him.

"How do you know he's still alive?"

"I don't. I also don't know that he's dead." He took my hand. "Evy, I want to let the past go. I want to focus on now. On you and the boys and keeping a lid on the pressure cooker that this city has become."

"But you need to know first."

"Yeah, I do. Does it make sense?"

"It makes perfect sense. You know I'd give you the name if I could." So damned true. Rufus hadn't sworn me to secrecy. Sometimes I thought he'd told me so I would tell Wyatt, and then it would be out. But this wasn't my secret to tell, and if Rufus wanted absolution, he needed to see the priest himself.

"I wish I'd been able to know your family," I said.

"You'd have loved them. We were a very stereotypically boisterous, food-loving Greek family. My mother was an excellent cook. Her stuffed grape leaves were the best in the country." His voice cracked under the weight of so many memories, so much loss.

I wrapped my arms around him, and we held each other for a while. Enjoyed this brief moment away from the rest of the world and the dangerous lives we led. For a few minutes, we were the only people who existed. The only people who mattered.

Movement in the corner of my eye caught my attention. I pulled back, startled that someone had approached and gotten so close without either of us noticing. My heart jumped at the familiar blue eyes staring back at me.

"Phineas?"

He smiled. Phineas el Chimal looked exactly the same as when he'd left five weeks ago and seemed none the worse for wear. He wore casual clothes and didn't look tense or worried. Only relieved.

"You're home," I said and launched myself at him. He caught me in a tight hug, and I inhaled the mountain stream smell of him, the scent of flying and freedom.

"I'm home," Phineas said. He pulled out of the hug, probably because of the warning growl from my overprotective boyfriend. "I heard about Tybalt, Evy. My sincere condolences."

"Thank you. Not that I don't like you being back, but why did you come home? Did you find more Coni?"

His expression shuttered. "No. I had no luck in that search. I did, however, find something that will help in our struggles with the Fey."

"What is it?"

"Allow me to show you?"

Wyatt and I followed him down a gravel path toward an older section of the cemetery. A handful of garden crypts stood here, aged and mossy, beneath the shade of an ancient weeping willow. Phineas paused next to one of the crypts.

"If you pull a dead body out, Phin, I swear—" I began.

"My surprise is very much alive," Phineas said. "I need you both to keep an open mind. I believe my companion holds the key to defeating Amalie."

I glanced at Wyatt, whose nose was wrinkled in a way that suggested he smelled fresh dog shit. He looked more suspicious than alarmed though.

"Okay, I trust you," I said to Phin. "What's the surprise?"

"Brevin," he said.

I didn't know the word, which turned out to be a name. A small figure walked out from behind the crypt. About four feet tall, his body inhumanly thin, like he'd been pulled and stretched. Silver hair. Pointed ears and sharp, angular eyebrows.

I'd seen a creature like this once, many months ago. It had sought to destroy me, to destroy everyone I loved, and to stick a demon in my body when it could no longer have Wyatt's. This wasn't Tovin, because Tovin was long dead.

"An elf," Wyatt said, a dangerous growl in his voice. "A fucking elf holds the key to defeating the Fey? Are you serious?"

"Perfectly," Phineas said. "And I believe that once you hear Brevin's story, you'll agree."

To say I was stunned would be an understatement. My first death had been machinated by an elf, his entire purpose to bring a demon over from the other side of the Break where they'd long ago been banished. Everything I am today is thanks to that fucking elf.

This was one story I couldn't wait to hear.

Author's Note

A lot goes into publishing a novel, and sometimes I think even more goes into self-publishing one. But I absolutely must start with Jonathan Lyons and Anne Groell, who gave Dreg City a chance and who championed it no matter what. I hope this book does them both proud.

Nancy, you are outstanding as a friend and as an editor. Your patience, support, and your hilarious emails kept me sane when I wanted to throw it in, and I thank you for that. Melissa, my best friend in the world, one of my biggest fans, thank you for everything you do. Nick, my biggest fan, for giving me the confidence to try something new.

To my sister and my parents, you mean the world to me. You let me play in imaginary worlds, and you never look at me askance. I love you all so much.

Thank you to all of the bloggers and reviewers who have supported me all these years. I'd try to name you all, but I'd probably forget someone, and I don't want to forget anyone, but you know who you are.

Thank you to my writer friends, especially Kelly Gay and Alison Pang, and the members of the League or Reluctant Adults. We are part of a fantastic community of UF writers, and I'm grateful for the support. More thanks to Howie Weinstein, Bob Greenberger, and all of my Shore Leave/Farpoint writer friends. You guys are invaluable to me.

Robin L., you created a fantastic cover. Thank you for being so true to these books and coming up a beautiful representation.

And a shout-out to everyone else who helped get this book into your hands: Nancy M., Melissa H., Mario A., Jed C., Karen K., and Gabrielle. Thanks to everyone who answered one of my bazillion Facebook or Twitter questions about self-publishing.

NEW: For everyone who poked and prodded at me to get this in print, this is for you.

48601563R00186

Made in the USA
Middletown, DE
22 September 2017